DÉJÀ DEAD

AN AMERICAN IN PARIS MYSTERY BOOK 1

SUSAN KIERNAN-LEWIS

SAN MARCO PRESS

Books by Susan Kiernan-Lewis

The Maggie Newberry Mysteries

Murder in the South of France

Murder à la Carte

Murder in Provence

Murder in Paris

Murder in Aix

Murder in Nice

Murder in the Latin Quarter

Murder in the Abbey

Murder in the Bistro

Murder in Cannes

Murder in Grenoble

Murder in the Vineyard

Murder in Arles

Murder in Marseille

Murder in St-Rémy

Murder à la Mode

A Provençal Christmas: A Short Story

A Thanksgiving in Provence

Laurent's Kitchen

The Stranded in Provence Mysteries

Parlez-Vous Murder?

Crime and Croissants

Accent on Murder

A Bad Éclair Day

Croak, Monsieur!

Death du Jour

Murder Très Gauche

Wined and Died

A French Country Christmas

An American in Paris Mysteries

Déjà Dead

Death by Cliché

The Irish End Games

Free Falling

Going Gone

Heading Home

Blind Sided

Rising Tides

Cold Comfort

Never Never

Wit's End

Dead On

White Out

Black Out

End Game

The Mia Kazmaroff Mysteries

Reckless

Shameless

Breathless

Heartless

Clueless

Ruthless

Ella Out of Time

Swept Away

Carried Away

Stolen Away

The French Women's Diet

1

EVERY LITTLE BREEZE

I moved to Paris the day I turned sixty.

Frankly, it was not the happiest day of my life.

Not by a long shot.

My father, who was French and whom I barely knew, had recently died and left me an apartment in the eighth arrondissement.

I was surprised to have been left anything. I can count on both hands and still have fingers left over the number of times I'd laid eyes on my father. A big bear of a man with twinkling blue eyes and silver hair, Claude Lapin was always pleasant to me if not particularly affectionate.

I was raised in the US by my mother and perhaps as a result wasn't all that interested in getting to know *cher Papa*. Not that my mother was bitter about how things ended with Claude. Let's just say she was philosophical.

At times angrily, self-abusively philosophical.

I'm sure a lot of my ambivalence about getting to know my father had to do with how Mom felt about him, but also because of my innate resistance to travel and meeting new people. It may be difficult to believe that a teenager wouldn't be interested in visiting Paris from time to time but I was born with a brain anomaly that makes handling new situations difficult for me.

At my age now I've got several mechanisms in place that help me overcome my affliction—for the most part. But when I was younger, it was just easier to stay home with Mom.

The apartment building I inherited in Paris was created in the classic Haussman style with massive double doors off a narrow street which nonetheless featured a steady stream of traffic.

The Paris realtor I spoke with on the phone from Atlanta where I lived told me the apartment would easily sell for a million euros. She said that price had more to do with its location which is a five-minute walk from the Champs-Elysées than any specific features of the apartment itself.

The first time I stepped across the threshold of the apartment—all of two days ago—I understood what she meant.

It was not at all extraordinary. The bathroom looked prehistoric with snaking coiled hoses instead of a shower nozzle and a pre-World War II ceramic tub and sink. The kitchen was so small I don't fit all the way in it. I can only assume my father and stepmother—both of whom used to live here before he died—must have dined out all the time.

It has two small bedrooms and a bathroom off the main bedroom which doesn't have a toilet in it. *That* is situated down the hall by the living room. (So when the French say "bathroom" they mean that literally.)

But for all its dubious attributes—at least from an American's point of view—I have to say it feels spacious. The windows are tall and wide. And the view from the living room is classically Parisian showing an expanse of rooftops as well as the façade of the building across the street which is studded with black wrought iron Juliette balconies and window boxes full of geraniums.

Standing in my living room—or *salon* as the Paris realtor called it—I can look through the tall windows at night and see the twinkling lights of traffic and the tip of a wider boulevard that leads deeper into the city.

But a million euros? I've translated that into dollars at least once a day since I heard the number. Let's just say I can definitely use whatever the exchange rate is on a million euros a whole lot more than the pleasure of seeing an Instagram-worthy picture out my living room window.

As I sat down and tried to fight my jet lag—still with me after two days—and my swirling emotions, I sipped a cup of tea made with a teabag I found in one of the kitchen drawers.

My eye caught the shelf where the television must have been on the far wall. The shelf was empty and needed dusting.

My stepmother Joelle Lapin lived in this apartment with my father for nearly ten years and you can see her touches everywhere—especially the spot where she ripped the decorative hooks off the wall in the bedroom, taking the hundred-year-old wallpaper with it.

An angry woman, my stepmother.

She took an instant dislike to me and I'm really not sure why. We've never even met. When I found out my father had left the place to me I offered to rent it to her so she could go on living here but she declined.

Now that I think about it, maybe the reason for her enmity had to do with the fact that I didn't go to my father's funeral last month.

But I had a pretty good excuse.

I was busy attending my own husband's funeral.

2

THE SECRETS WE KEEP

Bob and I landed at Charles DeGaulle Airport on the last Tuesday in August when the weather was so hot my silk blouse clung to my ribs in the back of the taxi.

Born and raised in Atlanta, Georgia, I have the need for climate control programmed into my blood. Even though I'm a Southerner, I do not do heat well. Maybe it's because I'm half French but my physical constitution wilts when the temperatures rise.

I'd been to Paris a few times with my mother when I was younger and I speak the language passably. My mother was a high school French teacher and felt it was a matter of pride that her only child speak French. Plus, there was the fact that my father was French.

My parents divorced soon after I was born—both clearly having realized what a mistake the union was. I'd toyed with the idea of calling my father while I was in Paris on this trip. At various points in my patchwork career I've worked as a skip tracer and a private investigator and I have to say finding people is something I do well. Because of Bob's job I didn't need to work, but I took a few cases here and there over the years to keep my hand in and also because I enjoyed it.

Finding people is like a big puzzle or a game you're playing with people who don't know they're playing with you.

Runaways are the easiest to find—even though they don't own property and try to "stay off the grid." But unless they come to a bad end fairly quickly—not unusual unfortunately—they're fairly predictable in their habits. If the kids have a cell phone, I can track them practically before their parents hang up with me. If they don't have a cell phone, all I need is the name of a single friend—preferably one who has a phone—and it's nearly as fast.

Adults are trickier because I'm sure they feel they have more to lose. A noncustodial parent who's fled with his kids will do serious time if he's caught and so that desperation makes him much more wily.

In any case, I try not to get caught up in *why* people are running away. That's the hardest part, not getting involved. It was easier when I was younger but at my age I tend to take sides.

Which is probably why I haven't taken all that many cases in the last few years. It all starts to feel personal, like the people trying to fall off the map need my help in letting them do that.

Or at least my blind eye.

Before Bob and I left for Paris I tracked down *mon père's* phone number and address *just in case*.

Once here, I found I didn't really have the emotional energy to call.

Jet lag walloped both me and Bob pretty good that first night. Travel is no longer like when we were young and could take a nap and shake it off. Now when we travelled together—which admittedly was rare—it took us days to recover.

I was pleased to see how excited Bob seemed to be about the trip. We hadn't had much time for vacations in the past twenty years, what with raising our daughter and Bob being a senior creative director at one of Atlanta's hottest ad shops. At sixty-four he was still going strong both in creative output and in the respect his peers had for him. But then, it's not typically the *men* who are let go in creative fields due to their age.

Our hotel was in the Latin Quarter. I'd booked it using an online travel site. In the process I learned that it's become harder and harder to find "quaint" or "old world charm" in the world's busiest and most visited city but I think I'd managed fairly well.

From the outside the hotel was definitely no-frills. A single doorway was set in a dark-stained stone building tucked into a maze of narrow lanes walking distance to the Seine and Tuileries Gardens and the boulevard Saint-Germain.

As I explained to Bob when he took his first skeptical look at the hotel, "When you live in a place as perfectly landscaped as Atlanta, it's nice to appreciate a more authentic setting."

I'm not sure Bob agreed with me.

Admittedly the hotel lobby was a little threadbare. A worn Isfahan rug covered a creaky hardwood floor and the couches and chairs looked as if they'd been there since the last world war.

The rooms were smaller than the pictures on the website had indicated. But our window opened onto a cascade of classic Parisienne rooftops, complete with pigeons and a patch of blue sky over the Seine.

After unpacking, we left our room and walked to the end of the street where we stood in front of the first restaurant chalkboard we came to. We had all week to find little culinary jewels. Tonight we just needed a meal, a glass of wine and a moment to reach across the table to each other and enjoy that moment when we realized *we were in Paris*!

That first night I had the duck *confit* and Bob made his way through a steak. I always thought it strange that anyone would come to Paris and order steak. I guess I think that the States—or maybe Brazil—has the market cornered on cooking steak but I suppose that's silly. These days you can get authentic sushi in Vidalia, Georgia.

In any case, Bob said the steak was excellent and the fact that he had it with steak *frites* instead of a baked potato made it seem more French. We laughed about that.

It was late summer and wouldn't be dark for several more hours so we walked back to our hotel in what felt like full daylight while every step required greater and greater effort.

We held hands on the walk back to the hotel. I stumbled once on the rough cobblestones and was grateful for Bob's steady arm keeping me from falling.

"Don't tell me you're drunk on one glass of wine," he teased, slipping his arm around my waist.

We made our way back to our room, pulled the blinds shut against the evening street noise outside and the late summer light, and fell into bed where we both slept like the dead.

3

PARIS IS (NEARLY) ALWAYS A GOOD IDEA

I woke the next morning to the sounds of my husband cursing.

Truth be told I was probably more than half awake before that. I think I was dreaming that I was in some sort of swamp or jungle. When I awoke I had a line of sweat tracing its way down my ribcage.

"What's happening?" I mumbled to Bob.

"Damn AC isn't working," he said from where he stood peering at the air-conditioning control panel of our window unit.

I guess the downside of finding a place loaded with old world charm means you might have to put up with less than first-rate air conditioning on a hot August night.

But we're American. I knew before I'd even swung my legs out of bed that there would be no "putting up" with anything.

"Get dressed," Bob said. "If they can't fix it by the time we get back from breakfast, I'll have them move us to another room."

I couldn't help smiling at his determined early morning focus.

I met Bob Baskerville in college at the University of Florida. He was majoring in advertising and at the time I was determined to be a librarian. I say "determined" as if that will count for something since I didn't finish my degree and so wasn't qualified for any library science jobs going forward. But after I had Catherine and a few years went by and the world of the Internet opened up, I found a different kind of researching—one I could do from my own living room. I pretty much never looked back after that.

Bob was a good provider and because he was outgoing and accommodating, he moved up the ladder quickly, first as an advertising copywriter and then into creative supervision which he was born to do.

I have to say we've been happy. Or at least happy enough. We adore our only child and we're so familiar with each other that I feel a peace that I can't imagine I'd have any other way.

We stopped at the hotel reception desk so Bob could request our AC unit be fixed. I didn't remember seeing the desk clerk yesterday so maybe it was his day off because I'm pretty sure even I would have remembered him.

The man pushed his face into a scowl of displeasure when Bob made his request. Because the French don't typically smile for no reason, many Americans misunderstand the French attitude and believe the French are all anti-American snobs. I knew better, but still I'd have to say that in this case they might not be wrong. This guy didn't like Americans.

"I am sorry, Monsieur," the clerk said dismissively. "It cannot be fixed until after the weekend."

"Then we'll need a different room," Bob said firmly.

I was already heading to the dining room for breakfast but I stopped and looked at Bob.

"You go ahead," he assured me. "I'll pack us up and move us."

I don't know about you but the idea of my husband

scraping all my bathroom cosmetics from the shelf into my carry-on was less appealing than missing breakfast. We both went back to the room, packed up and moved our things to the new room.

This one didn't open up onto the street and so there was no issue with street noise if we'd been inclined to open our window in the evening. And the AC unit in the window hummed reassuringly.

I could tell by how the desk clerk behaved that he thought we were typical Americans—demanding and hard to please. All my smiles and thank-yous had done precisely nothing to erase that assessment and so I decided to just stop trying with him. It was what it was. The temperature outside was in the high nineties. There was no way these Americans could endure a night without air conditioning.

After breakfast in the hotel, we set out for a morning of shopping and exploring. Bob had heard about a recent opening of a museum which focused on the liberation of Paris and since he was a bit of a history buff—especially World War II—that was a must-see.

But first we walked to a nearby park.

I have to say it's lovely when you just aimlessly walk, not really knowing where you're going or what you want to do. It's so different from how we tend to live our lives: so driven and goal-focused.

Truthfully I can't remember the last time Bob and I took a proper vacation. Because of his agency work there was always a client issue or a product launch that was screamingly urgent that always took precedence over family plans.

Plus, Catherine didn't travel well when she was younger, although thank God, she didn't inherit my affliction—and yes, it's intensely genetic. One in fifty chance, I read somewhere. So I'm beyond grateful that she dodged *that* bullet. No, she didn't travel well for the same reasons many children don't. They get bored, they don't like to sit still on buses or airplane seats, they like their own food and their own beds.

Honestly, I can totally relate.

On our way to a park I'd read was nearby Bob and I stopped at two *boulangeries* and picked up *croissants* and *palmiers.* I had the idea I might want to nibble on them later back at the hotel. That was before I remembered how hard it was to be hungry in Paris. Food was everywhere—and such a wide variety of enticing food—and so much better than what I could find back home.

The closer we got to lunchtime, the higher the temperatures climbed. We walked into the park and found a bench under a huge oak tree and managed to eat six of the *palmiers* as we watched two little boys play under the watchful eye of their Asian nanny.

"Catherine would love it here," Bob said as we watched the children play. I wondered if he was thinking of her as a child. Catherine had been a fairly serious child, loving and sensitive but because we never managed a sibling for her, I always worried she was lonely.

Like her parents before her, Catherine went off to college and met the person she would eventually marry. Bob always believed we were lucky to have found each other so soon in our lives and because I have a few friends who never did find their significant others and also because I thought it would be a little rude to disagree with him, I never vocalized the thought that I might not have minded being on my own for a couple of years before meeting him.

But what was the point of thinking that? We had Catherine and a happy, solid marriage and I wouldn't have done anything to change whatever led up to my achieving those things.

When I hear myself thinking *solid*, a voice in my head automatically says *boring*. But boring is fine with me. If boring means trustworthy and dependable, then it's just fine.

We watched the children until they and their nanny left the park and then we left too. Right outside the park we found a bookstore—something that had become harder and harder to find back in Atlanta—and while we had little hope of finding a book in English, we went in and browsed for nearly an hour.

I bought a handful of bookmarks and notecards with watercolor depictions of Notre Dame Cathedral and the Eiffel Tower. I wasn't sure what I'd do with them beyond sticking them on the fridge when I got home. But they were so romantic and pretty, I had to have them.

After the bookstore, it was past one o'clock and we both found we could probably manage lunch. We walked until we found a restaurant with a terrace but it was too hot to sit outdoors so we settled for a table inside by the window where we could look out onto the street with its wide avenues and green shade trees.

As we waited for our meals to come—a *salade Niçoise* for me, *boeuf bourguignon* for Bob—I felt a sense of peace. I thought I could be happy sitting in that little restaurant for the rest of the afternoon, it was so tranquil. Bob was hunched over his cell phone but I'd expected that.

"You're missing the view," I said to him after ten minutes had passed and he was still texting and scrolling.

"I saw the view," he said absentmindedly.

"Crisis back at the agency?" I asked, feeling the beginning threads of annoyance.

"No, no. Just checking on things."

When our meals came, he put the phone down if not away and gave me a forced smile. There was something in the way he smiled at me that made me feel like I was one more thing ticked off his to-do list but I quickly scolded myself for the thought.

After lunch, I was tempted to order dessert but I knew I'd need *some* sort of appetite for dinner tonight and so I resisted.

Bob signaled for the check.

"Interested in hitting the museum?" he asked with a yawn.

"It's Tuesday. They're all closed today. Besides, you look like you're having trouble keeping your eyes open."

"It's this damn jet lag," he said ruefully. "I must be getting old."

"Never."

He reached over and took my hand.

"Have I told you lately how gorgeous you are?"

I felt a flair of pleasure at his words. Honestly, it had been a while since he really noticed me. That's another great thing about leaving town. Your partner is forced to look at you pretty much non-stop.

"I'm sure I look terrible," I said, pushing a tendril of dark hair behind one ear. I keep my hair colored and I play a little tennis. I watch what I eat and I try to stay fit. At least for my age.

"Not for a minute," he said, his eyes glittering as he regarded me. "But I *am* ready for a nap. Do you mind?"

The waiter put the check on the table and Bob pulled out his wallet.

"Not at all," I said. "But if you don't mind I think I'll do a little shopping. I saw a boutique a few blocks back with this adorable macramé purse in the window I think Catherine would love."

Bob laughed. "How fortunate our daughter is to have a mother who knows her well enough to know exactly what she'll love."

"Well, I don't know about that," I said, pleased again at his words. I gathered up my purse.

He dropped three twenties on the plastic tray on top of our bill and stood up, pausing long enough to lean over and kiss me on the mouth. Once we were on the sidewalk outside the restaurant, he looked both ways and frowned.

"Which way is the hotel?" he asked.

I laughed and held out my hand.

"Give me your phone. I'll plot a walking course from here to there."

He grinned. "What would I do without you?"

"I shudder to think," I said, my heart swelling with pleasure as I tapped in the address to the hotel.

4

LANGUAGE BARRIER

The purse was perfect for Catherine. A pale melon-colored macramé clutch with a simple clasp. It was just different enough to get the admiration of the other moms in Cameron's carpool but not weirdly different. I took my time in the shop. I could tell the salesperson was watching me.

My French language mastery is basic and my accent immediately recognizable as American. I'm not saying I don't make most Parisians cover their ears in horror at my pronunciation but I can at least make myself understood.

Plus I'm not like a lot of Americans who get their feelings hurt because French people don't throw open their arms to embrace me as a relative or long-lost friend. Honestly, how they react to strangers is not unlike how I do myself. I'm hesitant to say that's a result of my being half French and more, again, because of this damnable affliction I have.

Our dinner reservations were for a place that one of Bob's people at the agency had recommended off Quai Saint-Michel by Notre-Dame. Because the French are happy to eat late, I was pretty sure I could stop for a coffee and a *pain au chocolat* and not worry about ruining my appetite for dinner.

There was a café not too far from the hotel that I'd seen on our walk this morning and I thought it would be perfect for my late afternoon snack.

When I got there I saw that I was not the only person who had that idea but there was a vacant table on the outer terrace.

I sat down and signaled to the waiter who looked at me but didn't react otherwise. I wasn't worried. He'd come over in his own time.

I settled my packages by my chair and checked my phone in case Bob had awoken from his nap and might be interested in joining me for a coffee. There were no messages from him. I turned off roaming at least for now since I knew the charges would be astronomical and resolved to enjoy a completely phone-free, Wi-Fi free moment.

When the waiter finally came over I ordered a *noisette* and my *pain au chocolat* and then just relaxed and watched the people walk by—or skate or scooter or pedal by.

Of course they were all young people. I used to be in a hurry too, I thought. I tried to imagine where they were all going that was so urgent. School? Not at this hour. Home for dinner? Again, wrong time. I looked around the café and saw several people had glasses of beer and peanuts so it was possible the scooters and bikers were hurrying to get some place so they could sit and chill out with a drink.

Seemed rather oxymoronic but then, it's important not to judge other cultures. I'm pretty sure mine couldn't stand up to very close scrutiny either.

After paying for my coffee, I turned my phone back on to see if I'd received any messages. Still nothing. I texted Bob alerting him that I was about to arrive in case he wanted to get in the shower first and reminded him we had reservations for eight o'clock.

I checked my watch. It was just before five. Plenty of time to shower, change and walk very slowly down the boulevard Saint-Germain until it dead-ended at Pont de Sully near the restaurant. It was a hot day but my weather app said it promised to be a gloriously pleasant evening.

Tonight would be perfect walking weather and that was something I never got to do in Atlanta where one had to get in a car even to walk the dog.

Not that I had a dog but if I did the dog park or any walking trails weren't located anywhere near where we live in Buckhead.

We had a dog when Catherine was small. He was a mutt, a lab mix and I quite enjoyed him but Bob hadn't been raised with animals—possibly it was all the teasing he was sure he'd attract with his last name Baskerville. He complained about the poor animal for the entire time we owned him.

I think we were all at least half relieved when it finally made its trek over the rainbow bridge. All except Catherine of course, but by then she was away at school and remarked on poor little Chewie's passing with a chirpy "Oh, well. Sorry, Mom."

I never did know why she was sorry. Except she obviously saw Chewie as company for *me* when she left.

I picked up my shopping bags to head back to the hotel.

I wasn't hit as hard as a lot of people I knew with the whole empty nest thing. For one thing, Catherine went off to college only an hour away at the University of Georgia and was home most weekends. And also, I'd come to my limit on being able to come up with nutritious meals for three—well, *two,* since Bob as often as not would work late.

After she left I found myself looking forward to those evenings where it was just me and a tub of yoghurt or a fried egg sandwich. Of course I missed her. But still, it was nice not to have to fuss.

I glanced at my phone to see that while my text was delivered, Bob hadn't responded. That had to mean he was still asleep. I picked up my pace. If he'd been asleep all this time, he would be groggy half the evening and have trouble sleeping tonight. I put a call in to him as I maneuvered down the street.

The call went to voice mail which made me believe he must be in the shower.

There was no way he could sleep through a ringing phone!

Before I crossed the street to the hotel, I saw a flower kiosk on the corner. The old woman manning it was about to close up but I could see she still had some tulips left. We made eye contact and she nodded at me in greeting.

"How much?" I asked.

"Five euros, Madame," she said, already picking the flowers out of the canister and shaking the water drops from their stems. She wrapped them in pale green tissue paper and I handed over the money.

"*Merci*, Madame," I said, turning toward the hotel and already thinking where I would put the flowers so I could see them when I woke up in the morning.

I crossed the street and entered the hotel. As soon as I did I remembered our dealings that morning with the desk clerk. My memory of him was that he was a little weasel of a man with a bad comb over and worse teeth which, thankfully, he didn't attempt to show me with a smile. He would've been hard to forget, even for me.

The reception area was at the top of a platform of three broad steps inside the hotel. I crossed the lobby but before I reached the first step I noticed someone was coming down, forcing me to step aside.

He was coming down quickly and he brushed hard against me and my bags. I was instantly annoyed although I had nothing in the bags that was breakable. But as soon as he was next to me, I could smell him.

That more than anything made me look up at his face. He had somewhat wolfish features with beady eyes but was otherwise unmemorable.

He wore a black denim jacket with some kind of embroidery on the epaulets. Once he was past, I hurried up the remaining steps to the desk. I didn't look behind me since I could hear the bell in the door ringing to indicate the man had exited.

The weasel-looking desk clerk was not at the desk so I banged the bell on the table. He appeared immediately from the backroom, a look of utter disgust on his face. Again, I reminded myself that I was not in America and the French had a right to do things differently.

"*Numero dix-huit*," I said with a smile.

I knew smiling was frowned upon in France but I was not going to change my habit just because I was in Paris. I'm from the South. We smile. About everything.

He passed my room key over to me and I walked to the tiny elevator off to the side of the lobby. I wrestled my way inside, clutching my handbag, armful of tulips and boutique purchases, wondering how in the world anyone managed to use these lifts if they were even a few pounds overweight.

After the swelter of the day, I couldn't wait to get into a shower and change clothes. Once out of the elevator I quickened my pace down the hall. Our new room was the second one from the end. As I neared it, I saw that our door was open.

I slowed, confused. I looked around and then glanced down at my key to make sure it was the right one.

Had Bob stepped out? Maybe to get ice?

Regardless of the fact that I knew there was a perfectly reasonable explanation for why our room door was open, my heart was pounding loudly in my ears.

"Bob?" I said as I pushed the door open wider and looked around the room.

From where I stood in the doorway I could see that Bob was in bed. My initial reaction was annoyance but that quickly gave way to fear.

Would he have fallen asleep with the room door open?

"Bob!" I said sharply, entering the room and dumping my purchases on the desk chair, my eyes sweeping the dresser top where Bob's phone and wallet were.

I turned to the bed, fully expecting to see my husband beginning to rouse himself from where he lay.

Instead, he was perfectly still.

His unseeing eyes stared at the ceiling.

His neck and chest, bathed in blood.

5

LETTING GO

I have no real memory of the next several hours.

In many ways it was like I was in a dream. I think my senses shut down at the sight of Bob on that bed. I'm sure that was shock. But my body—probably trained from years of private investigations—did what I'd been programmed to do.

I turned and stepped into the hall and dialed 999, knowing at some level that I had contaminated a crime scene.

A crime scene.

Standing in the hall with my phone in my hand I wasn't yet thinking in terms of who did this to him. My body just went through the motions of what on some level I knew I needed to do—notify the authorities and remove myself physically from that room.

I say "physically" because my mind has pretty much relentlessly replayed that moment when I saw Bob on the bed.

I didn't remember when the police showed up or what they did when they arrived. I don't remember being put in a police car and driven through the early evening streets of Paris to the police headquarters.

I didn't remember being ushered into the freezing cold interview room that I now found myself in.

I didn't remember the faces of anyone I interacted with.

Well, of course I didn't remember the faces.

Maybe it was the cold or just enough time had passed but I finally woke up from my daze and felt the chill on my skin and smelled the sandwich and coffee in front of me on the metal table. A young police officer was in the room with me. She was watching me and I realized that she considered me a suspect.

In the death of my husband.

The thing about shock is that it protects you. Whether it's a broken arm or the realization that you have suddenly lost a precious loved one, it protects you—at least for a little bit—from the cold biting agony of how your life has now irrevocably changed.

Tears filled my eyes and I stared at the sandwich and the coffee cup.

Because I wasn't sure how much of this nightmare was real, I asked the policewoman, "Is my husband...?"

But I couldn't finish the question. If for one second I had a hope that it was a case of mistaken identity, that I'd walked into someone else's room, or I hadn't gotten a good look at the body on the bed, just the fact that Bob wasn't here with me now would force me to realize the bitter truth.

If it wasn't him on that bed lying in his own blood, then where was he?

"Someone will be in to talk with you soon," the policewoman said in slow French.

I closed my eyes. Now that the protective shock was gone, I needed to focus on not thinking about what I saw.

Except that was exactly what the police would need from me now. For Bob's sake, I needed to try to remember.

~

Those hours sitting with the policewoman did not rush by in a blur. They crawled by with every minute an agonizing revisitation of what I'd seen in that room.

When the detectives finally came to talk to me, what I had to tell them would be critically important.

For Bob's sake. For Catherine's sake.

My body began to shake at the thought of Catherine and the thought of having to tell her what happened to her dad.

"You are all right?" the policewoman asked me, no trace of real concern in her voice.

She thinks I did this to him.

Of course she would. I'm the spouse. I'm the one who found him.

I'm the prime suspect.

I looked at the clock over the door. It was two in the morning.

When the door finally buzzed, I jumped out of my skin but the policewoman just walked to the door and opened it. Two men entered. I knew they had to be the detectives on the case. I was surprised to see that they were both middle-aged.

It was rare to see an older detective in Atlanta. Maybe because of the popularity of all the TV shows, most detectives were in their late twenties, early thirties. Older detectives tended to opt for promotions that kept them in the office in supervisory roles. In my experience, that tired old TV trope of detectives not wanting "desk duty" was baloney.

You didn't usually get killed driving a desk.

The policewoman went back to staring at me, her arms crossed as both detectives came into the room and sat down opposite me.

They looked very similar to me. Both had brown hair, medium height, brown eyes. One had more of the traditional hawkish French nose than the other but not clownishly so. There was nothing extraordinary about either of them. If I met them on the street after today I would never in a million years recognize them again.

"Madame Baskerville?" one of them said. "I am Detective Roman Pellé. This is my partner Detective Jean-Marc LaRue."

I nodded at them, knowing this was not a hand-shaking moment. I tried to see by their eyes if it was just possible that one of them was going to say "*Thankfully you called us just in time. Your husband is in the hospital and will recover.*"

Neither of them said that.

"What happened?" I croaked, realizing I hadn't used my voice in several hours.

"We were hoping you could tell us that," Pellé said pleasantly.

I looked from him to the other one. If this was good cop bad cop, then Pellé was definitely playing the good cop.

Which meant he was the lying cop.

I looked at LaRue who narrowed his eyes at me as though trying to determine if I looked like a husband-killing murderer.

His demeanor was at least honest.

"I came back to the hotel after an afternoon of shopping. The door to our room was half open." I wanted to say "ajar" but didn't know the word for that in French.

"I came into our room and found...and found my husband on the bed." I swallowed hard. I knew they were watching me closely for any signs that I had committed this crime.

Pellé nodded as if I'd answered correctly. "Did you touch the body?"

"No."

"Surely that is unusual? Your husband is lying on the bed in obvious distress? And you didn't go to him?"

"He...wasn't distressed when I saw him," I said, taking in a long breath.

After that they asked me when we came to Paris and why we came to Paris and if we were going through a bad patch in our marriage and if I was angry at him for any reason. I expected them any minute to ask me where I'd hidden the murder weapon but I guessed they'd get around to that in their own time.

They asked me about our lives back in Atlanta, where Bob worked, what I did with my time, how many children we had, where they were, when we married, and so on and so on.

It went on like that for hours until finally—because I was just so tired—I caught myself answering without realizing it. My mouth was moving but I wasn't thinking about what was coming out of it. I knew that was dangerous. Even though I was innocent, they would try to move me to the front of the line as far as suspects were concerned. It stood to reason.

I was sure Paris couldn't be that different from Atlanta in that regard. Case clearance rates were always an important factor in promotions and raises or even just job pride. A crime that wasn't solved in the first forty-eight hours stood much less of a chance of ever being solved.

And unsolved cases didn't look good in your employment file if you were a detective.

I wasn't sure because of the whole cultural differences but if I had to guess I'd say that two fifty-plus year old men still beating the bushes as detectives probably hadn't managed their careers very well.

But maybe that's just my view of things.

Which understandably was a little dark at the moment.

6

A LONG TIME COMING

The clock over the wall said it was five in the morning. The policewoman had left twice, both times to get coffee and water. She was gone now and returned with a bag of *canelés* that she set in the middle of the table.

The first thing I thought of was, *this is a trick*.

If I reach for a roll they'll take it as evidence that I'm not stricken with grief by what happened to my husband.

My stomach growled. I had no idea how much longer they would keep me here and I'd missed dinner. I was already babbling with no real memory of what I was saying. I needed to keep my strength up.

I reached for a *canelé* and ate it in two bites. I'm sure they saw that as callous, the uncaring American stuffing her face with pastries hours after she killed her husband.

I couldn't help that. I needed the carbs. I needed to stay strong.

"I've told you what I know," I said wearily. "Can you tell me now what you think happened?"

Both of them looked at each other. Pellé selected a *canelé* and put it on a napkin in front of him but didn't eat it.

"Your husband was killed by a serrated knife slash across the throat," he said as he indicated across his own throat the direction of the cut.

I felt the *canelé* begin to inch its way up from my stomach.

"When?" I managed to say.

This wasn't some backwoods berg. This was Paris. Their medical examiner would have made at least a rough estimate of time of death by now. Even I knew that Bob walked back to the hotel at two in the afternoon. Unless he got lost which granted was possible it would have taken him fifteen minutes to arrive at the hotel. I found his body at around five thirty. That meant the window for time of death was two and a half hours.

But they already knew that.

"We won't know until after the autopsy," LaRue said.

I turned to look at him, registering that I didn't like him. Even if he wasn't silently accusing me of killing my husband, I think I wouldn't have liked him no matter how I met him.

Now that I knew about the serrated knife, did I know as much as they did?

What *I* knew was that unless the killer was already in the room waiting for Bob somebody must have come to the hotel room door, Bob answered it, was attacked and fell onto the bed where he bled to death.

I was pretty sure if I asked these two *why* they thought Bob was killed they'd turn the question around on me.

They weren't looking outside this interview room for the murderer. Case clearance rates are very serious matters to two guys circling the drain on promotion probability rosters.

"I assume you've asked the desk clerk about the time I left and returned to the hotel," I said.

They said nothing.

"And I can give you the name of the shop I visited and also the café."

Although honestly, I knew neither of those people would

have any reason to remember what time I was at their shop or café.

"I bought flowers from the old lady across the street from the hotel," I said. "She was just packing up so that should help determine the time."

Again, the two of them just stared at me.

"I didn't kill my husband," I said, clenching my jaw. "You are wasting time when you could be canvasing the street and talking to other people."

"Is that so?" LaRue said.

It's official. I hate this guy.

"I saw someone leaving the hotel," I blurted out, hoping against hope this information wouldn't blow up in my face. "He was leaving as I was arriving yesterday evening."

"Surely that is not unusual for any of the forty-plus guests staying at the hotel?" LaRue said to me.

"I would have thought all forty of those people are possible suspects," I said tightly. "But this guy didn't look like a guest. He was scruffy-looking and unkempt. Ask the desk clerk. He'll remember him."

Except the desk clerk hadn't been at his counter at the time this guy walked past me.

Pellé opened his notepad to a new page.

I knew what was coming.

"Can you describe him?"

And there it was.

"I didn't get a good look," I said.

Except of course I *had* gotten a good look. I'd gotten such a good look that the scruffy bastard and I had even locked eyes. I remember feeling repelled as I looked into those eyes and I even remember vaguely wondering *what kind of hotel is this that someone like him is staying here*?

But recall his features I could not.

I couldn't tell the detectives the truth. I couldn't tell them I'd looked right into the guy's face as he was leaving the hotel.

How could I tell them that and then fail to describe what he looked like?

"It's all a blur," I lied.

They waited. Nobody spoke for several long moments.

"I'm afraid we must keep your passport for the time being," Pellé said. "You cannot go back to your hotel. Do you need help finding another room?"

I thought he was a breath away from saying *Enjoy your time in Paris* but he didn't.

"I don't need help," I mumbled, just glad to be allowed to leave.

When I stood up, Pellé did too and reached out a hand as if to assist me. Our eyes met and I swear there was something in them I hadn't seen before.

In fact there was something in them I hadn't seen from a man other than Bob for at least twenty years.

I swear I didn't imagine it.

Welcome to France, I thought in numb amazement as I made my way out of the room. Pellé walked behind me to show me the way out.

We stopped in the lobby.

"I am very sorry, Madame," Pellé said solemnly, "for your loss."

It was the first time anyone had registered what had happened to me and tears streaked down my cheeks. He put a warm, supporting hand on my shoulder and I actually felt a bit stronger as a result of it.

"We will be in touch," he said before nodding and turning to disappear back down the hall.

I turned toward the door. When I stepped out, I felt a sudden spasm of fear and sickness engulf me. Bob wasn't waiting anywhere to hear my story or to put his arms around me. He wasn't anywhere in the world anymore.

I was in Paris all by myself.

I was in the world all by myself.

Pushing those thoughts away, I hadn't taken two steps when my phone began to ring. My first thought was that it must be the police calling me to come back inside.

I pulled out my phone from my purse and saw a number on the screen that I didn't recognize. It was an international number.

"This is Claire Baskerville," I said robotically.

"This is Joelle Lapin," a cold flinty voice said on the line. "I am calling to inform you that your father has died."

7

HOMEWARD BOUND

That last week in Paris was without doubt the worst of my life. There were several more lengthy conversations with the two detectives, as well as with people from Bob's agency back in Atlanta. And the funeral home. And Bob's attorney. And my stepmother.

And Catherine.

If I took all the horrible things that happened that last week and piled them together, including the moment I looked on that hotel bed and saw Bob, I'd have to say that that brief, tragic transatlantic phone conversation with my daughter would cap them all.

Just listening to her cry, her shocked voice asking *why*? over and over again was enough to break my heart in every way a heart could shatter.

And the thing was, of all the questions the police asked me and of all the useless facts that ricocheted around in my own brain about that day, I have to say that the *why* equation was the single biggest question that did not look like it was going to get answered.

Bob died in a foreign hotel room. Brutally. Senselessly. Deliberately.

And nobody knew why.

There was nobody in the airplane seat next to me, for which I was grateful. I was flying home business class and had already swaddled myself in the airport-issue blanket, a glass of orange juice on the folding tray table in front of me.

It seemed to me if you lived a whole long life—a complete and detailed life of surviving childhood and your parent's usually well-meaning attempts to raise you and you made it through adolescence with the world's constant attempts to publicly humiliate you and you clawed your way through college and first love and final love and managed to do what was necessary to have a successful career and raise your own kids—it seemed to me that when that life was snuffed out the very frigging least anyone should know is *why*.

I didn't know what to tell Catherine about that or anybody else back in Atlanta who might ask me. I didn't know what to tell myself when I sat during a million different moments in the day and, God knows, the night without him and found myself not knowing why I didn't have him anymore.

Why? Why wasn't he still in my life? Why wasn't he going to continue being my husband and Catherine's father? Why wasn't he going to go into retirement and deal with all the fast-approaching indignities of old age with me? Why was he gone?

It seemed to me that that was the least the Paris police could do since it happened on their watch.

But once the police were at least moderately satisfied that I hadn't killed my husband, they seemed to stop caring about who might have. They did come up with a theory that it was a robbery gone wrong. I'm sure they counted on me being so beside myself with grief that I wouldn't notice the fact that I'd seen Bob's wallet on the dresser.

The robbery must have gone seriously wrong if the robber didn't even take a wallet left out in plain sight.

My mind went back to the question of police department efficiency statistics. It wasn't unusual for a tricky homicide with no convenient murderer to arrest to be shelved as an unsolved case to then wither in the stagnant icebox of cold cases while the police got on to more exciting, *i.e. easier to solve* cases.

So the *why* question would continue to be asked, at least by me and Catherine for as long as we both lived. But as far as I could see we were the only ones asking it.

In the five days since the police grew bored with me and finally released Bob's body to be transported back to the States, I'd seen Detective Pellé two more times. Each time was shorter than the last but the less suspicious he became, the nicer he became.

I couldn't believe I was sharing this flight home with Bob. But instead of sitting next to me in business class he was in the airliner hold in a wooden box.

Bile began to burn in the back of my throat and I felt an uncontrollable shudder sweep through my body.

The flight attendant came by to offer me another blanket which I took gratefully. We would land in Atlanta in two hours. On the one hand I was relieved to be back in the States and I desperately wanted to hold Catherine in my arms. But on the other hand, I dreaded seeing the devastation in her eyes. She was close to her dad. As an only child, and an only girl, of course she was.

Thank God she had Todd. I didn't love Todd. He rubbed me the wrong way and I thought he was gratingly paternalistic with Catherine. Bob used to say that if Catherine didn't mind, I shouldn't. But I couldn't help how I felt. I could only hide how I felt.

It was impossible to sleep on the flight home. Every time I closed my eyes, I saw that hotel room.

I picked up a magazine from the seat pocket to distract myself and promptly thought of my father.

How coincidentally bizarre was it that Claude would die the same week as Bob?

I shook my head in bewilderment. Joelle said he'd had a massive heart attack so at least there was no hint of foul play. He'd been a heavy smoker and it was frankly a miracle he'd lived to the ripe old age of eighty-eight.

I tried to plumb my emotions to see how I felt about his death but honestly I already had a full plate in that regard and I hadn't really known him.

My stepmother had been acid-tongued on the phone the three times I'd been forced to interact with her. She wasn't happy about my inability to attend the memorial service she was preparing for him.

I don't know what she expected from me—surely she couldn't have anticipated too much more after the nonentity I'd always been in their lives—but clearly she had.

She'd mentioned something about their apartment which made it sound like Claude had left it to me in his will but that was patently absurd. Joelle, on the other hand, didn't seem to think it was absurd at all.

She seemed to think it was nothing short of a crime. Her third and final phone call to me this morning was to tell me that she would have her things out of the apartment by the end of the week. I told her it wasn't necessary but she wouldn't hear me.

Honestly, I didn't have the emotional bandwidth to argue with her. So I guess it looks like I have an apartment in Paris.

Which is just about the last place on earth I ever want to go again.

8

THE FIRST CUT IS THE DEEPEST

I met Catherine and Todd outside the international terminal of the Atlanta airport at seven in the evening. Catherine looked exhausted. Her eyes were red-rimmed and when we greeted she didn't so much hug me as cling to me.

We stood there in the middle of the frenetic hustle and bustle of the second busiest airport in the world and held each other. It was going to take a long time to begin to buffer the agony of losing Bob but as we stood there holding each other I felt like we'd taken the first step in that direction.

They'd brought the baby with them although he was asleep in Todd's arms. Well, I call him the baby, but at three Cameron wasn't a baby anymore. As soon as I saw him the first thing that came to my mind was the fact that Bob was never going to know who Cameron grew into. He was never going to take him fishing or impart grandfatherly advice to him. He was never going to know the man Cameron would someday become.

It occurred to me that I had a lot more of those kinds of observations to look forward to in the months and years to come.

The drive from the airport to our condo in Buckhead was a

quiet one. I'd made arrangements for Bob to be transported from the airport to White and Fowler, the funeral home I'd contacted from Paris. I think in a way Catherine had been expecting to connect with her father at least though his coffin but I knew that wasn't going to be a good idea and was glad it wasn't an option.

When we got home, I was hit with a whole new set of sickening emotions. It was bad enough to lose Bob in a foreign country. But here I was surrounded by his things. And worse than that, I was surrounded by those things that he'd just placed there as if he would be back at any moment to pick them back up.

I know everybody who loses someone suddenly goes through this. Funny how knowing that doesn't make it any easier.

The section of Atlanta where Bob and I lived was a subset of the more upscale Buckhead neighborhood. Surrounded by multi-million-dollar homes and townhomes, we benefited from the top-end landscaping and beautifully designed parks and streets.

Just not the astronomical property taxes.

As soon as we entered the condo, Catherine took Cameron up to the guest room to put him to bed and Todd went out to pick up a few things for the morning, mostly breakfast items for Cameron.

I forced myself not to look around my home and see signs of Bob. There would be plenty of time for that in the coming months. Plenty of time for me to focus on his things, his special touches, to find something of his and be reminded all over again that he was no longer in the world.

Once Todd got back, he poured both me and Catherine bourbon and waters and then went into the kitchen to make omelets for our supper. I have to say I'd never seen this side of him—the caretaking side. And I have to say his taking charge the way he did this first night was a godsend.

Maybe Catherine wasn't so misguided after all.

I rolled my bag to our bedroom but didn't bother unpacking. Catherine was waiting for me in the living room. I'd already told her everything I knew to tell her but the grieving process tends to involve a lot of repetition. I'd learned that in just the brief time I'd been bereaved.

Catherine pulled her legs under her on the couch and sipped her drink. She looked more like Bob than she did me. She had light brown hair, big blue eyes and full lips. I have dark hair. Or at least I did several decades ago before I began coloring my hair to cover up the gray.

"And then on top of this, your father dies too," she said to me, tilting her head as if to gauge how that was affecting me.

"I know. But you know I didn't really know him."

"And the cops still don't know who did this?"

"They think it was a robbery."

"Burglary," Todd said as he stepped into the room with a drink in his hand. "When it's a break-in, it's considered a burglary."

I'm sort of surprised he'd have the face to correct me since I'm sure he knows I used to work with law enforcement and so of course knew the difference. I was further amazed at how little his conceit mattered to me. At least tonight.

"Right," I said. "Burglary."

"And they have no suspects at all?" Catherine asked, her voice trembling with tears. I knew she probably needed to ask me this all over again but I was pretty sure it wasn't going to make her feel any better.

"I think one of the detectives told me they had a lead about a thug who operated in the area."

That was a lie. There was no lead, no thug and no helpful detective telling me jack squat. But I also knew how helpful it was to hear that somebody was doing something to get to the bottom of why a beloved father would not be sitting around the Christmas dinner table ever again.

"Omelets are ready," Todd said solemnly.

"Thank you for doing this, Todd," I said mechanically. I wasn't at all hungry. Catherine looked like she felt much the same but she smiled encouragingly at her husband and I again felt that fissure of annoyance.

Somehow we were both trying to make *Todd* feel better.

As we took our seats at the table, Todd poured the wine and began to talk about the Anaheim peppers he'd found at Kroger this evening which he'd put in the omelets. I knew it wasn't fair to judge him. He'd never been particularly close to Bob.

But he was behaving as if nothing remarkable had happened.

"What time is the service tomorrow?" Catherine asked.

The funeral home had only one available slot for Bob and that was tomorrow afternoon. His ad agency was handing most of the arrangements if not the actual bill. But they were hosting the reception afterwards.

Bob had been with the company for ten years and he was well-liked and admired. I was grateful for their help.

With all the feelings rippling through me, it was one less thing to have to think about.

9

ADIEU, ADIEU

The next morning the sky was clear and uncluttered by clouds—typical for Atlanta in August. I didn't dare open a window and let out any precious air conditioning, but as beautiful as it looked outside I knew the temperature would be unpleasantly warm.

As usual when I woke up I was overcome with the fresh horror of what had happened, compounded by the fact that I could look at Bob's empty side of the bed and at his bedside table with his Apple watch charger that he would never need again.

I forced myself to look away. I heard my bedroom door creak open hesitantly.

"It's just me," a small voice said.

The thing I've recently learned about children—even beyond what I already knew having raised Catherine—is that everything else takes a back seat to their most frivolous needs. Your leg is hanging by a thread? You may deal with it as soon as you make Madame Haley or Master Brody their PB&Js just the way they like it.

Cameron was thoughtful and sweet but he was still a child

and therefore fully qualified to distract you from the gloom and tears that threatened even for the most dire reasons.

You can't fall apart when a child needs you to read to him or play Old Maid with him. That's just a rule of life.

And thank God for it.

"Come give me a kiss, Just Me," I said.

He climbed onto the bed and settled down beside me.

"I miss Grandpa," he said.

I smoothed his hair over his forehead. He didn't sound sad so he was saying what he believed he should say to me. He was trying to comfort me and I loved him so much for it that I thought I might start crying.

"I know," I said. "Me too."

Bob had been a good grandfather. But like a lot of men, he'd been less interested while Cameron was still so young. I'm not sure what kind of memories Cameron would have of his grandfather going forward.

Probably none that Catherine and I didn't invent for him.

The manicured lawns of White and Fowler spoke of serenity and peace even before you stepped through their doors. The memorial service would be held in the home's chapel although we didn't belong to a church. Bob wasn't religious and after getting Catherine through ten years of Sunday school, I'd fallen away too.

The first people I saw when I walked into the funeral home was the account executive team at Bob's agency Barter and Colum. I have to say I was surprised to realize how young they all were. I know advertising is a young person's business but because Bob had loved it with his whole heart he had always seemed just the right age for it.

Now that I saw his coworkers, I realized that at least some of them had to be thinking he would have been better off retiring and making room for someone with more energy and bigger ideas. Someone younger.

The woman who worked closely with Bob, Anita Jansen, hurried over to me when Catherine, Todd and I entered the building. Todd held Cameron in his arms. I hugged Anita and felt nearly every bone in her body through her silk chiffon blouse. She was probably fifty—getting a little long in the tooth for this business herself—and worked out religiously as though that and the surgeon's knife would fool everyone into thinking she still belonged.

"Claire, darling," she said, holding my hand so tightly I nearly winced. "What you've been through."

"Thanks, Anita," I said.

She tucked my hand through her arm and pulled me along to the double doors that led into what I imagined was the viewing room. There was nothing to view as I well knew. If the slit to Bob's throat could be camouflaged—which I had no doubt it probably could've—the Paris autopsy would be less easy to conceal. The body would be at the crematorium in any event. I swallowed hard and pushed the image away. I had a long day to get through.

I looked around the room and saw a huge twenty by sixty framed photograph of Bob standing next to Steve Jobs. I knew for a fact that Bob hadn't even spoken to Jobs at that event. But still, it was a nice photo.

I nodded at a few people in the room, people that Bob had worked with in the ad business, but mostly people from his own agency. I didn't know very many of them.

Over the years, the ones we used to socialize with—the ones our age—had retired, either by choice or not. Most of the crowd here today was young and Bob had long ago stopped bringing any of them home. What would have been the point? We were at least twenty years their senior. What would we talk about? Whether Ted Kennedy really killed Mary Jo Kopechne? They would have no idea who either of those people were.

One person I did recognize was Courtney Purdue who stood among a throng of other young and adorable women. She was quite pretty with long blonde hair styled in exaggerated curls to her shoulders. She wore a gorgeous dark velvet dress that hugged her every perfect curve. Bob had mentioned her a few times, even suggesting that he saw her as a younger version of himself.

Everyone milling about looked if not sad then at least taciturn. There were a few chuckles which suggested people weren't sure whether this was a funeral or a wake. The lack of alcohol should have tipped them off.

Anita took me to stand in front of Bob's photo as if she were in some way returning me to his side. I looked around and saw that Todd and Catherine had not ventured very far inside and were sticking close to each other.

"We're going to miss him so much," Anita said to me, squeezing my arm again. "He was a lion in our business. You know that, right?"

Maybe because Anita and I weren't really friends, I found her comments cursory. I know she was trying to say the right thing and let's face it, her company was paying for the reception afterward. But if she really thought I cared one complete crap about Bob's legacy in the advertising business, then she needed to stop drinking her own Kool-Aid and get out and mingle more with real people.

"Claire!"

I turned to see Abe Newman, our family lawyer. I'd talked with him briefly while I was still in Paris and had expected to see him here. I flushed with relief now, surprising myself at how glad I was to see him.

Admittedly, a part of that had to do with no longer being the oldest person in the room.

"Abe," I said as we hugged. "I'm so glad you could come."

"Of course. Of course," he said, frowning and looking at Anita.

"Well," Anita said suddenly, obviously skilled at taking a hint if nothing else, "I'll check to see if Bill's ready for his speech."

The president of Barter and Colum, Bill Colum—someone I knew not at all—would give the eulogy. I didn't care. I certainly couldn't do it without breaking down and it was nice that *someone* was going to say a few words about Bob.

I turned back to Abe. He was looking around the room and licking his lips.

"Is something wrong?" I asked and before the words were out of my mouth I knew that something was very wrong.

It takes a lot to unsettle an attorney—especially one as experienced and canny as Abe Newman.

"I need to talk to you," he said. "Can you come to my office tomorrow?"

"Yes," I said. "But I'd like a snapshot now."

"Claire," he said and shook his head.

"Is it..."

For a minute I couldn't even imagine what it could be. The only thing I could think of—and I knew he'd instantly laugh at the thought—was money.

"Is it about money?"

His face told me everything. Without words his face said how sorry he was that I was figuratively burying my husband today and after today I'd go out into the world alone and broke.

I honestly didn't know what to say. I'd hear the details of what there was to know tomorrow. I'd hear the how's and the why's and then I'd walk out the door and somehow learn to live with whatever he told me.

"Fine," I said hoarsely. "What time?"

"Whenever is good for you."

That was even worse. If Abe was willing to shuffle his schedule to give me the bad news he must really have very bad news for me.

I nodded and felt his hand rest lightly on my shoulder for a moment in a gesture of encouragement and comfort. After apologizing one more time, he turned and faded into the crowd.

I turned to see Catherine and Todd find seats midway into the congregation. There was a free chair next to Catherine. I wound my way to them and sat down, my heart pounding in my chest, my brain working overtime to stop the scenarios about my visit to Abe's offices tomorrow.

"It will be over soon," I said to Catherine as I sat down. That was a lie. With the reception right afterwards, this would all go on and on and on.

As I sat there, my hands folded in my lap, my eyes on Bob's laughing face in the glossy photo as I tried to imagine exactly how bad the news was that Abe had for me tomorrow I heard a small gasp and turned to its source.

The beautiful agency girls standing by the corner of the photo seemed to be especially attentive to Courtney who stood in the center. Unlike every single person in the room, his wife and daughter included, Courtney was seriously crying.

My first impulse was gratitude to see how much Bob must have meant to her but that emotion soon gave way to another less comfortable feeling. There was something about the *way* Courtney was crying and the way the other girls were consoling her that made me feel slightly nauseated.

Before I'd started doing strictly skip tracing work in the years after Catherine had gone off to college, I'd done quite a bit of private investigator work. Most of my cases centered on cheating spouses. After a few months I used to pride myself on my ability to instantly see the signs of infidelity.

Just obviously not in my own marriage.

10

DAYS OF WINTER

The afternoon sun filtered through the leafy canopy of the Linden trees that hovered over me on the bench where I sat in the Parc Monceau. The weather in Paris was much cooler than when I was here last—two weeks ago—and I was wearing one of my sweaters I usually don't get out of my cedar storage chest back in Atlanta until November.

I sat and watched the children squeal and laugh as they ran past me chasing balls, chasing each other, their nannies and minders walking quickly behind them.

I have no idea how I got through those last two weeks in Atlanta.

From Bob's memorial service to the endless reception at his agency afterward, my stomach plummeting with every sight that I caught of the distraught and tragically beautiful Courtney, to the meeting in Abe's office the next morning where he dropped the bombshell that not only was I completely broke but in debt up to five hundred thousand dollars—it had been a gruesome and interminable two weeks.

I discovered that it might take a full five weeks for a lab to create a mouth guard or nine months for a complete baby to form, but amazingly when the vultures get together on their laptops and smart phones to confirm the death of one of their debtors, things can happen lightning fast.

I hadn't been back in Atlanta three days before the truck arrived to clear out every stick of furniture in our townhouse.

In what then seemed like a sickening snowball effect, the creditors lined up behind the furniture truck. Abe had given me the name of a bankruptcy consolidator who would sell our condo—which, it was soon revealed, we were seriously upside down in—and both our cars.

The credit cards were the first things to go. There was now absolutely no money coming in. The pension fund and 401k's had been tapped out months ago. Bob had been able to keep the creditors at bay only because he was still employed.

Dead, he was a whole lot less attractive to them.

Abe had no real answers for me as to how we came to be in such dire straits. Oh, it was clear that Bob was spending beyond what he could afford and it was possible there was some online gambling involved that I had no clue about.

Just one of several things it appears I had no clue about.

So here I was. Sixty years old, five years from being eligible for Medicare. My healthcare benefits had evaporated with Bob's job. And I absolutely could not afford to buy insurance. The only income I could look forward to was my social security —but that was still two years away—and since I'd worked very little for most of that time—and not made a lot of money when I did—I wasn't expecting much.

At one point I actually thought about approaching Courtney to see if *she* knew where all the money went. I thought about that for about thirty seconds before deciding that knowing the truth wasn't worth her knowing how totally out of Bob's confidence I was.

She probably didn't know either.

A little girl's laughter made me turn my head. I watched her run and disappear around the far side of an Egyptian pyramid to my right. I smiled in spite of myself.

And so here I am. Back in, of all places, Paris.

On my birthday.

In all the bedlam of the last few weeks the fact of my approaching birthday had gotten lost. I really only remembered it when I found myself waiting for a taxi at Charles DeGaulle two days ago looking at my passport.

I'm sure anyone walking by must have been at least mildly disturbed to hear a sixty-something woman laugh out loud while waiting in the taxi line with her bags.

Or maybe like me they were all just too busy with their own problems to notice the singular travesties of their fellow travelers.

Catherine was horrified that I would even consider going back to Paris so soon. I was able to explain it by saying I needed to sort out my father's estate. That wasn't a lie. I did have a meeting with my father's solicitors to find out how I was involved in Claude Lapin's estate.

But mostly I was here because I have a roof over my head here. It was true I had the use of a guest room at a couple of benevolent friends' houses once the condo was cleared out. And I was grateful. Beyond grateful. Because of my disability, it's hard for me to make friends so I don't have lots of them. The ones I have are gold-standard.

But no matter how good your friends are, nobody wants to be living off them for any length of time.

I didn't have much anymore. But what I did have was one place that appeared to be mine. And so I borrowed the cost of a plane ticket from Abe, who I have to say was behaving slightly complicit and guilty, and I came back to Paris.

And maybe if I was honest I can admit that for a million different reasons I couldn't wait to get out of Atlanta. Maybe that was because I now saw my life there with Bob as the lie that it clearly was. Maybe it was because everyone at the memorial service knew the truth about him and his girlfriend —and I pray that our sweet Catherine didn't pick up on it although from the glower on Todd's face that day he clearly did.

In August, the weather in both Paris and Atlanta was beastly, all sultry steam and humidity. So I was surprised to see how much cooler the weather was in Paris.

I glanced at my watch and saw that I had forty minutes before my appointment. The map on my phone told me I was a comfortable thirty minute walk away.

While I had my phone out, I made a call, and then sat watching a little boy in a blue hoodie throw a ball into the air by the water lily pond. He made me think of Cameron.

"*Allo*?"

"Yes, *bonjour*, Detective Pellé," I said into the phone. "This is Claire Baskerville."

I'd decided to make Roman Pellé my unofficial police contact since he'd been at least moderately nice to me. He hadn't tended to look at me as a suspect—or not only as a suspect—like his partner had. In fact, unlike every male over eighteen in Atlanta he didn't look at me as if I were ninety years old.

Amazingly, he looked at me as if he could imagine me in my skivvies. Or less.

"Ah, yes, Madame Baskerville. How are you?" His voice was warm and earnest.

"I'm better, thanks. I'm calling because I was wondering if there was any more news on my husband's case?"

There was a pause on the line which I filled with my own assumption that he hadn't even thought about the case since before I flew home to Atlanta. This was no less than what I'd expected but hope must have been wedged in there somewhere because I felt totally deflated by that pregnant pause.

"Ahhhh. *Non*. I am so sorry. There are no new leads but we are always looking, yes?"

"Okay," I said, knowing full well that at least a modicum of smoke was being blown my way but not knowing what I could do about it.

"Are you in Paris again?"

"I am. I inherited some property here. So I'm here to sort it out."

"Ahhhh, *oui*? Then perhaps we could meet for a drink and talk about the case?"

I murmured something to the tune of *that would be nice* and I'd give him a call and I disconnected. Then I sat there and stared at my phone. He was flirting with me. It had been a while but the memory of it came back to me.

I listened to the sounds of the children laughing and then got up to make my way to my appointment.

One thing was for sure.

I was definitely not in Atlanta anymore.

11

SHOOTING STARS

I stepped into the offices of Dubois and Remey, my father's solicitors, and noticed that even if my father hadn't been particularly wealthy, his lawyers most certainly were.

It was a large office set on the second floor of a Haussmann style building on a narrow, manicured lane off the Champs-Élysées.

Inside it was quiet, carpeted, with only the sound of hushed voices as befitting a law office housed in a three-hundred-year-old building.

Today would mark the first time I'd ever laid eyes on my stepmother—the woman my father had married and lived with for the last ten years.

It was not a felicitous moment.

When I saw her I wasn't surprised to see that Joelle was beautiful. At forty-two she was nearly twenty years my junior. Her face was unlined as if neither frowns nor smiles would dare crease her perfect alabaster skin. She was auburn-haired, with almond shaped brown eyes and very trim in her vintage silk Chanel suit. In black, of course.

She sat beside me in one of the massive walnut chairs

facing the attorney's desk and never once looked at me. And while the attorney, Monsieur Jean Dubois—a sharp-featured man with shrewd eyes under a balding dome—*did* in fact register my existence, he did little more.

The preliminary notifications I'd received from his office had indicated I could move into the apartment even before everything was finalized with the understanding that it would only be officially mine after the reading of the will.

The vigor with which Joelle had moved out of the apartment, and her stiffness as she now sat in the attorney's office made it clear to me that she had no doubt as to what the outcome of the meeting would be. There would be no miracles for her. The law was the law.

And in France, the law favored the children of the deceased, not the widow.

After a brief exchange of small talk between the attorney and myself, he folded his hands on his desk and looked from me to Joelle.

"As you know, Madame," he intoned, "in France the spouse is not a protected heir."

I felt Joelle stiffen and found myself wondering why she was even here today.

The attorney turned to me.

"Because you are unfamiliar with French laws," he said condescendingly to me, "you might not know that because your father and Madame Lapin had no children themselves, if not for you, she would have inherited everything."

I was stunned that he would present the information like that—nearly accusatory and in front of Joelle.

"Madame Baskerville had been in infrequent contact with my late husband," Joelle said.

The fact that she spoke surprised me. But it at least explained why she was here. She was hoping to present her case.

But Monsieur Dubois wasn't having it. He looked very much to me like a *the-law-is-the-law kind* of guy.

"Tsk," he said to Joelle, pursing his lips and shaking his head at the same time. "It was the very matter of estrangement from adult children that triggered the necessity of these inheritance laws in the first place. Do I need to outline for you the nightmarish circumstances that are played out every day in America or the United Kingdom as a result of emotional parents excluding some of their children from inheriting while favoring others?"

Joelle made a sound of disgust and turned away. I saw her hands clenched into fists as if to restrain herself.

The attorney turned to the file folder on his desk and flipped it open.

"Claude Lapin's assets include an apartment in the eighth arrondissement," he said solemnly. "Which has been appraised at one million three hundred thousand euros."

I felt my pulse begin to race. That was even more than my realtor was estimating.

"In addition to that he had stocks, bonds and a savings account totaling..."

Dubois squinted at the document and I swear he did it for effect.

"...three million one hundred sixty thousand euros."

I was shocked. I assumed Claude had a little bit of money working but I wouldn't have guessed that much. I glanced at Joelle but she hadn't moved except for a vein throbbing under her left eye which revealed her agitation.

Dubois closed the folder and looked at Joelle.

"As the surviving spouse and as Monsieur Lapin wished, you inherit a quarter of Monsieur Lapin's estate. That comes to one million one hundred and fifteen thousand euros."

I glanced again at Joelle to see if this made her any happier.

But if anything, she was now red in the face, her fists clenching even tighter.

"And as Monsieur Lapin's only child, Madame Baskerville, your portion, which includes the apartment's value, comes to three million three hundred and forty-five thousand euros."

At first I didn't think I'd heard him correctly. I knew I had the apartment and I was expecting possibly a little something more—maybe a collection of silver spoons or a mid-range painting. Maybe yes, even some money.

But nowhere near the range of three million euros.

I was rich.

The sound of Joelle's chair scraping against the hardwood floor filled the room as she stood up and for the first time she looked at me. Her neck was corded tight and another visible vein throbbed there. Her eyes bore into me.

Yes, I was rich, I realized, as I watched her turn and stalk out of the office, the carpet muffling the angry thuds of her Dolce & Gabbana kitten heels.

Rich, and absolutely hated.

12

BLOWING IN THE WIND

The first thing I did once I walked out of the attorney's office was go to a bank and open a checking account in my name. The solicitor had given me an advance on my inheritance—forty thousand euros—which I deposited. I then emailed him the account number for the rest of the money to be deposited.

The feeling of relief as I walked out of that bank with forty thousand euros attached to the debit card in my wallet was nothing less than titanic. I'd only known I was broke, alone and destitute for two weeks, but they had been a life-changing two weeks.

The next thing I did was go to the first café I came to. I ordered a half bottle of good red wine and a fragrant bowl of *poulet Basquaise* redolent with peppers and spices.

I watched people walk by in a numb fog of relief as I ate with a hunger I didn't know I had.

While it was true that Bob died in this city, in many ways I feel as if he had left me long ago back in Atlanta where he was living a double life with Courtney. Although I had mixed feelings about Paris, I was surprised to realize that my feelings about Atlanta and my life back there felt more definite.

And not in a good way.

I had a place to live for the next few weeks at least. I would take the time to get my affairs in order, develop a game plan and maybe even try to recover a little bit.

I left the café and walked back to my apartment building on *rue de Laborde*. My thoughts came back to the memory of Joelle sitting in that solicitor's office with me. As wonderful as my father's money was for me—and it was a life saver—it was extremely uncomfortable to sit there and watch Joelle's face harden by the second as the solicitor droned on and on and in the end gave her only a fourth of Claude's estate.

But surely she'd known that would happen? Didn't she and my father talk about these things? I knew the French were weird about money but honestly!

On the way home I went to the Monoprix store near my apartment and felt a surge of gratification as I loaded my cart with groceries and sundries—yoghurt, wine, baguettes, chocolate and a half dozen *Kouign Amann* from the bakery, bed sheets, new towels and a French press coffee maker.

As I was heading toward the cash register with my trolley I saw a young man standing in one of the aisles who looked vaguely familiar. He looked up and nodded to me but then turned away. I wondered if he lived in my apartment building. If I'd been standing closer I might have been able to recognize his scent—if he wore aftershave or bathed infrequently.

Because of my condition I tend to work extra hard on distinguishing smells and sounds to make up for it.

Over the years it hadn't been as much of a handicap as people might think. When I was younger, it was only the school environment that caused most problems. At school, I kept to myself because other kids always saw me as shy or stuck-up, which meant they didn't reach out to me. That was actually helpful. I was able to get through high school without offending too many people.

But I often wondered how different life would have been if not for my face blindness. I think my natural personality is basically outgoing but had been perverted by the inability to remember anyone's face even seconds after I'd seen it.

When Catherine started school, the problems with my disability resurfaced. Before then, remembering a face was relatively unessential. Who really expected you to remember the cashier at Publix when she popped up at the mall? But just as when I was in school myself, the manifestations of my affliction reared its ugly head when Catherine was school age.

Meeting parents, *remembering* that you'd met them—or worse, had had a meal with them—without then walking right past them the next day, and remembering which little girls were Catherine's friends—and they all dressed and wore their hair alike—was a daily struggle if not a downright impossibility.

There was a minefield of potential humiliations every time I stepped into the after-school care center and braced myself for greeting the dozens of people I was supposed to know on sight but absolutely didn't recognize.

On the other hand...perhaps because of my disability, I have other gifts like my enhanced sense of smell. And while I can't remember a face that I saw even two minutes earlier, I can look at a document or phone number and can recreate it in my mind in complete detail. For a skip tracer, that is a valuable asset.

I left the aisle with the mystery young man behind me and stood in line at the cash register where I paid my bill with my brand new debit card and packed my purchases into my new lime green grocery cart and wondered if my US creditors would somehow be able to see me spending this money.

Could they get to it?

As I walked back to my apartment it occurred to me that, while it was entirely possible that I was still in shock from the dreadful turn my life had taken in the last month, shopping still had its restorative benefits.

While I knew I wasn't trying to start a new life here in Paris I did realize that as I conveyed my purchases down the street that for just a few moments I felt briefly, inexplicably, happy.

13

A RISING TIDE

The table lighting was reflected on the tin tiles stamped with ornate patterns overhead. Roman noted that the hardwood floors were polished to a gleam and gave the inside of the bistro an intimate, cozy feel. Heavy toile café curtains framed the large windows facing the street and the gilded antique framed mirrors on the dark walls presented a touch of understated elegance that announced this was a classic Parisienne brasserie.

Roman looked at the remains of his *coq au vin*. It had been *superbe*. Maybe the best he'd ever eaten. He glanced at Jean-Marc who was scowling at his cell phone.

Roman had to admit that lunch hours were much more pleasant now that he was a detective. Last year this time as a *Brigadier-Chef* he'd be grabbing a Quick Burger to eat alone at his desk.

He eyed his partner across the table. Possibly the company was a bit better back then. But he knew what LaRue had gone through in the last few years.

What he was still going through.

"You will never guess who's back in town," Roman said as

he tossed his credit card down on the bill on top of Jean-Marc's card. "Claire Baskerville."

Jean-Marc frowned. "Why?"

"Seems she inherited some property here in Paris."

"People seem to be dropping dead all around Madame Baskerville," Jean-Marc observed.

"She called me to ask for an update on her husband's case."

Roman hadn't worked that many murders with LaRue before now but there'd been something about the Baskerville case that had seemed strangely personal for Jean-Marc.

"I thought we gave that to her when she left Paris with his body," Jean-Marc said, his mouth twisted into a grimace.

"It appears she believes there's more to it."

"Americans," Jean-Marc said with disgust.

"In any case, I thought I might meet up with her to make sure no feathers are ruffled."

Jean-Marc's eyebrows shot up into his forehead. "Why do you care if her feathers are ruffled?"

Roman shrugged.

Jean-Marc waved to get the waiter's attention.

"She's like every other American," Jean-Marc said in irritation. "She expects to push a button and *voila*! she gets all her answers."

"That is probably true."

"And you have nothing new to tell her."

"I'm just being nice."

"Do you have time for that?"

"I do have a personal life, Jean-Marc."

"Ahhhh."

"What does that mean?"

"Nothing. Good luck with your *personal life*," Jean-Marc said with a sneer. "Just don't be surprised if she doesn't thank you for it."

The waiter came to take their cards and Jean-Marc crossed

his arms and stared unseeing over the heads of the other diners.

Roman wasn't totally sure the Quick Burger hadn't been the more enjoyable experience after all.

14

OVER THE RAINBOW

The next morning I was able to make my own coffee and warm up a croissant that I'd bought at the store yesterday. While I was still pretty chuffed at my newfound wealth, I was wary of getting too comfortable. At eight euros a pop every time I sat down at a café to rest my feet and have a coffee I could easily go through a hundred euros in a week.

Those two weeks in Atlanta being homeless and broke were scorched into my soul. The thought of having no income or assets at my age was still positively terrifying.

I knew someone a few years ago who'd lost her job at a research firm—a position she'd held for nearly five years. She had a PhD and more experience than anyone twice her age but the best she could find after nearly two years of job hunting was a cashier's position at Wal-Mart.

I'm not saying ageism is a thing but it totally is.

In any case, my friend had experience and skills and loads of credentials.

Me, I have forty years of being a housewife and a mother.

With those credentials, even if I were thirty years younger, I don't think *I'd* hire me.

And at sixty? Not a chance.

I checked my phone and saw an email from Abe hinting that the US government might garnish my social security when I was eligible for it.

Can they do that?

I scrolled through the rest of my mail and found a more cheerful one from Gigi my Paris realtor who wanted to meet up with me and do a walk-through of the apartment.

A million three hundred thousand euros?

I glanced around the living room and tried to see it through Gigi's eyes. Nothing about it suggested to me that it might fetch that kind of money. Certainly not compared to the condos or townhouses in the upscale zip codes in Atlanta.

But this was Paris and clearly the rules were different.

I sent her a reply saying I wanted to get the place ready to go on the market.

The sooner the better.

Later that afternoon, after a long bath and a nap, I wrapped up some kitchen trash and went into the hall to try to find the building garbage cans. The downstairs door in the lobby floor was opened with a magnetic key fob and the outside gate was opened with a code. Only my apartment door used an actual key and this I slipped into my pocket.

My apartment was on the third floor which in American is really the fourth floor since the French don't start counting until the second floor for some reason I'm sure I'll never understand. There is an elevator in my building but it's rickety and tiny and honestly scares me to death every time I step into it. So instead I cling to the banister and walk very carefully down the steep stairs. They're slippery and it wouldn't take much to miss a step.

I made the decision that if I didn't have suitcases or groceries, I would always take the stairs which were brutal but still felt safer than the elevator.

Lately my mind had been swimming with a myriad of thoughts—most of them unsettling. I couldn't believe that Detective Pellé—Roman—had basically asked me out. I could be wrong about that but I'm pretty sure I wasn't. After the initial surprise, and even though I've only been a widow for four weeks, I realized that I might want to take him up on it.

Not because I was looking for someone romantically—I'm honestly a thousand years away from ever thinking about dating again—but because I knew meeting him under the guise of a date was a way of getting information from him that he might not normally feel comfortable giving. I couldn't get away from the idea that there was more to Bob's case than the detective was saying. Don't ask me how I know. It's a gut feeling.

And except for those situations where beautiful blonde social media specialists were sleeping with my husband, my gut feelings are pretty reliable.

There are two apartments on each floor in my building. The other apartment on my floor is vacant. I believe the mysterious young man I saw yesterday at Monoprix lives on the second floor as does an elderly couple. That just left a single apartment on the first floor—French first floor, American second floor. As I reached that floor, I could see the apartment door was open.

I slowed my steps but I needn't have. It was clear the occupant was waiting for me.

"*Bonjour*!" she said, stepping out into the hall.

An elderly woman, her height clearly shrunk by her advanced age, stood in the doorway and waved to me. Her hair was curly grey and she had large expressive velvet brown eyes.

She wore a turquoise cashmere sweater around her shoulder clasped by a bejeweled peacock brooch.

I tucked my garbage bag under one arm and we shook hands. She smiled expansively at me which was so unusual in France that I was tempted to believe she must be German or Belgian.

"I am Geneviève Rousseau," she said in English. "Will you come in?"

I hesitated for a moment, then set my kitchen trash on the floor outside her door and followed her inside.

Geneviève's apartment was similar to my own but of course unlike mine it was properly furnished and looked like it had been for decades.

A green velvet Chesterfield sofa anchored the salon in front of a chocolate brown antique coffee table on gleaming herring-bone hardwood floors. Natural linen curtain panels hung from the fifteen-foot windows that allowed a steady stream of golden light from outside. The ceiling was inset with ivory panels as was the framed mirror over the fireplace.

It was as close to a classic Paris apartment as I'd ever seen.

Geneviève's living room faced the interior courtyard, not the street as mine did. I couldn't help but wonder if she had to pay more for that.

"I have tea ready to pour," she called to me over her shoulder as she went to her kitchen.

What would Bob think about all this?

I was surprised as the thought popped into my head. I'd done a pretty good job of either not thinking about him or only thinking about him in sudden angry bursts. It hurt less to be angry at him. I cried less when I was angry with him.

I instantly shook all thoughts of him away.

When Geneviève returned with the tea tray, I stood up to take it from her. I hadn't seen any sign of a male presence and assumed she lived here on her own.

"Thank you so much for inviting me in," I said as she poured tea from the hand-painted teapot into two delicate teacups. "Did you know my father?"

She clucked her tongue and looked at me sadly.

"I am so sorry about your father," she said. "I liked Monsieur Lapin. Very much."

I noticed she didn't say how much she liked *Madame* Lapin.

"Did you know them very well?" I asked as I added milk to my cup.

"*Non*, not well. Madame Lapin was not friendly." She shrugged as if to say that wasn't any big deal but I could imagine Joelle being a bitch—mostly because I've only known her four weeks and I've personally experienced her being nothing but a bitch.

"You are alone in Paris?" she asked.

Here comes the hard part, I thought, taking a fortifying breath.

"I'm recently widowed."

I'd come up with that phrase as the thing to say rather than *My husband is dead*. Somehow *recently widowed* sounded like words with no real meaning. At least that's how they hit me right now.

"Oh, *chérie*, I am so sorry! So much tragedy all at once!"

I didn't bother telling her that I didn't know my father very well.

"So you will be living here alone?"

"I'll be selling." When she frowned, I hurriedly added, "Oh, it's beautiful and I love the neighborhood. But...you know..."

"But you have a life back in America, of course."

It's funny but when she said it like that it made me think how I really *didn't* have a life back in America at all.

"Where did you learn to speak English so well?" I asked.

"My husband was British. He is gone now these past ten years but I practice with American television."

"Oh, that's cool."

"You have a very unusual last name. Baskerville. Like the Sherlock Holmes story."

"My husband's ancestry was English. Yes, it's a memorable last name."

"We will have to get you a dog!" she said, clapping her hands with excitement. "To have a hound of the Baskervilles, of course!"

I have to say it was not the first time I'd heard jokes about my name but it obviously caused her such delight that I found myself laughing along with her as though I'd never heard the reference before.

I think that says something about how you look at the world when even a tired old joke can seem funny.

Or maybe it had more to do with the fact that it looked like I'd just made my first real friend in Paris.

15

RIVER DEEP, MOUNTAIN HIGH

I'm not sure whether it was something Geneviève said or just the prospect of going back upstairs to my apartment for another long boring afternoon, but after I left her, I decided to go out.

I ran back upstairs to get my purse and then hurried down the stairs to drop off the trash (Geneviève told me it was behind the nonfunctioning fountain in the inner courtyard), and then stepped out onto the street.

The breeze was blowing in sharp gusts and I felt little spritzes of rain but nothing that immediately required an umbrella.

I think somewhere in the back of my mind I must have known that I intended to go back to the hotel where Bob and I had stayed. I didn't consciously realize that before then because I knew how anybody normal would react if I were to tell them I was going back there.

God knows, the last thing I wanted to do was remember or relive any moment of that terrible day.

But that hotel in that neighborhood felt like one big flapping loose end that was winding up and around my brain and threatening to trip me up the longer it stayed untied.

Regardless of what I'd told Catherine and Todd, Bob's murder was not solved. Not for a minute.

While it's true that like most citizens, I had fewer resources than the police did for tracking down perpetrators of crimes—and even fewer here in France—I had one thing they didn't have: tenacity.

Or was it obsession?

Whatever it was, there was no benefit to me to forget about this case. The exact opposite in fact. The longer I went without knowing what had happened to Bob that day and why, the more I knew I would never be able to move forward.

I'd never be able to make new friends, settle into whatever new life was waiting for me, reflect back on my old life with Bob—none of it—until I got some answers on what happened to make it all blow up in my face.

The whole Courtney thing was a completely different matter. I'm not saying it doesn't complicate my feelings because it does. I'm not saying I don't still love him because one event can't kill my love. Not right away anyway. In some ways it would be easier if it could. But since he's dead and gone, it's my memories that are important for me to keep.

And those are up to me to preserve.

In whatever way I can.

It took me less than forty minutes to walk from my apartment to the *pont Alexandre III*, across the Seine and into the Latin Quarter. As soon as I stepped into the neighborhood of the hotel I felt my gut tighten as if I were about to be attacked.

I went to the first available bench along the *rue Jacob* and did a few breathing exercises to calm myself. But once I sat down my phone rang. My first thought was that it must be Catherine calling from the US. It wasn't.

I recognized Joelle's number. I was tempted to dismiss the call but curiosity got the better of me.

"Hello?" I said.

"I need to see you tomorrow," she said abruptly. "At Café Dominique on rue Etienne Marcel. Noon."

"Sure," I said as she hung up on me.

I looked at my phone and instantly got a bad feeling about why she was calling. I knew she didn't want to be friends. She probably wanted her apartment back and maybe some or all of the money Claude had left me.

In spite of the strange phone call from Joelle, within ten minutes I was steady enough to continue on. It was late afternoon and already the sun was sinking behind the buildings. I was wearing a wool jacket and took a second to button it up, glad of the cashmere scarf knotted at my throat.

I walked down the broad avenue and squared my shoulders. Around the next corner was the hotel. I stumbled just a little over a rough patch in the cobblestone and remembered tripping last month and Bob had been there to support me. The memory made me go weak in the knees and I shot out a hand to steady myself against a nearby stone wall.

The fact was that the loss of him was still so fresh that my mind and my heart were no longer working in tandem. The heart was leading the way and the mind had abdicated all responsibility.

That is never a good thing.

I walked around the corner and across the street to the hotel and straight up the front stairs—just like I did that fateful day four weeks ago.

I walked inside and went straight to the reception desk and saw the weasely desk clerk watching me come. I could see by the look on his face that he was unpleasantly surprised to see me. He put down the phone he'd been talking on and gave me a grimace.

"May I help you, Madame?"

As I've said before, I'm no good with faces so I compensate with other abilities. But there are a couple of instances where I *will* remember a face. A clownishly huge nose or dramatic snaggle teeth, outlandishly big breasts or very bad pitted skin —these are things that will tag my memory and help me remember a face.

As I looked at this man I noted, as I had the first time I saw him, that he was exceedingly ugly.

I don't mean to be hateful by that observation. It's just a fact. His ugliness was a helpful tool in my being able to identify him again if I ran into him somewhere other than behind this hotel desk.

I can't say that about ninety-nine percent of the people I meet.

"I'm sorry," I said. "What is your name, Monsieur?"

He blinked as if surprised at such a bold question.

"Bernard Santé," he said.

"Monsieur Santé, I was hoping you could tell me what you remember about the day my husband was killed."

He said nothing.

"I can't imagine you would have forgotten much about that day," I continued. "Since I assume people aren't murdered in your hotel every day. Or at least I would hope not."

"*Je suis désolée, Madame*," he said. *I am sorry, Madame.*

"A man came from my husband's room," I said, regardless of the fact that I didn't really know this to be true. "You might have seen him."

"I see many men, Madame."

It was clear he was not going to help me.

"I would like to see our room, please," I said.

Actually I had no idea I was going to ask that and I was not at all sure I even wanted to see that room again. Surely it would have been scoured of any and all evidence that I might be able to see.

"There is a guest in that room."

Was he trying to cover for someone? Did he know more about the murder than he had told the police?

"You will please excuse me a moment, Madame," he said and then disappeared into his office.

I waited, shifting from foot to foot. I finally went to sit in the lobby for a few minutes and then came back to the desk and banged the bell. I was starting to wonder if he was ever coming back when I heard the sound of heavy footsteps coming through the door.

I turned to see two strange men in suits approaching from the street.

16

THE LESS WE KNOW

Well, this was awkward.

I walked out of the hotel without saying a word to either Detective Pellé or Detective LaRue. While it was true I didn't recognize their faces and they didn't bother showing me their badges this time, I had no problem guessing who they were.

Roman Pellé was a little taller than LaRue and stood slightly behind his partner. He looked almost sheepish, his shoulders slightly hunched, his hands clasped behind his back.

Even though I knew he was in his mid-fifties he *looked* like the junior partner. He tended to duck his head as if not completely sure of himself.

LaRue on the other hand...how could I ever forget that scowl?

"Why are you back here?" LaRue asked as soon as we were outside.

I gave him my best withering look which, to be fair, might not have held up since it's the look I see most often from just about every waiter at any restaurant in Paris.

"I will handle this, Jean-Marc," Roman said in a low voice.

LaRue snorted and muttered that he'd see Roman back at the station. I waited until he climbed in the police cruiser parked by the curb and drove off before turning to Roman.

"Why did the desk clerk call you?" I asked.

He gestured with one hand to indicate we should continue walking.

"I know a decent *brasserie* near here where we can talk," he said.

As I walked I felt my irritation rise with every step. It wasn't until we were seated at a table in the back of a very nice French *brasserie*—complete with brass chandeliers, wood paneling and brocaded bench seating—that Roman addressed my question.

"My understanding," he said, "is that the clerk felt inadequate to handle what he thought would be an emotional woman."

"He's a hotel clerk. Surely he's handled every imaginable customer service crisis."

"I do not know, Madame Baskerville. All I know is that he called for police assistance."

The waiter came and Roman ordered a coffee. I ordered a whiskey, neat.

"Why did you go back to the hotel?" he asked once the waiter left.

"I was hoping to get some answers about what happened."

"Madame Baskerville," Roman said with a pulse of frustration in his voice, "I told you what happened. Your husband was attacked by a burglar who overreacted."

"But then why wasn't my husband's wallet taken?"

"When your husband unexpectedly fought back, his assailant panicked and defended himself with a knife."

"And you still have no idea who this mysterious assailant is? What about fingerprints? DNA?"

The waiter returned with our drinks and set them on the table. I felt like drinking the whiskey straight down but was pretty sure I already looked unstable to Detective Pellé. I sipped the drink and felt it burn all the way down my throat.

Roman sighed. "I know you want answers. I understand that. You have been through a terrible shock."

"Not as bad as the shock my husband had," I said, feeling tears threaten. "What about the killer's DNA? Surely he must have left some! Don't you have the usual suspects you can round up? They can't all have an alibi for the time in question."

"Madame Baskerville," Roman said with a sadly indulgent smile. "*Claire*. We have processed the crime scene, of course we have. And we have spoken to all the usual suspects, as you say in the area. Trust me, if we could have solved this case by now, do you not think we would have done it? There was no DNA, no fingerprints. There were no footprints except for your own."

I felt disappointment at his words but it was only what I'd expected. I sipped my drink and looked around. The restaurant was nearly deserted at this hour—too early for dinner, too late for lunch.

Impulsively, I pulled out my phone.

"Do a selfie with me?" I asked.

Before he could answer I scooted my chair over so we could both be in the frame together. I wish I could've gotten a picture of the expression on his face.

I have to admit the request did come out of left field. But Pellé had already looked at his watch twice while we were sitting there so I knew he couldn't stay much longer and I needed the photo to help me remember his face in the future.

Although he didn't touch my shoulder he draped an arm around my chair and leaned in close to me. I took two quick photos.

"Thanks," I said. "I guess that must seem strange."

"Not at all," he said, a smile playing on his lips.

Once I moved my chair back I thought I could detect that he seemed a little more relaxed. And all it took was one innocent selfie like we were two friends out enjoying a drink together to do it.

So I went and ruined the mood.

"Did you find the murder weapon?" I asked.

He made a noise of frustration and ran his hand through his hair.

"Do you really find this helpful? I should think it would make you relive the horror of that day."

"Yes, Detective Pellé. It *does* make me relive the horror. For some reason you think if I don't think about it I'll feel better. That's not how it works. Have you never lost anyone to violent crime?"

"No," he said, tilting his head to regard me with a sudden intensity.

"Trust me," I said, fighting tears, "the only thing that will make me feel better is knowing that the man who killed Bob is held accountable. Nothing else."

"And you must trust *me*, Madame, that knowing who did this will not ease the pain."

I finished the rest of my drink in one gulp.

"Maybe not," I said, placing my empty glass carefully on the tabletop. "But I can't *not* do it."

Later I walked home from the restaurant in the fading light of the early evening, not caring if I got mugged. So of course I didn't get mugged. It's only when you're petrified you'll be accosted that you ever are.

I knew Pellé was unhappy with my persistence about Bob's case but I also got the idea that he sympathized too. Before we parted, I got him to say he'd take another look at the case file to see if there was anything he might have overlooked.

The fact is, I knew the forty-eight-hour rule still held and he could look through all the case files he wanted—or tell me he was going to—but it was way too late for it to do any good.

The only other thing I thought that he might be able to do for me was to let *me* have the file to look. I didn't ask. We were getting along so well I didn't want to ruin everything by asking.

Not yet anyway.

17

POISONING THE WELL

The next morning, while I waited for Joelle to show up at the café, I took out a notebook I'd bought at the stationery store Gibert Jeune on Quai Saint-Michel. I can lose myself for hours in that store and I now have more notebooks and postcards than I can ever use in a lifetime. But still I keep buying them.

Joelle had been very specific about which café she wanted to meet at and I wasn't sure that wasn't because she needed to be sure of my exact location coordinates to accurately set up the sniper. I mean, I really didn't know this woman beyond the fact that she hated and resented me. Plus she was French so I had even less insight into her than I might have had.

I ordered a coffee and watched people walk by for a few moments. Then I wrote down in my notebook the few things I thought I could safely believe about the case so far.

First, the police believed that Bob was killed by a burglar and second, no fingerprints or DNA were found at the scene.

I stopped writing and looked out unseeing at the street traffic.

That was just barely believable.

No.

It wasn't believable.

I saw Joelle coming down the sidewalk. I had to admit she was beautiful. Even from fifty feet away I could see her fury though. I was frankly surprised that people on the sidewalk didn't step off the curb to avoid her but nobody was looking at her but me.

For all my newfound belief that French men find older women attractive, my father had still opted to marry someone forty years his junior.

She marched over to my table and tossed down her gloves.

I guess that answers the question about *do we hug or double cheek kiss*?

"I will make this quick and less painful for both of us," she said, pulling out a chair but shaking her head at the waiter to indicate she would not be ordering anything.

On the one hand I was relieved to know Joelle wouldn't be staying. On the other hand I began to get definite vibes of a developing hit-and-run scenario.

"I would suggest you not get too comfortable in my apartment," she said.

"I told you I would be happy to rent it to you, Joelle," I said. "Or sell it to you, come to that."

She curled a lip—impeccably painted with pink gloss to reveal her perfect white teeth beneath.

"A question has been raised as to your paternity," she said.

Up until this moment I did not care two hoots for my paternity. I can say that honestly. But that paternity had recently allowed me not to live in fear of abject poverty—which I'd gotten a healthy preview of back in Atlanta—and so the thought of losing any benefits of that paternity sent a sudden charge of fear straight through me.

Just as Joelle had planned.

I saw the evil smirk on her face as the faint lines around her mouth relaxed just a bit. She would never be so unladylike as to openly gloat but it was clear she couldn't hide the pleasure of watching me squirm.

"And I suppose it's you who has raised that question?" I said, carefully putting my notebooks away.

"Claude told me the story many times," Joelle said. "I think I didn't really hear it until I was talking to my lawyers the other day."

I wasn't going to be her straight man for this so I bit my tongue to prevent myself from asking the obvious question my brain was screaming to know.

What story?

"He used to say he felt sorry for your mother." She shrugged and flicked off invisible lint from her flawless cashmere camel coat. "An American schoolteacher with nothing in her life but the memory of her summer with a handsome Frenchman."

"A summer that led to a wedding," I interjected.

A flinch shimmered across her face as she regarded me.

"Which was quickly annulled," she said.

"I'm pretty sure it was a divorce."

"In any case, when your mother became pregnant Claude allowed her to believe that he thought it was his."

"Why would he do that if it wasn't the truth?"

She ignored my question. "Didn't you find it strange that Claude was so uninvolved in your life?"

"Again, my question is why would he allow my mother to believe the child was his if it wasn't?"

"Because he was a decent man. Because he was married to your mother at the time and felt it was the honorable thing to do."

"At what time? At the time my mother became pregnant with me by another man?"

"*Exactement.*"

"You know how crazy that sounds, right? And desperate?"

"It is the truth."

"So you're saying my parents were married and my mother got pregnant but I am not Claude Lapin's child."

"*C'est ça.*"

"Fine. I assume this is all about what I inherited from Claude, so great. Prove it."

"That will not be hard. My lawyers are already working on it."

"Good for you. But I'm curious. If not Claude then who is my father?"

She smiled.

"I imagine that would be the man who raped your mother in the toilets of the Cluny Museum."

18

THE SHORT END

I know Joelle was waiting for a reaction from me and I was determined not to give it to her.

"You're saying my mother was sexually assaulted while married to my father."

"It is a matter of public record," she said with a shrug.

"If there was a question about my paternity," I said hoarsely, "then why did Claude leave everything to me?"

"He didn't. The State did that. And once the DNA test proves that you are not his child, you'll be stripped of everything."

Again, I worked very hard at not letting my face show how I felt. Because how I felt was like death.

"A DNA test?" I said.

"Oh, don't worry. We will not need to inconvenience you."

I knew what she was going to say before she said it.

"I have someone who was able to locate a social media ancestry website that your mother subscribed to. You are familiar?"

I didn't respond. I was afraid I might throw up if I opened my mouth.

My mother had given me a *23andMe* test as a gift one year for my birthday. What she'd done with the results I hadn't bothered to follow up on. Not that it would have mattered. I vaguely remember my ancestry being a project for her that summer. It kept her busy and engaged.

And now it was coming back to bite me on the *derriere*.

"It seems these clubs are very popular on social media," Joelle said. "Your mother posted the results of your DNA test in order to find any distant relatives for you. So we have your DNA, Madame Baskerville. Once the test is performed on Claude's remains, we will have our answer. Once and for all."

After my meeting with Joelle I didn't feel much like hanging out at cafés and people-watching. I went directly back to my apartment to get on the Internet.

Was it really possible that my mother was attacked during the months she'd lived in Paris with Claude? Of course it was. Was it likely that she could've been raped—with my paternity in question—and never even hint at it to me?

I don't know. My mother had been a talker. If she somehow managed to keep from me what had happened to her all those years ago, she would certainly have told *someone*. A therapist maybe although this was back in the sixties and turning to therapists unless you were wealthy was rare in those days—especially for trauma or PTSD.

As soon as I got back to my apartment I opened up my laptop and went to my usual news archive sites and punched in the year before I was born and the key words *Paris, France*.

An hour later I'd found nothing. There weren't even that many reports of sexual assaults for that year and I had to believe that many had just gone unreported. Joelle said it was a matter of public record but perhaps she was just saying that. I reminded myself that it all could be a lie.

But she'd seemed awfully confident for it to be a total lie.

I got up to make myself a cup of tea. I'd done a good job of not thinking too much about my mother on the walk back from the café and then when I was focusing on the archived news articles.

But the thought that she'd been attacked in this city—a city she continued to love her whole life long—was enough to bring tears to my eyes. My mother passed away five years ago but she'd been a live wire right to the end and while we didn't often see eye to eye there wasn't a day I didn't miss her.

I pulled a stale *canelé* out of the bread box and brought it and my cup of tea back to my laptop.

It was true that my mother wasn't around anymore to tell me what really happened but there might still be someone who knew the truth: my mother's best friend, Lillian. The two of them had taught in the DeKalb County school system in Atlanta for forty-five years before retiring together to adjacent condos in Jacksonville, Florida.

As far as I knew, Lillian was still alive.

I searched for her on Facebook first. I know my generation tends to use Facebook more than the Millennials or my mother's generation. But Mom had loved social media and there was at least a ghost of a chance that Lillian did too.

If she didn't, I only had about fifty other ways to track her down to her cozy little condo in Florida.

I found her in under thirty seconds.

She was listed on Facebook as *in a relationship* with her hobbies as needlepoint, gardening and karaoke. Even though she and my mom had been lifelong friends I'd only met Lillian once—at my mother's memorial service in Jacksonville.

I flipped through a few of her posts—mostly shared cat

videos and Christianity memes—and then wrote a somewhat lengthy private message to her telling her what I needed from her—confirmation that my mother had indeed been attacked all those years ago.

19

DOG DAYS

The next morning I got up, made coffee and looked at the news and my email account. The only email I had was from Gigi the realtor who wanted to come over to take pictures of the apartment that afternoon to see how much work needed to be done to list it.

Gigi seemed to think it would sell fast. She wrote a long chatty paragraph about the real estate market in Paris and finished by asking me if I knew any other American expats in Paris?

Ever since my meeting yesterday with Joelle, I hated the unsettled feeling I now had about living here. I finished my coffee and checked Facebook but there was no response from Lillian. I rinsed out my coffee cup as well as the French press and went to look out the window in the living room. I could see a couple of parents walking and holding the hands of their adorable children. My heart caught for a moment because I couldn't help but think of Catherine. It seemed like centuries since she was that age.

I took a long time to dress and was reminded of Parkinson's Law about a trivial task expanding to fill the time allotted for it. I always thought that sounded pretty depressing since my whole life long I never felt as if I had enough time. But here I was spending the morning trying to decide between two pairs of earrings to wear and neither choice made a difference since I would see nobody who would care how I looked.

I bent over to retrieve one of my ballet flats from under the bed and it took me a good five seconds before I could stand all the way straight again. Which made me think of Courtney. She could probably do gymnastic back flips and I couldn't comfortably fish out a slipper from under the bed.

I'd always done yoga and Pilates but lately I did them less to look toned in a swimsuit and more to make sure I was steady on my feet.

Not very sexy, I thought. *I do yoga now so I won't fall over.*

After I dressed, I sat on the sofa for a few minutes to figure out what to do next. I decided I could probably afford a restaurant lunch. The thought of that perked me up—or possibly just the thought that I had some direction did—and I quickly made sure the cooker burners were all off, locked up the apartment and set out.

Since it was only midmorning and a little early to be contemplating lunch even in Paris, I decided to just walk and see where I ended up.

Two hours later I was once more standing in front of the Hotel L'Ocean.

I honestly think it was because I did not know where else in the world to go to try to get closer to Bob—the Bob who was a loving, attentive husband. And the Bob who now needed me. Because one thing I knew, the Bob who ended up on that hotel room bed needed me.

Not in the real sense of course. He was way beyond that. But he needed me to find out what happened to him. And the only thing I knew to do was to come here.

I couldn't go to the police and I had no other starting point.

I also knew I couldn't go inside. Whatever reason that weaselly hotel clerk had for calling the cops yesterday, he would assuredly still have. And as polite as the cops had been yesterday, especially Roman, I was pretty sure they'd be less so today.

Not that that mattered.

But it wouldn't help either.

I sat for a time across the street from the hotel on an iron bench. From where I was sitting I could see the old woman with the flower kiosk and also the front of the hotel. It was midday on a Tuesday. I watched a young couple come out of the hotel—holding hands—but that was all.

I had no idea what I was looking for. But that didn't bother me. When I'd done surveillance as a private investigator, I often didn't know what I was looking for. I just waited and watched and sooner or later I saw something that made my vigil worthwhile.

I checked Facebook on my phone to see if there had been a message from Lillian yet. And then forced all thoughts of my mother and Joelle from my mind. As best I could.

I'd tried hard all morning not to think of Joelle and her evil plan to impoverish me in my old age but it was hard not to reflect on it. If Mom really had been assaulted then I had to find out if I was the result of that assault.

If Mom *wasn't* assaulted I still had to find proof that I was the result of her union with Claude.

The street that led to the Hotel L'Ocean held a couple of chain sandwich stores in it, a laundromat and an outdoor café. But at the end of that street there was only the hotel and what looked like vacant office buildings surrounding it. On the other side there was a stretch of more empty buildings before you came to a small park and finally the Seine.

I watched a few people buy flowers from the woman at her kiosk but today didn't look like a booming sales day for her. I was hungry and was just about to go find a restaurant before resuming my unofficial stake-out when I saw what I'd been looking for.

It wasn't the front door of the hotel that snagged my attention but movement at the side of it. The hotel was flanked by two alleys. I assumed that the cops had scoured both for any sign of the missing murder weapon but I made a mental note to check them myself after I had lunch. But for now my attention was diverted by the diminutive appearance of a small Asian woman who appeared at the entrance of one of the alleys.

I was up and crossing the street before the woman knew I was zeroing in on her. When I reached the alley I could smell the waft of cigarette smoke which told me what she was doing out there.

Unfortunately, at my age I don't move as quickly as I used to. I saw her fling her lit cigarette out the entrance of the alley and begin to turn toward the interior of the lane.

"*Bonjour*!" I called. "*Excusez-moi*!"

Maybe because she was used to obeying orders, the woman stopped. I hurried over to her and stood for a moment, trying to get my wind back.

"*Pardonez-moi*," I said to her breathlessly. "*Est-ce que je peux vous demander une question?" May I ask you a question?*

She bowed her head but didn't move away so I took that as a *yes*.

Physically she was indistinctive in just about every way except size. She had long black hair tied in a low-slung ponytail and nondescript facial features—all of which were pointed downward as she stared at the ground.

In spite of the smoke, I detected the scent of lavender blossoms but that could have been the stack of freshly laundered pillowcases she held in her arms.

"My name is Claire Baskerville. And you are?"

She didn't lift her face. "Marie," she said in a small voice.

"*Bon*. Marie. I need to ask you a few questions."

She rubbed both hands nervously up and down her pant legs. It occurred to me that she was probably afraid of being accused of stealing or otherwise doing wrong. That couldn't be helped.

"My husband died in the hotel where you clean," I said and then cursed myself for phrasing it as though her cleaning might have had something to do with him being dead.

She looked at me with a stricken expression on her face and I knew for sure I'd never seen her before. I realized that because she had a large birthmark on her right cheek. I might not remember faces, but I'd remember something like that.

"I just want to know if you remember seeing any strange men that day?"

What a stupid question! She probably sees strange men every single day in her job!

She shook her head, tilting her head to hide her face again.

"Did the police talk to you?"

The fear came back in her eyes at the mention of the police and she shook her head.

I knew it! They hadn't questioned the hotel staff!

"Did you see anything that day that was weird or different? Anything at all?"

"No, Madame," she murmured, her eyes darting down the alley to the back door that I could see must lead into the hotel.

"How many maids work the hotel?"

"Me and Trini," she said. "But Trini go back to Russia."

"When? When did she go back?"

"Long time. They hire new girls soon."

I thought about that for a moment. Was Marie the only maid working the hotel? That sounded like slave labor for the size of the place. But the pertinent information for me was that there didn't seem to be any other maids to interview.

"Is there a cook in the hotel?" I asked.

"No cook," she said and edged away from me toward the side door of the hotel.

"Okay," I said with resignation. "Well, thank you." I was about to give her a tip but she turned and ran down the alley before I could open my purse.

I felt a sudden heaviness in my arms and legs and turned to survey the street from this perspective. The closed-up offices on the street looked like they hadn't been inhabited for months if not years.

Were the desk clerk and Marie the only ones holding down the fort for a twenty-room hotel? How did they manage? Was it really a hotel? Or a front for something else?

My stomach growled, reminding me that I had been about to find lunch. I decided to stay on the street and walk to the end of the block to see if there were any restaurants down there. I reminded myself that I still needed to come back and search both alleys. But food first.

I crossed in front of the hotel, ducking my head in case the desk clerk was watching through the picture window from the front desk.

As I reached the entrance of the second alley, I heard a gut-wrenching sound. I stopped and felt chills go straight through me.

It sounded like a sick cat and I like cats. I turned slowly to try to gauge where the noise had come from and realized it was coming from the alley.

I held my breath to see if the sound would come again.

It did. Only this time there was no mistaking it for a sick cat.

This time it was an agonized bleat for help as clear as anything I'd ever heard.

I took two steps into the alley, straining to see to the end.

Two more steps. Then four.

And then I began to run.

20

THE DEVIL'S PLAYGROUND

It was a man. He was on his back and by the time I reached him he was no longer calling for help.

I dropped to my knees beside him and opened my purse for my phone. My purse slipped from my hands and fell into the puddle of blood he was lying in. I saw my lipstick, a coin purse and cell phone come flying out.

My hands shook as I snatched up my phone and quickly dialed 999 for the second time in four weeks. I spoke to the dispatcher and gave the address of the hotel.

Blood was everywhere and for a moment my eyes blurred and I thought I was looking at Bob.

"Help will be here soon," I said in French to the man.

I could see that most of the blood appeared to be coming from a neck wound so I pressed on it to try to staunch the flow. The blood had pooled around both of us. I had a sickening feeling that it didn't matter what I did.

I reached down and took his hand. I prayed the ambulance would come soon. He looked to be in his early twenties. He had long brown hair and was dressed like a college student—not cheap but not really nice either.

I thought I remembered at some point that the man had been gasping and now I wasn't hearing anything. I knelt close to him and realized he'd died.

My heart was pounding in my chest like a set of pistons. I couldn't believe he was gone. So young and now his life was over.

I removed my hand from his neck and let go of his hand. Before I knew I was doing it I reached into my purse and grabbed a tissue and used it to pull out his wallet from his front jeans pocket where I could see it peeking out. I don't know what made me do it and later I'd tell myself it was because the police had been so useless and I had nothing but a hotel that I was forbidden to visit as my only lead so I was desperate for something, *anything* to work with.

I opened his wallet with the tissue to reveal his identification card. I didn't take it out of its sleeve but took out my phone and photographed it. Then I photographed his face and put his wallet back in his pocket.

My heart was pounding so loudly I'm surprised I heard the sound behind me but I did. It was a scraping sound against gritty pavement. I turned toward it.

A man stood several yards away at the back of the alley. He had dark hair, dark eyes and was dressed in jeans and a sweatshirt. Our eyes met.

"Monsieur!" I called to him. "*Attends*!" *Wait!*

He turned and ran.

21

NO HOLDS BARRED

They put me in the same interview room as before.

On the good news front, the detective team assigned to this homicide was the same team I already knew. So that saved time for everyone.

On the bad news front, it was the same team that I already knew.

This time they didn't keep me waiting. Either they knew from last time that it wouldn't help or they literally had no other leads but me.

I was betting on the latter.

I hadn't been arrested so I had my phone and my purse—ruined as it was with the victim's blood.

I had no doubt that these two detectives—unless they tried to pin it on me—were going to tell me this was a mugging. The only problem with that of course was that it was broad daylight and once again, like with Bob, the victim still had his wallet.

Roman and LaRue stepped into the room. They must have prepared a strategy in advance about how to question me because this time LaRue took the lead while Roman stood back and gave me sad facial expressions as if to say *why are you here again*?

"You came back to the hotel," LaRue said as he seated himself across from me. I noticed he had an ugly purple knot over his left eye.

"Clearly," I said, reminding myself why it was I didn't like this man.

"I'm sure Detective Pellé requested that you refrain from visiting the Hotel L'Ocean."

"He might have," I said. "Except I'm also sure this is a free country and I can go where I like."

Whoa! Where did that come from?

I think the detectives had the same reaction because LaRue's eyes widened in surprise.

"How do you know the victim?" he asked.

"What makes you think I know him?"

His identification card had revealed that the victim's name was Reynard Coté. He lived in Clichy. And I was right. On his ID under "Occupation" it said "Student."

"Can you please walk us through how it is you have discovered another body within four weeks?"

I thought that was pretty insensitive when you consider that one of those bodies was my husband's but I told myself that letting this putz get to me was ultimately unproductive.

"I went back to the hotel to see if I could talk to someone who was there when my husband was attacked," I said. "And I talked to a maid who said nobody ever questioned her."

I thought I saw something flinch in LaRue's cheek when I said that, which made me think it was true.

"So you *didn't* question the hotel staff?" I asked.

"I will ask the questions. Please continue," he said cracking his knuckles and glaring at me.

"So I went to the hotel to talk to anyone who might know something since the police don't seem to know anything and as

I was leaving I crossed in front of the alley and heard someone call for help."

"The medical examiner said he was dead for hours," LaRue said.

"Then you clearly don't need my statement," I said. "I'm only telling you what I know."

"Continue," he said folding his arms across his chest.

"I heard someone call for help so I ran down the alley and saw Monsieur Coté lying on the ground."

"How did you know his name?"

"What?"

"How did you know the victim's name?"

Crap. How could I have said that? I must be tired. And hungry. I really don't manage well on an empty stomach.

If I tell him something snotty like the name was a wild guess he might think everything I say was a lie. On the other hand, what benefit has telling the truth been up to now?

"Just a wild guess," I said sullenly, my stomach growling loudly.

LaRue stared at me and said nothing. I know that the silent treatment is a tactic not just reserved for marital contretemps but that the cops often use it to positive effect.

"Am I wrong in assuming the victim had his throat slashed like my husband?" I asked. "Do you not think that is significantly coincidental?"

Roman spoke before LaRue could.

"It is not unique being slashed across the throat," he said. "Ninety percent of all Paris homicides or muggings use a knife in this way. We are not like the US. Most citizens do not own guns."

"So you went to the body," LaRue prompted me impatiently.

"Yes. I saw...what I saw and called 999."

"And then what?"

"I don't know what you mean."

"You just knelt in a puddle of blood of a strange man while you waited for the authorities to arrive?"

"I saw a man," I said before I could stop myself. Again. Hunger. Not good.

Both detectives stared at me. LaRue narrowed his eyes suspiciously.

"What man?"

"Brown hair, average build. He appeared maybe ten yards away. I called to him but he ran off."

Roman nodded encouragingly. But I was going to severely disappoint him in about fifteen seconds because I'd just given them my best shot. Brown hair, medium build. There was no way I would be able to pick him out of a line-up.

Even though our eyes met, the second he ran off, his features dissolved from my memory like butter on Teflon.

"We picked up a man in the area," Roman said. "He had no good reason for being there and he has a record."

"We'll need you to identify that he was the man you saw," LaRue said.

"I can't," I said.

"Are you saying you didn't get a good look? Sometimes your memory will jog when you see the face again."

Not in my case.

"I didn't see his face," I lied. "I just saw someone running."

The thing about prosopagnosia which is the scientific name for my condition is that it is impossible for anyone to believe it's real unless they suffer from it. That's because face recognition is one of the most basic abilities that we're born with.

If you don't have face blindness, you can't imagine not being able to remember a face you've just seen.

I didn't expect the detectives to understand that. It was easier just to say I didn't get a good look than to admit I saw his face but couldn't remember what it looked like.

22

OCEANS AWAY

In the end the police interview didn't take nearly as long as the first one. Plus I didn't appear to be considered a viable suspect in Coté's death.

I found a *boulangerie* on the way home since I was way out of the mood for a sit down meal by then. I bought a *pan bagnat* as well as two sugar *crèpes*. There was a grocery shop on the corner of the street leading to my apartment where I bought bottled water and a couple of apples.

I missed the fact that back home in Atlanta if I was in the mood for peaches I could find them even though peach season was long over. But the apples that I bought were crisp and juicy. There was definitely something to be said for in-season produce, I thought as I punched in the code to my apartment and made my way inside.

A young man was standing by the mailbox looking through his mail and glanced up as I passed. Honestly, I wasn't at all sure it was the same man I'd seen at Monoprix two days earlier but French people don't smile or nod at you for no good reason. The fact that he had done both at the store meant he knew who

I was. The fact that this guy was doing it too, meant *in all probability* it was the same guy.

You see? This is how I must live my life with this infuriating affliction.

"Good evening," he said. "You are the new owner in apartment *cinq*?"

"I am," I said. "Claire Baskerville."

"Luc Remy," he said as we shook hands. "Welcome."

"Thank you. It's a beautiful building."

"Very old, I think, yes? Different from what you are used to?"

He spoke French slowly which I appreciated.

"Yes, but in a charming way," I said. "Well, I'll no doubt see you around."

After another bout of nods, I made my way through the lobby and to the elevator. I was so tired that I decided even if the contraption plummeted me to my death in the dark bowels of the basement, it would be worth it.

Upstairs in my apartment I ate my sandwich and drank half the bottle of wine that I'd bought at Monoprix before I finally began to unwind after everything that had happened that day.

I took out my phone, carefully avoiding the photo I'd taken of the body, in order to better examine Coté's identification. I was too tired to do it tonight but tomorrow I would get on the Internet and try to find out who he was.

As I was clearing up after my dinner, my thoughts went to the man Luc who'd stopped me outside the lobby downstairs. Something about my interaction with him had stayed with me but because my day had been so eventful, it had been hard to pinpoint what it was. As soon as the wine let me unclench a bit I realized what it was.

Amazingly, Luc was reacting to me the way men used to do before I became old and decrepit. Now, as a matter of fact, I don't see myself that way. In my mind, I'm thirty years old forever. Maybe even more like twenty-six. But the rest of the world no longer sees me like that.

Bizarrely, Luc had smiled at me like men used to. Not that he was coming on to me, I didn't get that vibe. But he was enjoying talking to me. In fact, now that I thought of it, he behaved like Roman had yesterday at the café.

Thinking about all this inevitably made me think about Bob. But unfortunately it made me think about the Bob who wanted to reach past me to a woman half my age. I'm not saying Luc or Roman wouldn't prefer Courtney to me, but they didn't make me feel like I was too old to be desired.

Bob and I had always stayed romantic. Our sex life might have been predictable but it was alive. He didn't stray because he wasn't *getting it* at home. He didn't stray for any other reason than she was young and he could. That may not be fair to Bob but of course at this stage there's no hope in getting his side of things.

I opened up my laptop and saw that I'd missed my appointment with the realtor. I wrote her back, apologizing, and rescheduled for tomorrow.

I thought of that poor young man who died in the alley today and wondered who he was and who at this moment was getting the terrible news.

I went to take a long hot shower after which I put on my favorite comfy pajamas and did a few basic yoga poses before climbing into bed. Before I clicked off the light, I saw the photo of Bob that I'd placed by my bedside.

It was a picture of the two of us, taken the year before up in the Blue Ridge mountains at a friend's mountain cabin. He had his arm draped over my shoulders and he was looking at me as if I were the only woman in the world.

I turned off the light. I know I needed to forgive him. I know

I needed to remember him for the kind, mostly honorable and decent man that he was for all those years with me.

I'm trying.

23

FUNERAL FOR A FRIEND

Nico stood with his back to the wall of the alley and watched.

At this time of night—well past two in the morning—the only ones walking around were those looking to score—drugs, women, or women in search of clients. With the tourists all asleep in their Airbnb's and hotel rooms, even the pickpockets and muggers were off the streets tonight.

He felt a quiver of unease.

There was an argument to be made that he'd screwed up.

And that argument had already been made to him very clearly.

He touched his bottom lip with the fresh cut that the razor had made when the Big Boss had indicated his displeasure over the bungled hit.

But I'd fixed it. I got the right information and then I made it right.

He pulled out his phone to make sure he hadn't missed the call.

There were no missed calls.

A thin ripple of frustration and doubt clenched his gut.

I got it right, didn't I? He can't blame me for the American.

But of course Nico knew he could.

The sound of a police siren pierced the air and Nico instinctively leaned back into the wall, the shadows hiding his face. But the siren was a long way away.

Suddenly his phone rang.

He pulled it out of his pocket so quickly he nearly dropped it and for a moment the image of the phone smashing onto the pavers at his feet sent a shiver of fear through him.

"*Allo*?" he said.

"Sloppy! Sloppy! Sloppy!" the voice shouted at him, each word sounding like a hatchet chop across the face.

Nico was bewildered and then a terrible thought gripped his bowels.

Had the kid survived?

"He wasn't dead yet when the American woman found him," the voice snarled.

Nico felt his stomach turn over in fear.

"Is he...did he survive?" he asked, his voice nearly a whimper.

"Do you think you'd still be alive if he had?"

Nico felt a sheen of sweat spread across his face. So he *did* die. At least there was that.

"You need to take care of her," the voice said. "No screw ups. You understand?"

Nico nodded and then realized the Big Boss couldn't see him nod.

"Yes," he said hurriedly. But by then the line had disconnected.

24

HANDS ACROSS THE WATER

The next morning after my usual French press coffee—accompanied this time with the *pain au chocolat* I picked up at the *boulangerie* yesterday—I settled down at my small dining room table with my laptop.

I'm not sure why I'd taken a picture of the body except I know that that's what crime scene investigators do. Reynard—it seemed silly to keep referring to this kid as "Monsieur Conté"—looked happy and confident in his identification picture.

Yesterday had been a less than good day for me on several different levels but for the parents of this young man it was the worst day in the world. I wasn't sure what I was looking for except that I had no other leads that were even remotely connected to Bob's murder and while I fully expected to discover that Reynard's death had nothing to do with Bob's, it was a little coincidental that he was killed in the same way just a few yards away.

I opened my browser window on my laptop. In the States, I have a series of websites that I used to locate people through a variety of public records including address histories, phone numbers and recent background checks. It was a little trickier over here but of course France had private investigators too. And they have much the same resources that I use in the States.

It took me less than fifteen minutes to find a phone number at the address listed on his identification card. I didn't hesitate about calling; one thing I've learned in my sixty years on this planet is that you don't get anywhere by being shy. If worse came to worst I could always hang up although hanging up on a newly bereaved mother was not how I wanted to start my day.

The woman who answered didn't sound middle-aged. I can sometimes be wrong about that sort of thing but not often.

"Hello? Is this Reynard Coté's mother?" I asked.

"I am his sister. Who is this?"

I had assumed that the family had been fielding a lot of calls from consoling loved ones and friends.

"My name is Claire Baskerville. I am sorry to trouble you during this terrible time but I am calling to extend my deepest condolences."

The French are formal at the best of times but never more so than when someone dies.

"*Merci*," she said. "Thank you. I am Adelle."

"I don't know if I should be calling you," I said, "but I was the one who found your brother yesterday."

I heard a sharp intake of breath.

"In the alley? It was you who called the police?"

"Yes, that's right. I just wanted to—"

"My mother would love to meet you, Madame Baskerville. She and I both would love to meet the woman who held Reynard's hand at the end."

When the ambulance driver asked me if I had touched the body, I'd told him I'd gripped his hand. It must be in a report somewhere and somehow the family had heard.

My own eyes filled with tears and I said haltingly, "I would love that too."

We arranged for me to come by later that day and I hung up feeling better than I had in a long time. Even if this wasn't a lead that would take me closer to finding out what happened to Bob, it was someone else's sadness that I could relate to and that helped make me a little less sad.

I had a few hours before heading out to meet Adelle and her mother who lived in Clichy which was a bit of jog from the eighth arrondissement. I'd need to take the Metro.

As I settled down at my computer I noticed a text from Catherine had come in. I felt bad about not keeping in better touch with her but I knew that Todd was being very attentive and of course Cameron would do his best to distract her too.

<*Send photos of the apartment*> Catherine had texted. <*Cam's preschool teacher says he's the smartest in his class!!*>

She included a series of emojis that were too tiny for me to read but I assumed were illustrations of how proud she was.

<*That's great!*> I texted back. <*Tell him Gran is SO proud of him!*>

I felt a sudden wave of sadness cascade over me—which felt so much better than the anger I have been feeling every time I thought of Bob.

If only I can forgive him, I thought sadly as I turned back to my computer.

So I can finally mourn him.

I typed in the address of a few websites that I used back in the day when I was trying to access certain sites not openly available to the public. I was hoping to find a way to access the guest registry of the Hotel L'Ocean during the week that Bob and I stayed there. I came to a few frustrating dead ends but finished with a hopeful heart. While I hadn't gotten into the registry there were still a few more avenues to try.

Just before I was about to close up my laptop and go meet Adelle and her mother, I got another idea and typed Adelle's name into one of my *find-people* search engines.

What I got was a whole lot more than I could have expected.

I stared at my computer screen in disbelief.

It seemed that Adelle Coté was employed as a certified forensic tech in a DNA laboratory.

25

MARKING TIME

LaRue got up from his desk and turned to Roman. When his partner looked up, LaRue mimed that he was going into the hall to make a phone call. He knew he could count on Roman to cover for him if necessary. He realized as he left the room that that was a feeling he hadn't experienced in a while.

Ever since Chloe's accident, he'd worked alone. Five years without a partner. It had been the Chief who'd finally decided it was time to team up again and get back to working suspicious deaths, not just common homicides. Work, as his chief called it, that was "more fulfilling."

LaRue snorted as he entered the hallway.

Fulfilling. The last thing he needed was something that made it more difficult for him to attend to his more lucrative side job.

LaRue walked down the hall and slipped outside and scanned the sidewalk. Police vans were parked or were pulling into the Prefecture of Police of Paris transportation garage. A few uniformed police were standing, looking at charge notebooks and talking to each other. One looked up and nodded at him.

He was well known on the force.

After thirty years how could he not be? That was a long time not to show up on anyone's radar. In fact, lately it had taken real skill to become invisible after all those years.

After Chloe.

He swallowed hard and instinctively pushed thoughts of her away. He dug out his phone, dialed the number and waited.

"Hotel L'Ocean," the voice answered.

"It's me," LaRue said gruffly.

"*Oui*?" the voice said.

LaRue felt an irresistible urge to reach out and strangle this creature. He took a moment to rein in his revulsion.

"I'm coming by tonight," he said.

"One moment please. I must attend to a guest."

His phone went mute but before LaRue could react, a voice called to him.

"Hey, Jean-Marc!"

He turned to see Hugo Beaumont, a detective from Robbery Division, waving at him.

LaRue lifted his hand. There had been a time, a thousand years ago, when they had been friends.

"*Ça va*, Hugo?" LaRue said, his face stretching into his best attempt at a smile.

"Not bad. Join us at *Les Choses* for drinks later?"

LaRue nodded. "Okay. Sounds good."

Hugo hesitated as if he would say more. LaRue got the distinct impression that the man knew he had no intention of joining them for drinks.

"Great," Hugo said. "See you then."

He turned and walked away. There was something in the way he walked that reminded LaRue of Reynard.

Instantly he got an image of Reynard laughing.

Which was strange because he was sure he'd never seen Reynard laugh.

Thinking of Reynard made him think of the American woman who'd found him.

And how he really needed to get rid of her.

"I don't have the packet yet," the desk clerk said, suddenly back on the line. "It wasn't delivered."

LaRue cursed. "Then when?"

"In the morning. Definitely."

"If not, bad things will start to happen," LaRue growled.

He was about to hang up when the desk clerk said, "Detective?"

"What?"

"I was just wondering about the problem with the American couple last month."

"What about it?"

"As you know, the woman was here asking questions."

"You don't need to worry about anything except getting my money."

"Except I was just wondering..."

The desk clerk hesitated as if pausing for dramatic impact.

"She still doesn't know you were at the hotel that day, does she?"

26

HIGH HOPES

October in Paris was chilly, bright and clear.

I felt an anticipatory breathlessness as I waited at the Café Danielle in Montmartre for Adelle to arrive.

I knew that more and more police departments were farming out the kind of work she did. That was certainly the case with the Atlanta police. Paris would no doubt also have a huge forensics department with separate labs for firearms, serology, toxicology as well as DNA analysis not to mention fingerprint examination, trace evidence and so on. They would need to send a lot of that out in order to handle the massive workload.

One thing I knew beyond a shadow of a doubt was that my chance of getting any information on an active case from the Paris police without an inside contact was exactly nil.

But having a contact with one of the forensic outfits that the police frequently farmed out to? That would be almost as good.

I spotted Adelle when I stepped into the terrace section of the café. I'd never met her before of course but I could tell she was looking for someone.

She was young, no more than thirty, with dark eyes and hair which hinted at a Middle Eastern background. She was slim and wore jeans and a black leather jacket and gold hoops on her ears.

"*Bonjour*, Adelle?" I said as I joined her at her table.

"*Bonjour*, Madame Baskerville," she said. We shook hands.

"Please call me Claire," I said. "I'm so glad you could meet with me."

"I am sorry my mother could not make it. She is very appreciative for what you did for Reynard but she wasn't up for going out."

"Perfectly understandable."

The waiter came and took our coffee order.

"I want to thank you again for what you did for Reynard," Adelle said, her eyes full of sadness. "He was a troubled young man but we loved him dearly."

"Of course."

I could tell by the way she looked at me that she was hoping for information on Reynard's last moments. I'd steeled myself for this. It's what I would have wanted too.

"I heard a noise," I said, opting not to make it any harder on her than necessary by revealing that her brother had been calling for help. "I ran down the alley but he had already become unconscious."

Adelle took out a tissue from her purse and held it to her face, her eyes were far away as she listened.

"I called 999 and told Reynard that help was on its way."

"You held his hand the ambulance medic said."

"I did. His hand was warm. And although he didn't squeeze my fingers I felt he knew I was there. I continued to talk to him until I realized he wasn't breathing. I'm sorry I didn't perform CPR—"

Adelle waved away my words. "I know how he died. CPR would not have helped."

I knew that. At the point I got to him nothing would have helped.

"I'm so sorry for your loss."

It was important to me that Adelle offer up the information about what she did for a living. I needed certain things from her but later when she reflected back over how the suggestion had been made it would be important that she didn't recall that it had come from me.

The fact that her brother was murdered meant we had a connection and one that I was pretty sure she wasn't aware of yet. It was time to nudge her in the right direction.

"I know a little bit of what you and your mother must be going through," I said as I stirred a couple of lumps of sugar into my tiny coffee cup. "I lost my husband in much the same manner just four weeks ago."

Adelle's mouth fell open.

"That is terrible, Claire. I am so sorry." She instantly looked as if she was doing a fast calculation in her head and coming up with an answer she most certainly did not want to arrive at.

"In fact, he was killed in the Hotel L'Ocean, right off the alley where Reynard was killed."

Adelle was looking downright ill by this time so I had no doubt she knew what murder I was talking about.

Could her company have been the forensic crime techs that worked Bob's murder scene?

Does Adelle know more than I'd even dared hoped for?

I was only expecting to be able to use her for some of my own laboratory and forensic needs going forward. It hadn't occurred to me that she might be personally familiar with Bob's case.

"It is a terrible thing," she said, motioning to the waiter for the check.

So not today, I thought feeling a needle of disappointment invade my gut.

I reminded myself that these things take time. Connections worth anything had to be cultivated. Come to that, friendships didn't happen after one coffee either.

I laid down ten euros to cover both checks but Adelle insisted on paying for her own. She didn't want to owe me even for the cost of a cup of coffee. I might have felt the same in her position, which was why I felt slightly terrible for having to remind her that I was the one with Reynard at the end. I feel bad about that. I truly do. I hated to use him or Adelle's grief but serious problems call for serious tactics.

I couldn't afford to let her go until I had at least set the hook.

"I'm just glad I was there with Reynard at the end," I said shamelessly as she stood up with her purse in her hand.

I gave her a meaningful look.

She hesitated.

"I wonder," I said taking a chance that I was about to go too far, "could it be possible that Reynard's death and my husband's death are somehow connected?"

Adelle stared at me and then something in her face seemed to collapse.

"I have your number," she said.

I smiled encouragingly at her.

And I have yours, I thought as I watched her walk away.

27

THE SCENIC ROUTE

The next day it rained. Because it was late October, it was also cold. Those two factors would have normally jettisoned most of my plans in favor of staying cozy, warm and dry. But in spite of the weather I felt driven to get out and do something.

I didn't blame Adelle for not coming clean on what she did for a living. She had every reason to want to hold her cards close to the vest. I would too if I were in her shoes.

The biggest question I had was what kind of access did she have within the Paris police department that might help me get more information on Bob's case? And if I were to outline what I knew about the hotel crime scene, could she point me in the right direction to finding some answers?

Feeling very much like those preprogrammed baby turtles who turn unerringly toward the sea right after being hatched, I left the apartment after breakfast and made my way back to the Latin Quarter.

If all roads lead to Rome, do all Parisian back alleyways lead to the Latin Quarter?

How is it that no matter how I start out in the morning I always find myself walking in the direction of the Île de la Cité?

Of course I know the answer to that. Something was seriously not right with my world and the only answer I can possibly find to assuage that had to be back at the scene of the crime.

It's literally all I have to go on.

Along the way I stopped at what I was now starting to think of as my favorite *boulangerie* and got my usual—one *pain au chocolat* and a small bag of *palmiers.* I carried the sack to the bench that was catty-cornered to the hotel. I wasn't in anyone's direct sightline from the hotel—like the desk clerk's—but I could comfortably sit and watch the hotel for hours unmolested if I wanted to.

I also had a decent view of the side alley where I'd talked to the maid Marie. I now knew there was a back side entrance into the hotel and if Marie used it for smoking cigarettes, it could be used for other things as well. As of yet, I didn't know what. But again, I often don't know what I'm looking for until I see it.

The only person who had an unobstructed view of me, if you didn't count people in the upstairs apartments of the building behind my bench, was the old lady at the flower kiosk. I say "old lady" because she's got grey hair twisted into a bun at the nape of her neck and her face looks like she's got Sharpei in her gene pool but honestly she's probably my age.

Every time I looked over at her, she wasn't studiously *not* looking at me but that only meant I hadn't caught her at it.

After I'd finished off my little mort of pastries and was feeling a bit chilled by the sudden disappearance of the sun behind a bank of clouds, my eye caught movement in the alley.

Someone had come out of the side door of the hotel and was in the alley. That was the only possibility since I'd not seen anyone enter the alley from the street.

I debated waiting where I was but quickly realized that

wouldn't tell me anything. This wasn't the alley where I'd found poor Reynard and I hadn't yet explored this one to see if, like the other one, there was another way in or out.

I gathered up my things and hurried across the street, taking care to stay out of sight from the front window of the hotel. I went to the mouth of the alley and looked both ways before slipping into it. Whoever I'd seen in the alley was gone.

Smells seemed to pour off both buildings and pool into the space between them, roiling up from the wet stone floor at my feet. A rat was startled from something it was gnawing on thirty feet ahead of me and scurried for its bolt hole in the side of the hotel.

There were no windows, no fire escapes, no pipes or ledges. No point in looking up. It was deathly quiet. The alley, sandwiched between the two buildings, was cut off from all sound.

I hadn't gone more than a dozen yards before I realized that this alley did in fact terminate in a dead end. The good news about that was that it meant that whoever had been in the alley a few seconds ago had come from—and gone back into—the hotel.

I'm not sure what that information told me but it was good to know.

I walked down the alley and saw the door that led into the hotel. There were no words on it but there was an electronic keypad which told me it was locked from the outside. I tried the doorknob anyway. Yep. Locked.

I took a few steps past the door and saw a stone wall jutting out that hid a dumpster.

I felt a small adrenaline rush when I saw it.

I'm ashamed to say that after years of doing private investigator work, I have a regrettable Pavlov's dog reaction to the sight of dumpsters.

It's true that dumpsters are where people put things they don't want anymore.

But they're also where they put things they don't want found.

Mind you, dumpsters are disgusting but that's why people feel confident putting their secrets there—because most normal people won't go looking in them.

Cue the not normal ones, I thought as I hurried to the dumpster.

Twenty minutes later I left the alley with nothing to show for it except a desperate need for a wet wipe.

I still had the question of who had been in the alley from the hotel—because clearly he or she came and went from there —and what were they doing out there? Whoever it was, they weren't out there long enough for a smoke. Were they just tossing garbage in the dumpster?

I made my way back across the street and as I did I noticed that the florist was watching me. Without thinking about it too much, I approached her.

She watched me come.

I must have been holding my hands in a way that announced that I was contaminated—because just as I stepped up to her kiosk she handed me a rag. I took it gratefully. It occurred to me that she knew what I was doing in the alley.

Because clearly she'd dove into a few dumpsters in her time too.

"*Merci*," I said. "Filthy work, treasure hunting."

She narrowed her eyes at me.

"Anything in particular you are looking for?" she asked.

"Not really. You know what they say, *One man's trash*."

I'm not sure they have that saying in France but she seemed to get my drift. She nodded toward the alley.

"I have found some very useable bed sheets there," she said.

"Why would they throw away perfectly good bed sheets?" I asked innocently.

"They would if they are too badly stained to use again. Just last month they threw out a brand new hand towel."

"Really."

She shrugged. I've noticed that more than half the time the way the French communicate is nonverbal.

"It is true I couldn't get the blood out of it but that doesn't bother me."

I swear she knew who I was and what I wanted. The way she looked at me, the fact that she practically lured me over here to give me the rag, she knew I wanted something and she might have something to sell.

And I don't mean flowers.

If I had found a bloody towel in the dumpster I would've taken it. Even though the dumpster would surely have been emptied many times since Bob's murder.

It would still have been valuable as a possible clue.

But this towel the florist had found?

That was different. Because that towel could have been thrown out the day my husband was murdered.

28

BELOW THE BELT

LaRue slammed the car into gear and pulled out of the parking spot in front of the police headquarters on 36 quai des Orfèvres on the corner of Pont Saint-Michel where it overlooked the Seine.

"Whoa! Jean-Marc," Roman said, bracing his arms against the dashboard. "The LeMans is not for another year yet."

"Sorry," LaRue muttered.

He drove in silence down the busy lanes, mindful of Roman beside him. He'd had too much on his plate to spend much time getting to know Pellé. He knew he was fortunate in that the man was easygoing and turned a blind eye when he needed to.

Again, a lot of that has to do with my past reputation but some of it, no doubt, has to do with the whole Chloe debacle.

Five years ago the idea that Roman wouldn't report him for malfeasance because he felt sorry for him would've killed him. Now, he was just grateful. It was vaguely sickening—during those moments when he allowed himself to feel anything about it at all—but that was where he was now.

"I don't like the American woman interfering," LaRue said. "Someone is going to get hurt."

He turned to look at Roman who was looking at him with an incredulous look.

"She is harmless, Jean-Marc. She is just looking for—"

"I know what she is looking for! Answers about her dead husband! But we have told her what happened and still she will not let it go!"

"She will. Her grief is still new. Or perhaps it is her guilt."

"Guilt?"

Roman shrugged. "I think she feels guilty that she is not grieving him. Something has happened. I don't know what. Perhaps secrets were revealed."

"His secrets?"

Roman shrugged again. "She is not a broken-hearted widow. She is an obsessed one."

LaRue frowned. "Not grief but guilt." Then he shook his head. "It doesn't matter what drives her. She needs to go."

"She will go. When life here gets too inconvenient, she will go. This is not Atlanta. There are no drive-through fast food restaurants or twenty-four-hour nail salons. She will give up."

"I wish I had your confidence. She does not strike me as someone who gets her nails done at three in the morning."

"I'm making a point."

"I can't afford for her to...dig around."

"She's just a woman. Even if she found out about...things, what could she do? Go to her embassy?"

"Report me."

"That won't happen. Trust me. She'll tire of all this and go home." He sighed dramatically. "Although I wouldn't mind her staying a little longer."

LaRue gave him a sideways glance. "She is a bereaved widow," he said.

"Yes, but she won't always be."

"Thinking of transferring to Atlanta?"

Roman laughed. "She inherited an apartment in Paris, remember?"

"Which the realtor that I spoke to last week told me she intends to sell."

"Well, you never know," Roman said directing his glance back at the streets they drove through.

LaRue focused on his driving and worked to keep the American woman out of his head. He had secrets that would be devastating if they were revealed. Just the fact that he was at the hotel the day her husband was murdered could be easily confirmed if she knew enough to try.

Was that her next step? What happened then? When she discovered he was at the hotel that day?

Things could get messy for him very quickly and *that* he could not allow.

There was too much at stake.

What Roman said made sense and it felt logical. But right now how LaRue felt wasn't sensible or logical. All he knew was that no matter what, he would not let another American step in and ruin his life.

No matter what he had to do to stop it.

29

PAYING THE PIPER

I'm not good at haggling.

I was determined to pay what I needed to in order to get the towel from the florist but I was not eager to pay more than I needed to. Again, those two weeks in Atlanta seeing my impoverished future had an indelible effect on me.

I wouldn't ask her how much she wanted for the towel. I would tell her what I was willing to pay.

And then I would pay her whatever she asked.

"I'll give you fifty euros for it," I said.

Her eyes widened and she glanced at my purse.

"Five hundred," she said.

"For a towel someone threw away?" I said with affected astonishment.

But I wasn't willing to walk away without the towel and she knew it.

"Seventy-five euros," I said, making it as easy as possible for her to say *one hundred* and put us both out of our misery.

"One hundred," she said.

I began to reach for my purse but she waved a hand to stop me.

"I do not have it here. Come back in two hours. I will have it then."

I nodded.

Honestly, putting things into perspective, there were worse things in life than having to kill two hours on a lovely afternoon in the Latin Quarter.

~

I walked away from the florist as she began to shut down her kiosk, presumably for the afternoon.

Because it was no longer tourist season, the streets weren't as crowded as they'd been even the month before.

I stopped at a café for a hot chocolate and watched the people walk by. I wasn't sure what the bloody towel would tell me but it was more than I had at the moment. Plus, now that I knew someone with access to a forensics laboratory, there was a possibility of getting the blood stains tested.

If they turned out to be Bob's, then the next step was to find out who put the towel in the dumpster. And answering the question of why Bob's blood would be on a hand towel?

Honestly, the more I thought about it the more outlandish the whole idea seemed to me. Was it a bathroom hand towel or a kitchen towel? I should have asked. If it was a kitchen towel the blood was probably beef.

It was just that I had absolutely no other avenues to explore. It was *something* in a very big world of nothing. Besides, at least ninety percent of what any investigator does is go down blind alleys, grasp at straws and pay shifty people a hundred euros for blood-stained dumpster towels all on a wild hope it might actually lead to something.

As I sat at the café I saw a woman in her late thirties walk by holding the hand of a little girl around nine years old and I felt my heart squeeze. They looked so happy. The little girl even skipped and I found myself trying to remember if I'd ever seen Catherine skip at that age.

I was consciously aware to a certain degree that trying to find out who killed Bob was a comfortable barricade against thinking about having lost him. If I was focused on blood stains and DNA tests I wasn't thinking about how he and I used to be with Catherine when she was little or how he used to look at me when we were both younger.

And it keeps me from thinking about this past year—all those thousands of innocent exchanges with him over unimportant things that now seem glaringly significant.

Was he really at that conference with the creative team in DC last November? Did he really stay an extra night up in the mountains in April because he was trying to woo a client?

Or woo someone else?

No, it was vastly better that I focus on blood stains than think about any of that.

My phone rang and I dug it out of my purse. It was Catherine.

"Hey, Mom. Bad time?"

For a moment it occurred to me that she might be trying to be sensitive to the fact that I was in mourning. She might be worrying that I was over here in Paris weeping into my pillow every night.

A normal widow would be.

"Not at all, sweetie," I said, signaling to the waiter to bring me another hot chocolate. The sun was still high in the sky but that didn't stop the cold chill from snaking its way through the serpentine streets of Saint-Germain-des-Prés and finding its way under my cotton sweater.

"I was just calling to see how you were doing," she said.

"I'm fine. How about you?"

"I feel like I'm on a roller coaster," she said. "One minute I'm in tears and the next minute I'm so angry at Daddy for losing all your money I could scream."

It was bad enough that Catherine knew about the money. There had been no way to keep that from her. The last thing she needed to know was that her beloved father was cheating on me too.

"I know," I said. "I don't suppose we'll ever know where it all went."

"But how are you going to live? Mr. Newman said Daddy even hit your 401k."

"Well, I inherited some money from my father, as you know," I said evenly, pushing thoughts of Joelle from my mind. "And I intend to be careful and invest it."

"Todd can help with that. He's really good at that sort of thing."

"My thoughts exactly," I lied.

"When are you coming home?"

"Just as soon as I can sell the apartment Claude left me."

"It sounds so weird hearing you call your dad by his first name."

"I know but he was never really a dad to me."

"Except in the end," she said. "When it counted."

That surprised me to hear her say that. Up until now I just assumed that Claude had had his feet held to the fire about the inheritance. French law is very inflexible on that point. But I'm sure there are ways. Maybe I should give him a little more credit.

Especially since I'm sure Joelle had probably spent the last few years of his life haranguing him about it.

"Wow. Are you out in a café or something? I hear traffic."

"I am. It's chilly here so I'm having a hot cocoa and watching the world go by."

And waiting until I can go pick up a piece of blood-stained evidence that might lead me to the identity of the man who killed your father.

"Very cool. Well, I must run. Cameron went down easily enough but now I've got a sink-full of dinner dishes to deal with."

We said our goodbyes and as I hung up an image came to me of Catherine on the school playground back in our Dunwoody neighborhood of Atlanta. It was a very strong, vivid image of her laughing.

And skipping to reach me where I waited in the carpool line.

After I left the café on Saint-Germain-des-Prés I walked east toward the river. I was glad I was wearing layers since the wind had definitely picked up. I passed a perfume store and was tempted briefly to go inside but a sour little voice in my head said, *What for*?

On that discouraging note, I walked past the dress boutiques, breakfast bars, Starbucks cafés and ice cream shops without turning my head. I'd once more ended up skipping lunch and reminded myself that if I found myself in a police interview room before the day was over I'd be sorry I hadn't eaten.

By the time I passed the boulevard Saint-Michel my feet were starting to ache. I used to be able to walk all day long—five miles easily—without even thinking about it. But those days were long behind me and I was tired.

Once I reached the river the looming towers of Notre-Dame Cathedral lured me and so I turned toward it. It was still undergoing massive renovation but I didn't have time to wander around it in any case. Even so I was sorry not to have the opportunity to go inside and sit down. The inner sanctum was always so cool and serene—even when packed with tourists.

But its gardens would serve just as well, I decided, and crossed over to the Île de la Cité and walked behind the grand cathedral.

I remember coming to this garden with my mother when I was about eight years old—back in the day when she still thought there was some merit to my getting to know Claude.

There was nobody in the garden today except pigeons which wasn't at all surprising. In the past hour it had gotten downright cold. My brisk walking had produced a nice little rosy blush to my cheeks but had disguised the fact of the dropping temperatures.

I settled on one of the stone benches and while I could hear the sounds of traffic from both sides of the Seine, there was still a peaceful, eternal feel to the garden.

Again, as soon as I stopped moving, my mind began to go places without my permission. An image of Bob came to me and my first thought was a stab of longing which I quickly quashed with a wave of anger.

Frustrated that I didn't seem able to control these emotions from dictating how my moods would go, I forced myself to see that if I could just find out the truth of how he died, it wouldn't matter so much that the mystery of how he *lived* would be something I would never unravel.

Suddenly, I detected a scent very near me. It was an unpleasant odor and I instantly stiffened.

Before I could decide what to do—turn and look or just run—an iron hand clamped down on my arm anchoring me to the bench.

"Don't run," a guttural voice warned me. "I'd prefer not to hurt you."

30

CLOSING RANKS

"Who are you? If you want money—"

My voice was trembling and for a moment I forgot the French word for "money."

He didn't let go of my arm and I didn't turn around to look at him. Any moment I expected to feel the cold shock of a blade slide into my back.

"Not money," he said. "I will let go but you are not to run, *d'accord*?"

I nodded, thinking running had never really been an option anyway. He let go of my arm and instantly I felt it throb in testimony to how hard he'd been squeezing it. He walked around to the front of the bench and sat down next to me.

A part of me was afraid to look at him. He didn't know that I had no hope of ever identifying him but he might well try to harm me to prevent the possibility of it.

He was powerfully built with piercing blue eyes which were made all the more intense by the knit hat that he used to cover his hair.

"My name is Daigneault," he said.

Because I didn't know what else to do and because he'd hesitated, I introduced myself.

"My name is Claire."

"I know who you are," he said. "Why are you here?"

I didn't know if he meant Paris or the Notre-Dame gardens. For one mad moment I thought perhaps he was an overzealous security gardener and I wasn't supposed to be in the gardens. There was a gate that I walked through but there was no lock on it.

"I...I am just a tourist," I said feebly.

"You are not a tourist."

He licked his lips as if trying to make up his mind as to what to say and I found myself getting less terrified as the seconds ticked by. First, we were in a very public place. And second, well, no that was the only reason.

"I know someone," he said finally, "who wants to hurt you."

The fading fear instantly spiked back up. He must have seen it in my eyes because he said, "No. Not me. I am here to warn you."

That did not make me feel any better.

"Why would anyone want to hurt me? I don't know anyone in Paris."

"I think you should stay away from the Hotel L'Ocean. Or better yet, go home to America."

"If you're not the one who wants to hurt me," I said, choosing my words carefully, "then tell me how you know someone wants to."

"Can I not just talk you into leaving? *You're in danger*. Why would you not go?"

He was honestly perplexed as if what he was saying was the most logical argument in the world.

"Do you know who killed my husband?"

I just blurted that out and while I didn't expect a real

answer from him, I was shocked to see that he wasn't surprised at the question.

Is he connected to Bob's murder?

"All I can say," he said, looking away, "is that the Big Boss called it and all the soldiers fell in line."

I know my French isn't top-notch but I'd challenge even a native speaker to understand that one.

"Big Boss? You mean *your* boss?"

He shook his head but not very convincingly. I thought he must answer to this Big Boss and he was stepping out of line to talk to me. That was my guess based on nothing but gut and intuition.

"My husband was an advertising executive," I said. "Nobody would want to kill him."

He stood up but didn't walk away. Then he turned to me.

"You switched rooms at the last minute," he said, narrowing his eyes as if indicting me.

I'd already thought about this at least a million times.

"Are you saying my husband was killed accidentally?"

"Not *accidentally*."

"You mean there was a target but he wasn't it?"

"*C'est ça.*" *That's it.*

I thought about that for a moment. As painful as it was to think that Bob's death was random, it made even less sense to think it was deliberate. A break-in, as the cops would have me believe, was barely more believable but only just.

I studied Daigneault's face with a thought toward trying to memorize his features but I knew it was hopeless. He had a nice face but totally unmemorable. He didn't have a scar or tattoo or any other defining feature. There was absolutely no way my brain would hold his image in my memory after I walked away.

"Who was the hitman?" I asked.

He let out a frustrated huffing sound, something I'd heard

several Frenchmen do since I'd been in the country. It sounded like air being let out of balloon too fast and could mean anything from *How good that clams are on the menu today!* to *I believe I am having a heart attack.*

"Even if I were to tell you," he said, "you cannot go to the police with his name."

"Why not?"

"You just cannot. If you will not leave the country then you must be mindful of your surroundings."

"You mean don't let people sneak up on me in public gardens?"

His lips twitched in what I'm sure the French would call a near-smile but most normal people would call an involuntary spasm.

"*Exactement.*"

"I just want a name," I said. "I have no power. I certainly can't find him on my own from just a name."

Except I absolutely could.

He shook his head in frustration. "I don't want to be the reason you are killed, Madame."

"I hereby absolve you. Please. I won't tell anyone you told me. I promise."

He looked over my head and then down at his hands. Finally, he shrugged.

"Nico," he said.

I frowned. "Is that a last name?"

"It's just a name and I'm sorry I gave you that much. Now please, go home."

I pulled out my phone.

"Will you let me take your picture?"

I could see he was taken aback at the request and he didn't like it. But it was also clear that he wanted me to believe him. And so he agreed.

As soon as I snapped the photo I felt better. I felt as if this was one time where my brain and nonexistent memory would not have the chance to let me down.

He stood up and so did I. It was time to go get the bloody towel from the flower lady.

"Thank you for the warning, Monsieur Daigneault."

"Does it help?" he asked. "Knowing your husband's death was just a mistake?"

I think as soon as the words were out of his mouth he answered his own question but I gave him a sad smile anyway and thanked him again for his concern.

He turned on his heel and slipped out of the garden gate and was gone. I followed him, more slowly of course, my chest aching with a sadness I didn't know was hiding there.

I'm not sure what I was hoping to discover through all this but I found it impossibly sad to think that Bob was basically killed because we wanted a room with better air conditioning.

31

A DAY LATE

All the way back to the Hotel L'Ocean I thought about what Daigneault had told me.

I walked south from the *quai de Conti* which morphed into the *quai de Voltaire* along the river before turning onto *rue du Bac*. I have to admit to looking over my shoulder more than a few times on the way to the hotel.

If it was true that I was in some kind of danger why would Daigneault warn me? What was I to him? How did I know that *he* wasn't the one who killed Bob? Who was Nico? And who was this mysterious Big Boss?

I hurried down the last narrow avenue in time to see Madame florist waiting impatiently for me by her kiosk. It occurred to me as I walked across the street toward her that all she had to do was go home and smear some chicken blood on an old towel and collect her hundred euros.

The sun was wavering in the sky and my watch told me it was after five o'clock. I was starting to feel the effects of skipping lunch.

The florist had the towel wrapped in brown wrapping paper and shoved the parcel into my hands as soon as I reached her. A small part of me wanted to look inside the package before I paid her but only a small part.

I was weary and ready to put this day behind me.

I handed her the money and she gave me an abrupt nod and turned and walked away without another word.

Feeling more and more tired by the moment, I walked up the street to the Metro. As I sat on the train heading to the eighth arrondissement I found myself praying that whatever was on the towel wasn't from Bob. And yet of course if it wasn't, I was as far away as ever from finding who killed him.

Once I got back to my apartment building I was surprised to see the shadows had deepened all around me on the street. It didn't take long for autumn to steal away the light. There was nobody loitering about the mailboxes or in the building lobby and I was so tired by now that I risked the scary elevator rather than take the ten minutes of exhausting trudging required to ascend to my apartment.

I did rip off a corner of the paper on the train ride home and saw brown stains that could easily have been old blood stains which at least seemed to invalidate my fresh chicken blood theory.

I was briefly surprised at the feeling of comfort and respite when I entered my apartment. It was the first time it didn't feel totally strange to me. I was sure that was in part due to the fact that I was tired and knew a hot bath awaited me but it was still nice.

Once in my apartment, I dropped the package on the dining room table and went straight to the bathroom where I turned on both taps in the tub and dumped in nearly a quarter box of Epsom salts. Ten years ago it would've been rose or lavender flakes but needs change.

I stripped, leaving my clothes in a pile in the bedroom and eased into the tub, groaning in sheer pleasure and let the next thirty minutes and the hot water work on soothing my muscles. When the water finally grew cold, I got out, dressed in my yoga pants and a cashmere sweatshirt and went to the kitchen to find something to eat.

Ten minutes later I was in front of the huge picture window in the salon that looked out over the street with a glass of wine and a sandwich of cheese and pickles. I was briefly sorry I hadn't stopped at the *boulangerie* for what had now become a ritual sugar buzz in the evening but decided a second glass of the very good Sancerre would settle that account.

I opened up my laptop as I ate my meal. As soon as I went to my Facebook page I saw there was a personal message waiting for me but there was also a photo of Cameron dressed as Spiderman for Halloween. He looked adorable and I felt a pang of regret that I hadn't called him to ask what he was going to go as. I could see Todd's leg in the picture so I guessed he was the one who was taking Cameron door to door while Catherine stayed behind to dole out candy.

Finally I allowed myself to check my personal messages and saw that the one I'd received was indeed from Lillian. I held my breath and scanned the lengthy message.

<So sorry to hear about your dad and your husband. Wow that's a double header no one should have to face. I'm glad you reached out to me. Your mom was flat crazy about you and never stopped talking about you.>

I frowned. That didn't ring true at all. I loved my mother but she was one of the most self-absorbed women to walk the planet.

<I know she never wanted you to know the truth about what happened to her in Paris...>

Shit. So it was true. My mother was raped.

<...but if the truth will help you keep what's yours then I'm sure

she'd agree. Yes. It happened while she was married to your father but I'm pretty sure it was months before she conceived you with Claude. Hope this helps and that you know you're always welcome down here in Jax! Hugs, Lillian.>

I jotted off a hurried thank-you to her and closed out of Facebook. I sat for a moment staring into space, registering that such a terrible thing had happened to my mother and she'd never hinted to me that it had. Maybe I was wrong about her. Children often are. It must have taken a lot for her to keep the rape from me.

I got up and brought my wine glass to the kitchen and rinsed it out. I wondered briefly if I should just wait for the results of Joelle's DNA testing and respond accordingly?

I frowned at the thought. That was definitely not happening.

I sat back down at my laptop and sent off a probing email to Claude's estate attorneys. They didn't work for Joelle. They worked for Claude. Or maybe France. In any case, they would want the truth as much if not more than I did.

Once I sent the email I looked around the living room. I knew I had a few things of my father's right here in the apartment that I could get Adelle to test for me. There were a pair of his shoes in the closet that had somehow got left behind when Joelle packed everything up.

It's bad enough to lose my inheritance, I thought feeling a sudden soreness develop in my throat.

But if the DNA shows that Claude isn't my father then I not only lose my inheritance but I gain the news that I'm the progeny of a sex offender.

Leave it to me.

If I'm going to lose, I'm going to lose big.

32

STRANGE FRUIT

After washing up my dinner dish, I refilled my wine glass and went back to the website that I thought might help me get a glimpse into the Hotel L'Ocean's online registry. I'm no hacker but there are some basic tricks that can afford the casual observer a quick glance of certain files. I certainly didn't want to change or alter anything. I just wanted to see what was there.

Most hotels had online registries for various reasons, the biggest of which was to connect with their managing or corporate offices. I wasn't at all sure that the Hotel L'Ocean was big enough to have a corporate office but I was quickly able to see online that it wasn't a sole proprietorship either.

As my search function went through its lengthy process in an attempt to date the registry at the hotel, I looked out my window and enjoyed the sight of the lights twinkling golden below me. I felt very relaxed after my bath and fully human after my dinner.

As long as I didn't think of Mom and what had happened to her sixty years ago, I was fine.

In the middle of these thoughts came a knock on my door. I froze, all my muscles tightened.

Who would be visiting me at this time of night? And how did they get past the main gate below? And the locked lobby door?

I walked to the door and saw the gap at the bottom—big enough for skinny mice and fat cockroaches to easily come and go—and a shadow that intersected the wedge of lamplight the hall sconces produced whenever they detected any motion.

"Who is it?" I said through the door making a mental note to have a peep hole installed soon.

"It is me, Luc," came a deep voice.

I frowned in confusion before I realized it was the young man from the first floor apartment. As I twisted open the lock, I wondered why I kept referring to him as *the young man*.

I opened the door and he stood there—much taller than I remembered—smiling and holding a white bag.

"I have extra *mille-feuilles*," he said. "And they won't last. I thought you might like them."

I blinked and looked at him and then the bag.

"I can see you are ready for bed."

"Thank you. That is very thoughtful." I took the bag.

"*Bon soir*," he said with a wink and then disappeared down the stairs.

I closed the door and glanced down at my yoga pants and sloppy sweatshirt. I'm not sure why it mattered. It was ridiculous to think he would look at me *in that way*. I glanced inside the bag and caught a delightful whiff of sugar and vanilla.

I pulled one *mille-feuille* out and set the bag in the breadbox in the kitchen for my breakfast tomorrow. I took the pastry back to my laptop where I could see the search engine had settled on a hazy but readable snapshot of a hotel registry.

From the looks of the quality of the text I was pretty sure I was looking at something that was not supposed to be available to the general population. But then again you could say that about ninety percent of what I found out as a skip tracer.

I took a bite of the *mille-feuille* and scrolled through the document until I came to the week that Bob and I were at the hotel.

Just seeing our names on the list made my heart hurt. I forced myself not to dwell on it and ran down the line of names. There weren't many people staying at the hotel that week which I would have thought was odd since it was August and the height of tourist season in France.

I counted twenty people, mostly couples.

Any of these people could give false names and false places of origins. But I read them and reread them slowly all the same.

One name jumped out at me and that's a phenomenon I always look for. What thing niggles you even if you have no idea why? Whatever it is, it must be important.

A man named Ribault Costé was registered the same time that Bob and I were. If I were Reynard Coté and I wanted to give an alias on a hotel registry I think Ribault Costé sounds very much like the kind of alias I would use.

Was Ribault Costé really Reynard Coté? If so, then it meant that Reynard was staying at the hotel *the week that Bob and I were.* And if I put what Daigneault told me into the mix then maybe—just maybe—that meant that Reynard was the original target and Bob had gotten caught in the crossfire so to speak.

I know a lot of this sounds like grasping at straws and imaginary straws at that. But I swear that's mostly what detection is. Especially when you have no real clues or leads.

It was after eleven o'clock and I was officially exhausted. I swept the pastry crumbs from my sweatshirt onto the floor and made another mental note to find a carpet sweeper tomorrow.

I went into the bathroom to brush my teeth and get ready for bed.

Just as I turned out the light on the side of my bed, it

occurred to me that Luc had been flirting with me. As inconceivable as that was to me, it was the only explanation for his behavior.

Winking.

Pastries.

Half smiles.

It had been so long since a strange male flirted with me, I'd forgotten what it looked like.

The thing that woke me a little bit later from a very deep sleep wasn't a sound but a pungent odor as stark and palpable as if alarms had gone off in my ear.

I sat up in bed bolt upright and listened, my heart pounding.

And what I heard was as terrifying as anything I could imagine.

Someone was in the apartment with me.

33

OFF AND RUNNING

My mouth was dry and I felt a crawling sensation on my skin as I strained to hear any sound from the hall. My nostrils seemed to fill with the scent of grease or a heavy body odor. The smell got more pronounced as I heard the sound of a heavy tread on the uneven boards in the living room.

I looked wildly around the bedroom.

Was there anything I could use to defend myself?

I grabbed up my phone from the bedside table, pushed 999 and jumped out of bed, the sound of my heart exploding in my ears. My breathing coming in noisy pants that I was sure whoever was in the other room could hear.

I glanced at the bathroom door. But I knew that by the time I went in there and rooted around for something to defend myself with, the guy would be on me.

Should I hide?

There was no way he wouldn't find me in this small apartment. I crept to the half open bedroom door and saw him standing in front of the window in the living room, the moonlight illuminating him through the window. He was tall and dressed in black. A surge of nausea coursed through me at the sight of him.

I had a butcher block knife holder full of knives in the kitchen. But at ten steps away the kitchen might as well have been in the next apartment.

Even though my fear threatened to overwhelm me I was aware that I recognized his denim = jacket. I saw the odd embroidery on the epaulets and this time I could see it was a design of a coiled snake.

It was the man I bumped into at the Hotel L'Ocean.

My vision suddenly narrowed and I felt a cold fury pump into me.

Was this the man who killed Bob?

He stood in the living room and turned toward me, a knife glinting from one gloved hand.

I held up my phone. My hand shook.

"The police are on their way," I said to him in French.

"Then I guess I had better hurry," he said in a high, unctuous voice.

Without realizing I was going to do it, I flung my phone at his head and turned and ran for the kitchen. Out of the corner of my eye I saw him pivot in my direction.

I never made it to the kitchen.

A terrible pain exploded in my shoulder and propelled me forward into the dining table which slammed me to a stop. A white-hot agony shot into my scalp as he grabbed my hair and jerked me back into his chest.

My breath thrust out of me as he held me with my back to him, my hair wound tightly in his fist.

Through my blinding panic, some part of my brain registered that I had been in this position dozens of times in the past in classroom situations. I could do the required moves in my sleep but I had never done them in pain or convulsed in terror.

Without thinking, I drove my elbow hard into his chest

before my brain fully registered what it was doing. I used the momentum to rise up on my toes and smash his nose with my fist. Blood squirted out onto my nightgown and the back of my neck. It wasn't hard enough to do real damage.

But I'm sure he wasn't expecting this kind of fight from me.

I twisted around to face him and with both hands grabbed his knife hand and torqued his wrist as hard as I could. He yelped in pain and dropped the knife.

That was the moment we both heard the sounds of police sirens coming up my street.

He shot out an arm knocking me out of his way and I went down hard, my hip exploding in pain on the uncarpeted floor.

He was out the door and gone before I fully realized the fight was over.

34

TILTING AT WINDMILLS

I suppose I shouldn't be surprised that Detective LaRue was one of the boys in blue who came to my rescue.

I wouldn't be surprised if both he and Roman know where I'm living in Paris so that when the dispatch reported a distress call to my address, they were notified first.

This is all in my head because of course LaRue was saying nothing about why he was the one who had showed up. But I know he's a homicide detective and this, thankfully, was not that so why did he come out on a routine distress call?

And where was Pellé? I thought he and LaRue were attached at the hip. Why did Roman get a night off but not his partner?

The police arrived within five minutes of my attacker's departure although I have to say they were five very long minutes. In the meantime I managed to stagger to the door and lock it—although clearly that hadn't stopped my attacker from gaining access.

As soon as the police arrived they looked at the lock, determined that I must have forgotten to lock the door—*ridiculous*—

brushed it for fingerprints and bagged the knife—for all the good it would do since my assailant was wearing gloves.

LaRue stood in my living room as the forensic techs worked.

"He disengaged the lock," he said to me. "That suggests he was a professional thief."

"Do professional thieves often break in carrying knives?" I asked.

"It would not be unusual for him to be armed. It was fortunate for you that he dropped his weapon."

I'd already told him that I'd disarmed him. Clearly he chose to think I couldn't have done that.

"Can you describe him?" he asked.

It was the way he asked. Almost snidely. Somehow he knew I couldn't do it. I don't know how. But he knew.

"He was the same man I saw coming out of the Hotel L'Ocean when my husband was killed," I said.

"You mean the man you say you cannot identify?"

"I remember his smell."

I knew how *that* was going to be received and, true to form, LaRue snorted in derision. I tried to imagine on what planet he was any good at his job.

"But you cannot describe his face?" he said. It was more of a statement than a question.

"I know he had one," I said tartly.

No, I couldn't describe the guy. You'd think that terror would sear the man's features into my brain for all eternity but the prosopagnosiac brain doesn't work like that.

"Would you be willing to come to the police station and look at suspects' photos?"

That would be a supreme waste of time. I could look at a hundred pictures of the very guy who stood in my living room threatening to kill me and never recognize him.

It sucked but there you are.

"No," I said. "It wouldn't help."

"I guess you didn't get a good look?"

"It was dark," I said. "Do you hate all Americans or am I special?"

He looked at me in surprise which in itself was a surprise. Was he truly unaware of what a jerk he was being?

My scalp, my hip and my shoulder were starting to hurt in unison. I guess the excitement of the last hour had temporarily kept the pain at bay. Now it was demanding my attention. I moved into the kitchen where I got a glass of water and a couple of ibuprofen.

LaRue watched me as I took the tablets. I got the impression he was thinking of saying something along the lines of *how do you feel* or *are you hurt* but in the end he didn't. It was just as well. I was too tired and too uncomfortable to respond nicely to fake concern.

"I was hoping you could give me an update on the man I discovered murdered in the alley three days ago," I said.

He made a face. "That information is classified."

"I've worked with the police before. I know it's not classified."

"Perhaps we do things differently in this country."

"Oh, I can tell you right now you do."

I knew he was going to take that as an insult. I was hoping he would. People often unintentionally divulge information when annoyed. I pushed a little harder.

"Were you not able to find any DNA from the man's attacker? I'm not sure what sort of forensic resources you people have over here—"

He bristled. "We are as up to date in criminal forensic analysis as your country, I assure you. There was no match to any DNA left at the scene in any of our criminal databases."

I'm pretty good at picking out liars. It is a gift I've developed from years of working with bail jumpers and people who basically lie for a living. And this guy was good. If I didn't know for a fact that acting and dissembling were mandatory requirements for all good detectives, I might actually have believed him.

We didn't talk much after that. He focused on watching his people collect what little evidence there seemed to be in the living room while I took my throbbing head, wrapped up in a heavy throw and sat on the sofa until they were finished.

When it came time for them to leave, I swear LaRue actually seemed embarrassed about his cold manner up to now—as well he should.

"I feel certain your assailant will not return," he said.

Based on what? I wanted to say but held my tongue. I was tired and my shoulder hurt. I just wanted him gone.

It was closer to dawn by the time they finally left and I figured there was no point in going back to sleep. I folded up my blood spattered nightgown, took a long hot shower, made coffee and sat in the salon with a big mug of it. I stared out the window as the dawn turned to full-on morning, lighting up the trees, dousing the streetlamps, and energizing the shop owners to move signs and produce bins out in front of their stores.

So Daigneault was right. Someone wants to hurt me.

I wondered why I hadn't mentioned to LaRue that I'd been warned about being in danger. I wondered why I hadn't mentioned to him that someone told me that Bob's death was not a burglary gone wrong but a mistaken hit.

I wondered why but somewhere deep inside I think I knew why.

I imagine I'm going to have trust issues with men for the rest of my life.

As I got up from the couch to dress for the day and check the ibuprofen bottle to see if I could take another two tablets without falling into a coma or incurring brain damage, I saw from my phone screen on the kitchen counter that I'd missed two texts from Adelle.

<Im in the neighborhood if you are up yet.>

<Claire? R U there? I have something big to tell you>

35

A LEG UP

After I'd texted Adelle back I waited for her to show up and decided I no longer felt I was taking advantage of her.

How could I feel that way when her brother's death was probably involved with Bob's death too? Adelle had the necessary tools that were imperative to my getting the answers I needed. And to that end Adelle and I both benefited. It was as simple as that. Nobody was using anyone. That's what I told myself.

I dressed quickly in my yoga pants and sweatshirt, wincing as I pulled the top over my head. Daigneault's words yesterday in the Notre-Dame gardens continued to come back to me.

If what he said was true and Bob's murder was just an accident, then why didn't I feel better? If his murder wasn't deliberate then it wasn't personal. It was just a case of mistaken identity. Which meant I reminded myself that *nobody's* motives for his murder were going to add up because Bob wasn't the one who was supposed to die.

So how was I going to find his killer?

If I couldn't trust the clues I found, where did that leave me?

Adelle was at my door within five minutes of my answering her text. Her eyes were large with concern as she stepped across the threshold.

"You've got quite a crowd gathered in the lobby below," she said. "Your neighbors seemed to be discussing taking up a petition to evict you."

"Can they do that?"

"It's just a joke."

Ah. French humor.

I went to the kitchen to make a fresh pot of coffee but as I reached for the bag of beans I got a stitch of pain in my shoulder and moaned.

"You're hurt?"

Adelle came into the kitchen and took the bag from me.

"I'll do this," she said as I sat in one of the dining room chairs. "Do you have ice?"

"I thought the French didn't believe in ice," I said, massaging my shoulder.

What did the guy hit me with? A brick?

"And I thought Americans couldn't live without it," Adelle said as she tugged open my freezer and found ice cubes.

I watched as she broke open the tray and wrapped the ice in a dish towel.

"Are you going to tell me what happened?" she asked.

"The guy who killed Bob came here in the middle of the night to kill me too."

She gently positioned the ice bag on my shoulder and frowned. Adelle was a cool one, I'll say that for her. Must come from looking at all those bloody crime scenes for a living.

"What did the police say?" she asked.

I snorted which sent a jolt of pain through my shoulder. Adelle turned back to the kitchen and ground more coffee beans and spooned them into the French press.

"They've signed off on Bob's murder," I said. "They think it was a burglary gone wrong."

Adelle put the electric kettle on and joined me in the dining room while we waited for it to boil.

Because of my brain affliction I like to think I'm a better judge of subtle human expressions than most. I tend to watch hand gestures and facial expressions closely. Not that it helps me remember people later but these things tend to jump out more at me.

Adelle had come here to tell me something and now she was trying to find the words.

"What is it?" I asked, too tired to play games.

She pulled her leather satchel onto her lap and opened it. She drew out an eight by ten spiral notebook and flipped it open to the first page.

"What I'm showing you is highly confidential," she said. "I could lose my job."

My mouth went dry as I thought of all the things she might be about to show me. I reached out to take the notebook and saw it was a crime scene sketch.

Of our hotel room at the Hotel L'Ocean.

So it's true. Adelle was one of the crime techs at Bob's murder scene.

The drawing showed a dresser by the window, a nightstand and a double bed. A man's outline was drawn on the bed and I swallowed hard when I saw it. The door to the ensuite bathroom was next to the headboard.

"My company is often called in to help the police in August," Adelle said, "because so many people are on vacation during that month. I wanted to tell you when we talked yesterday but I knew I'd be crossing a line."

I studied the drawing. "What am I looking at?"

"I think the main thing I wanted to show you was this area..." She pointed to the wall behind the bed. "It's where I personally lifted a set of prints—"

"So the cops lied?" I said. "They said there was no DNA."

"No useable DNA, that is true," she said. "And the prints didn't match anything in any database."

My shoulders sagged in disappointment. "But if it was a hit man or a known criminal..."

"Right. The guy would certainly be in the ICD—the International Crime Database. It lists all missing persons, violent offenders, terrorists, foreign fugitives, or unidentified homicide victims."

"What if he wore gloves?"

"Okay, but in that case whose prints did I lift?"

"I see," I said.

"Are you familiar with chain of evidence?"

"Of course."

Chain of evidence was the documented continuity of possession to ensure the integrity of evidence collected at a crime scene.

"What are you suggesting?"

"Well, I'm not saying mistakes don't happen," Adelle said. "Of course they do. But let me ask you, do you trust the detectives on the case?"

"I...shouldn't I?"

"Look, Claire. We are no more crooked or dirty here in France than you are in the US but we're no cleaner either. There *are* dirty cops."

When I saw where she was going with this, I have to say it wasn't the first time the thought had come to me.

"But why would they deliberately contaminate or withhold evidence?"

"That is a whole other mystery, *n'est-ce pas*? Let's focus on one thing at a time."

"Why are you helping me?"

"Because I think it's possible, as you said, that my brother's death and your husband's death are connected."

I thought for one brief moment about telling her about the whole Reynard/Ribault thing that I'd discovered last night which at least hinted at the possibility that Reynard was in the hotel during the time of the murder.

Which meant, as Daigneault had suggested, *he* could have been the target all along.

But I didn't mention it. I'm not naturally a deceitful person but I fear I've developed a recent compulsion not to trust everyone. I would keep my discoveries to myself for a little bit longer before some of these clues began to form a picture that made sense to me.

"I have something I need you to analyze for me," I said.

"My company has a long waiting list."

"I've found something that might be important in Bob's death."

She frowned. "What is it?"

"A kitchen towel with blood on it."

"Blood on a kitchen towel isn't unusual. There are knives in kitchens."

"I don't really know what kind of towel it is," I said. "But I need to know if it's Bob's blood." I picked up the ice bag again. My shoulder was throbbing in all seriousness now.

We sat for several long moments not speaking. I needed her to think about my request and I needed not to ruin my chances of getting a *yes* out of her by talking too much.

"I believe Reynard was executed," Adelle said. "His wallet was still on him making me believe it was not a mugging as the police would have me believe." She snorted in disgust. "The thugs are outsourcing to stupider and stupider minions."

She got up to pour the hot water into the coffee press.

I hadn't gotten any sleep and my mind was now buzzing unpleasantly. As I waited for her to return with the coffee I tried to make the facts line up with what I thought I knew so far.

First—it seemed there was DNA found at Bob's murder site that didn't exist in any criminal database.

Second—the man who attacked me tonight was the same man who nearly knocked me down running out of the hotel the afternoon Bob was killed.

Third—Adelle's brother Reynard—the likely intended target of Bob's murder—was in the hotel that day and was successfully killed—*or as Adelle said, executed*—not far from there just a few weeks later.

Adelle brought two mugs of coffee to the table and I set the bag of ice on the floor.

What about Reynard? LaRue had said there was no usable DNA found at Reynard's crime scene. Did Adelle know that? Was it her company who did that analysis too? I decided to hold off asking.

For now.

"Was Reynard in trouble in any way?" I asked instead.

She sighed. "If you're asking me if Reynard could legitimately have been a target for a criminal element then the answer is yes. My brother was a delightful, charming man. And a drug dealer."

The pieces just kept clicking into place.

"I'm sorry."

"It is what it is," Adelle said sadly. "Let me have the towel with the blood on it. I'm sure this is just a way for both of us to feel as if we're doing something to solve these murders of the men we loved."

"Well, feeling better isn't nothing," I said. I got up and went to the bedroom and returned with my nightgown. I put it and the towel in the same bag.

"The guy who attacked me tonight," I said, "had the courtesy to bleed all over my favorite nightgown."

Adelle stood up and took the bag from me.

"If he's in the system, I'll know who he is by tonight."

36

SYMPATHY FOR THE DEVIL

Jean-Marc hurried up the front steps of the hotel, pausing to look both ways to see if anyone saw him enter. What with the two recent homicides in and around the hotel, he had every reasonable explanation for why he was here today. But by now looking over his shoulder was an ingrained habit.

Once inside, he saw the lobby was vacant as it always was this time of day. Normally it would have been empty last August at the time of the Baskerville hit but because Bernard was a greedy bastard with the brains of a centipede, he'd taken in more guests than he'd been warned to take in. And they'd all paid the price ever since.

Jean-Marc felt an uncomfortable thickness develop in his throat as he strode to the desk. He could hear the sounds of a soccer game on the television through the closed door of the office.

"Santé!" he barked, his irritation spiking. He'd texted the man that he was coming.

I should demand more, having to put up with his bullshit.

Bernard came out of the back room, a look of surprise on his face as if he'd not been expecting Jean-Marc.

"Were you involved in last night's attack on the American woman?" Jean-Marc asked.

Bernard widened his eyes innocently.

"I never leave my post, Detective. You know that."

"I wasn't asking if you *personally* did it," Jean-Marc said, holding out his hand for the envelope he knew Bernard would delay giving him until the last minute.

"I don't understand. Shouldn't *you* know who *personally* did it?"

Bernard pushed the envelope of bulging euros across the desk to him.

What was the sense in talking to this cretin? In the end, what difference did it make?

Jean-Marc stuffed the envelope in his inside jacket pocket and turned to leave.

"She was here again yesterday," Bernard said. "The American. She didn't think I saw her."

Jean-Marc froze.

"Who did she speak to?" he asked without turning around.

"The florist."

Jean-Marc frowned in confusion. "Who?"

"The old lady across the street who sells flowers."

Jean-Marc felt a thin pulse of appeasement. The American wasn't a professional. She had no contacts. She was just a bored housewife walking around Paris talking to street vendors. She was not a threat.

As he walked to the doors he got an uncomfortable feeling that someone was watching him. But when he looked around he saw no-one except the little Asian maid in the hallway with her cleaning cart.

He stepped out onto the street.

Harmless or not, enough was enough. The American

woman needed to *go*. The more she stuck her nose into her husband's murder the more she was going to stumble onto something that caused major problems for everyone.

Especially me.

His phone rang and he cursed when he saw the name on the phone screen and pushed *Decline*.

He would do what was necessary—didn't he always?—and he would do it regardless of the moral or legal ramifications.

But just this once he would do it in his own time.

Right now his problem was one American loose end. A devoutly recalcitrant woman who refused to accept what the authorities told her.

Last night she'd been lucky.

Next time it would be a different story.

37

WE'LL ALWAYS HAVE PARIS

I felt like an old woman, aching in all the places one could ache. A part of me wanted nothing more than to wrap up with a blanket, and a cup of tea on the couch.

But another part of me needed to get out of the apartment.

After Adelle left with the bag of items for her to analyze, I dressed gingerly for the day and went out.

The dark clouds roiling overheard had blotted out any real light or warmth from the sun. A breeze kicked up and the threat of rain was real.

I found a kiosk selling hot mulled wine and a bench with a good view of the Eiffel Tower and settled down.

Bob and I hadn't made it as far as the traditional tourist sites when we were here in August. I looked at the famous tower now and wondered why the thought of not seeing it with Bob didn't bother me.

I guess I was still angry at him. Or maybe I'd already taken several strides away from him emotionally and our life together.

I looked at the Eiffel Tower and I thought about how it had been here during the Nazi occupation and how the first time I'd seen it was with my mother. Someday I would show it to Cameron.

Maybe.

I felt a throb of sadness as I drew my limbs in close to my body and held the hot wine to my lips. But I didn't drink. Sitting here on this bench looking up at the Eiffel Tower made me feel as if the world had been spinning too fast and was now just beginning to slow down.

As if offering me the opportunity to get off.

Thinking of my mother inevitably made me think about Joelle and her quest to impoverish me. I didn't think what she was doing was personal. Even though she seemed to have all the charm of a Disney villainess, the fact was she barely knew me. The meeting in the attorney's office and then at the café were the only two times we'd laid eyes on each other.

But that didn't make it any better. If it did turn out that I was the result of a sexual attack, lack of money to live on would be the least of my troubles.

Who am I kidding?

Knowing the terrifying details of how I came into the world would be bad but losing all my money would be the worst. Without a doubt. How would I support myself? I couldn't go back to Atlanta. The creditors were pounding on my virtual door every time I opened up my emails.

Without an apartment here that I could sell—or live in if worse came to worst—I was out of answers.

An image of a granny suite in Catherine and Todd's back yard came to mind and I audibly groaned.

I startled a pigeon that had gotten too close and decided it was time to walk again. Another less than happy consequence of being sixty is that if I sit for too long I get up like a crone out of fairy tale and must massage my back for several seconds before I can fully stand up straight again.

Even in Paris, old age is not for sissies.

I walked just for the sake of walking—not an uncommon practice in Paris. I passed parks and cafés, children on scooters, businessmen on their smartphones, pigeons watching it all from the backs of park benches.

When it finally started to rain I pulled out my collapsible umbrella and continued to walk.

I checked my phone for the time and then put a call in to Adelle. I knew she was probably working but I wanted to explain the extra item I'd given her this morning in the bag.

I'd found a man's toothbrush in the bathroom closet with the initials CL on the handle and slipped it in with the towel and bloody nightgown.

When I got Adelle's voicemail I left a message telling her that the toothbrush wasn't urgent and I'd explain later. She should just hold onto it for now.

After I hung up I stood for a moment holding my phone to my chest and felt the cold breeze whip through me.

Hold onto it, I thought, *until I can send my DNA results to match with Claude's.*

At which time I will either lose everything or I won't.

As I left the park, something made me look over my shoulder at the Eiffel Tower in the distance. It looked impregnable. Like nothing could destroy it. Not time, not Nazis, not city fires or terrorists. It looked like how Paris always felt to me—timeless and indestructible.

It was then that I realized that I really, really didn't want to lose it.

38

BUSTING A MOVE

I arrived back at my apartment and hesitated at Geneviève's door but decided I needed to go upstairs and get on the computer.

I ached in every imaginable way physically and when I thought about the possibility that what little money I had might well be taken from me if Joelle had her way, I felt my stress level inching up by the second.

The day had begun with me wrestling the same man I was sure killed Bob and then wrestling in a different way with the very people who were supposed to be helping me.

After a quick sweep of the apartment to confirm I was indeed alone, I opened up my laptop. I'd left it open to the site where I'd tracked down the Hotel L'Ocean's guest registry for the week Bob and I had stayed there six weeks ago.

Was it only six weeks ago?

Looking at the registry made me think of how Detective LaRue had told me that there hadn't been any useable DNA at the crime scene in the alley. I found myself wondering again if the police had done the forensic lab work in-house on

Reynard's murder or had farmed it out like they had with Bob's murder.

Would Adelle have told me if her firm was handling it? Probably the cops thought it was a conflict of interest for Adelle's company to do it.

Deciding I was getting nowhere on the computer, I took a hot bath but couldn't relax. Understandably, every creaking sound I heard from the other room—instead of thinking it was the natural noise of an almost two-hundred-year-old building—I was sure was someone about to burst through the door and drown me in my bath.

Hardly conducive to a relaxing soak.

I finally gave up, dried off and pulled on my pajamas. It was Paris in October and that translated into sunny but cold days and just plain cold evenings. I passed the marble fireplace in my *salon* on the way to the kitchen but was pretty sure it was for looks only.

I wedged a chair under the doorknob on the front door and made a mental note to call a security company in the morning to set up monitoring and alarms.

On the other hand, if this place was going to be handed over to Joelle, I might want to save my money.

I poured myself a large glass of Sancerre and brought it back to the bedroom. I climbed into bed and took three ibuprofens which I washed down with the wine. I'm sure that wasn't healthy but at the moment I was more concerned about pain management than long-term health.

As I made myself comfortable in bed, I once more found myself running through everything I knew so far.

First, it seemed pretty safe to say that Bob was killed mistakenly for Reynard the drug dealer. They were both killed in the same way, in the same area and there was a good chance that Reynard was actually staying at the hotel during Bob's murder.

I wasn't sure how to confirm my theory about the whole

Reynard/Ribault thing so in the absence of any corroborating information to support I decided to just go with it. I know that sounds frivolous but often it's exactly the right approach to take. Once you commit to a direction, wrong or right, you at least start moving. If along the way you discover that your original hypothesis was flawed or wrong, you can always change it.

But if you have a gut instinct about these things as most cops and private investigators do, then trusting your gut on some half-truths to form a working picture is generally not a bad approach.

So I decided to go ahead with the belief that Reynard was staying at the hotel the same week we were. This also went hand in glove with the idea that Reynard was the intended victim instead of Bob.

My shoulder was still steadily throbbing. I'm not sure how I would've felt if all this had happened to me in my forties but I can tell you that fighting off a killer in your nightgown and getting bashed about will stay with you much longer when you're in your sixties.

As I was getting ready for bed I noticed my left eye was slightly blackened. I didn't remember how that happened but it could easily have been during the scuffle with Nico.

Even before Adelle confirmed to me that my assailant was Nico, I was sure it was him. He was the one Daigneault warned me was out to get me.

Who else would it be? Same smell, same jacket.

I wondered again why I hadn't mentioned to LaRue about Daigneault's warning. I reminded myself that Adelle thought one or both cops might be dirty.

If so, how was I ever going to find the truth?

I thought of Daigneault and wondered for the thousandth time why he reached out to me? Why did he want to help? Who was he and how was he involved?

I had a novel I'd been trying to read for the last couple of nights and picked it up to find my place when my phone rang.

Roman's face showed up on my screen and I felt a rush of relief. I was glad I'd linked his photo to his phone number. The more I reinforced the image of his face, the more it stayed with me.

"Hi, there," I said, picking up.

"Are you all right? I can't believe the one time I leave to check on my folks, this happens!"

I leaned over for my wine glass and felt suddenly safe. After all, even though he wasn't with me, if anything should happen, at least I wouldn't have to waste time dialing 999.

"Where do your folks live?"

He laughed and I realized the sound of it was already familiar. And nice.

"Meaux," he said. "Ever heard of it?"

"No. But I don't know France at all."

"I'd like to take you there some time. It's very small but like a lot of villages outside Paris, the old ways are still going strong. It is very charming."

"Sounds nice."

"Jean-Marc said you knew the guy who broke into your place?"

"Yes, but I'm surprised he told you that. He didn't believe me."

"You must have been scared out of your mind."

"I truly was." The effects of the wine were starting to make me sleepy. Combined with the rough comfort of his voice in my ear, I was feeling very pleasant.

"I can come over tonight if you want."

"I'm fine, Roman," I said. "Just really tired."

"Lunch tomorrow? And you can give me a blow by blow."

"I'm sure it's in Jean-Marc's report."

"I want to hear it from you."

"Lunch sounds good."

And it did. It really did.

"But can we make it the next day?" I asked. "I have a thing tomorrow."

After establishing where and when, we hung up and I tossed my book on the floor, feeling better than I had any expectation to feel. Just as I was leaning over to turn out the light, my phone lit up again.

It was Adelle.

"Are you still up?" she asked breathlessly.

Instantly I was awake.

"You have news," I said, sitting up straight.

"I do. Although not what you were looking for, I'm afraid."

"Tell me."

"The DNA on the towel was a match for human blood."

I knew it.

"Just not your husband's."

I felt a sick fluttering sensation in my chest at her words. I don't know why I was surprised. I knew upfront it was likely a dead end. In fact, I had nearly convinced myself that the blood had to be chicken or beef blood. So the fact that it was human should have been encouraging. But it wasn't. I felt dejected hearing it wasn't Bob's blood. I felt like I was back at square one.

"I am sorry, Claire. But it was always a long shot."

"I know."

"Are you coming tomorrow?"

Reynard's body had been released to his family yesterday and he was to be buried at Montmartre Cemetery in the morning.

"Of course," I said.

"I won't have much time to talk."

"Adelle, it's fine. Be with your family. We have the rest of our lives to talk."

"The towel wasn't a total dead end," Adelle said.

"What do you mean?"

"There was an awful lot of blood on it. Did you look at it?"

I hadn't really.

"Was there enough to suggest that the person who bled on it might not have survived?" I asked.

"Probably not that much. But it was more than a mishap with a razor or a kitchen accident."

But it wasn't Bob's blood so what difference does it make?

"Who would have access to the dumpster?" Adelle asked.

"Only everybody coming in and out of the hotel. The people who work there as well as the guests. And probably anybody walking by the alley. Plus the florist out front. So everybody."

"Don't forget the police too."

"You're really down on the police, aren't you?" I said.

"I just know some of them. They are not the vanguard of honor and integrity that you might think."

"Well, so the towel could have been left there by anyone. I don't suppose the DNA you found on it matched anything in your database?"

"Regrettably, no."

"Is there any way to see if Bernard Santé is in the criminal database?"

"Who?"

"The desk clerk at the Hotel L'Ocean."

"Get me something with his DNA and we'll see."

"It would eliminate him from the question of the towel if he is."

"That is true. Now we just have to sift through twelve million other people in Paris to find those who do not have criminal records to determine a match."

"I'll get you something with Bernard's DNA on it," I said.

"As for the name of the man who broke into your apartment, the sample matched an international criminal by the name of Nicolas Bourdeaux. He goes by *Nico*."

Just like Daigneault told me.

So now I knew for sure the name of the man who attacked me and who probably killed Bob.

"Can I ask you, Adelle, did your firm process your brother's death?"

She sighed. "We did although naturally I wasn't assigned to the case."

"And?"

"It came back totally clean of any prints or DNA. Except for yours, of course."

"You're kidding."

I was expecting there not to be a match to anyone in the criminal database. I wasn't expecting there not to be *any* DNA.

"It seemed strange to me too which is why I went on a colleague's computer and checked a copy of the report that was sent to the police department."

"Yes?"

"It turns out there *was* DNA found on Reynard," she said taking in a shaky breath. "And it matched Nico's in the ICD."

But LaRue said the report came back with no match to anyone!

"Why would the police lie about Nico killing your brother?"

"If Nico is a valuable asset to the police they may not want to lose him."

"Nico might be a confidential informer?"

"Yes, exactly."

"And the cops are willing to give him a pass on murdering someone because he's so useful as a CI?"

"It's ugly but very possible."

"I'm so sorry, Adelle." I didn't know what to say. Bottom line was that she had discovered her brother's killer. But because the police had either falsified or ignored her company's findings, Nico would not be held responsible.

We were both quiet for a moment and I felt another wave of discouragement. How was I ever going to find out the truth if the police were able to manipulate the facts for their own purposes?

"Do you want to tell me now why you included a toothbrush in the same bag as the towel and nightgown?"

Honestly, it was the last thing I wanted to do.

"No big deal and no rush," I said, feeling like that was the biggest lie of all. "It belonged to my father. There's been a question raised as to my...as to his and my..."

"Paternity?"

"Yes."

"I see. Someone is challenging the will?"

"My stepmother."

"I'll need your DNA."

I felt a rush of gratitude to this wonderful girl who didn't even know me. Tears pricked my eyes.

"I'll send you the link to my 23andMe results. Thank you, Adelle."

"Before we hang up, there's one more thing. I'm not sure how useful it is. Do you remember that set of prints I found in your husband's hotel room that weren't in the database?"

"Yes?"

"I double-checked my notes and discovered there was a partial thumb print that wasn't sent to the police."

"Why not?"

"They try to save money by giving us parameter limits as to acceptable findings levels. This partial wasn't enough on its own to match anywhere but with additional testing it might be possible to enhance it. Not guaranteed."

"And the cops don't think doing everything *possible* to identify every fingerprint at a murder scene isn't essential?"

"The enhancement testing is expensive. With budget cuts, operating costs..."

"Plus why waste money on the death of a single American tourist?"

"I don't know, Claire. Maybe."

"So you enhanced it?"

"I did. But then I had to erase any trace that I'd done it. So I have the facts but no evidence to support it."

"The print matched someone in the database, didn't it?" I said, my excitement mounting.

"It did. He's a petty thief and drug dealer, fairly well known in the Latin Quarter."

"Name?"

"Guy by the name of Paul Daigneault."

39

THE BITE IS WORSE

It rained the morning of Reynard's funeral.

As I walked up the hilly mound in the northerly section of Montmartre, I saw evidence of the feral cats for which the cemetery was famous. They were perched on ancient headstones, winding around obelisks and statues of angels, and generally glaring down at the mourners making the climb to bury their dead.

Adelle's news last night about Daigneault had kept me up most of the night trying to think how it fit in. The more I thought about it the more bewildered I was.

If Daigneault was involved in Bob's death then why did he contact me and warn me? Did he kill Bob and now he felt guilty?

I walked through the graveyard until I saw a small group of mourners gathered beside an open grave under umbrellas in the drizzle.

The closer I got I could also see Detectives LaRue and Pellé standing toward the back of the group trying not to look conspicuous. I was able to recognize Roman immediately now, thanks to regularly looking at his photograph and I assumed the scowling guy next to him must be LaRue.

Normally it might make sense that they would be here to see if anybody suspicious showed up. But if Reynard's death was an execution as Adelle thought, then that was unlikely. Serial killers and other nut jobs tended to go to the funerals of their victims for reasons known only in the dark recesses of their minds.

But if Reynard was killed because of a contract—or even a mugging as the cops seemed to believe—then the thought that his killer would show up at his funeral was idiotic.

So why were the detectives here?

I would be sure to ask Roman when we met for lunch tomorrow. I'm sure he expected me to grill him about their progress on Bob's case and I fully expected him to say that they'd either closed it or shelved it. He'd essentially told me that already.

I looked past the detectives to see Adelle with her family. I assumed the older woman dressed in black next to Adelle was her mother. I was shocked to see that she was my age. Of course Adelle was much younger than I was, but for some reason I tended to look at her as a contemporary which of course was ridiculous.

I scanned the crowd to see if there was anyone who looked suspicious to me. I knew I wouldn't recognize anyone—I wasn't looking for familiar faces. I was just looking to see if there was anyone who looked like they didn't belong.

Regardless of how beloved he was by his family, Reynard was a drug addict. His compatriots would be thugs and druggies. I don't know if those sorts of people pulled themselves together long enough to honor a fallen friend or if they just saw his death as another excuse to go get high. In any case, I didn't see any disreputable types or indeed any young people at all who might be Reynard's age.

I was so focused on the crowd and the surroundings of the ancient cemetery that I didn't see Detective LaRue striding over to me with murder in his eye until he was nearly on top of me.

He grabbed me by the arm and dragged me back toward the car park. I stumbled over a tree root and nearly went down but Roman was behind me and caught me.

"Jean-Marc!" he said to LaRue. "This isn't necessary."

LaRue let go of me and turned on Roman and for a moment I thought it was Roman who was going to get the brunt of LaRue's fury. But LaRue sorted out his priorities in time to zero in on me again.

"What the hell are you doing here?" he snarled.

"How dare you?" I said, rubbing my arm where he'd dragged me. "This is police brutality and abuse of your position. I have every intention of reporting you!"

"You're not in the US now," he said hotly. "The police in France actually have some jurisdiction. You are at the funeral of a murder victim. Are you a ghoul? Or did you have more to do with his death than you told us?"

I felt my vision cloud and the adrenaline rush through me at his words. I was literally seconds from slapping him. Something in my face must have broadcast my intention because Roman put his hands on my shoulders and turned me away from LaRue, leading me to the parking lot.

He called angrily over his shoulder, "You need to get a grip, Jean-Marc!"

I was so furious I was shaking but I let him take me away.

Within minutes we were sitting at a nearby café. It was cold but we sat outside anyway and let the alcohol warm us.

"What is his problem?" I said. "Is it just me or does he hate all Americans?"

Roman ran a hand across his face and I found myself feeling sorry for him. LaRue was his partner and from the things Roman had said, his *senior* partner. It might well be that the both of them hadn't managed their careers well but from everything I could find online, LaRue was well-respected by his department.

"He's got a problem with Americans," Roman admitted.

I looked at him in surprise. I hadn't really expected that LaRue didn't like Americans.

I understand, as a nation, we Americans can be a strong flavor and not everyone in the world likes us. But after the first few interactions with someone, I expect to be judged on my own merits and not my nationality.

"What happened?" I asked.

Because the fact is, you don't hate a whole country—and everyone in it—unless something had happened.

Roman looked around the café and then back at me, clearly uncomfortable.

"I probably shouldn't say. I mean everyone knows but nobody talks about it."

"About what?'

He sighed, his body posture softening.

"About five years ago his wife was the victim of a hit and run. She didn't die but she's been in a wheelchair ever since."

"I guess it was an American who was driving the car?"

Roman nodded. "A tourist in a rental car. Pretty easy to track down. But because we couldn't get him the night it happened, we couldn't test his blood alcohol."

"But you got him on the hit and run, right?" I said.

"Yes. He was arrested, tried and found guilty for leaving the scene of an accident."

"So the system worked."

"Except he knew people. He was back in the US and driving around free within a month of the trial."

"I was truly appalled. I know there is a separate set of rules for the rich but this was egregious.

"So Detective LaRue was understandably furious," I said slowly.

"He was obsessed. He really loved his wife."

"Past tense?"

Roman made a face. "It's not much of a marriage now. She drinks too much, she's addicted to her prescription drugs. She's angry. And she takes it out on Jean-Marc. Basically everyone on the force knows his life is a living hell."

"I'm so sorry."

"So maybe we cut him some slack. Maybe some of the senior guys look the other way if he's too rough with a suspect or is unconventional in interviews."

"You mean he uses abusive techniques."

Roman looked uncomfortable. "I wouldn't go that far. Just not regulation approved."

"You really like him."

"I respect him. He was a great cop before all this happened. A legendary cop. But this broke him. Nobody wants to accept that. Least of all Jean-Marc."

I sipped my whisky and shivered. I wouldn't totally let LaRue off the hook. He was after all responsible for his actions. But knowing what was done to him and his wife helped me to see a little better what he was struggling against.

I made a vow to make an effort not to take his treatment of me so personally in the future.

40

BLOWING IN THE WIND

The next morning I was up early to hit the grocery store for milk and yoghurt. Unfortunately, I wasn't prepared for the hundreds of different kinds of yoghurt in my neighborhood mini-mart. I was so overwhelmed I ended up buying none. I'd see if I could winnow down the selection by looking at some of the brands online later that evening.

Even without the yoghurt I was back in my apartment with my arms straining with two bulging bags of groceries, a *baguette* and a sack of sugary just-baked *chouquettes* that I absolutely could not resist at my local *boulangerie,* and a paper cone of hothouse violets that would look pretty in a vase on my dining room table. Unfortunately Joelle hadn't left any vases when she cleared out, so a jelly jar would have to do for now.

Once I put away my groceries and positioned the violets in a plum *confiture* jar that I found in the back of one of the kitchen cabinets, I made myself a cup of tea and settled down on the couch. I still had a good hour before I needed to get ready for my date with Roman. I nearly laughed when I called it that so I decided to refer to it that way from now on.

Because it made me smile.

The first thing I did was go to a newspaper archive on a genealogy bank website to see if I could find anything related to an attack at the Hotel L'Ocean in the past year. Adelle said the amount of blood on the hand towel looked more like it was the result of an accident than a murder attempt. I tried to imagine what kinds of scenarios that might include.

After an hour of searching on the computer I finally concluded that if there had been an attack on a guest or an employee at Hotel L'Ocean, it hadn't been reported to the media. Unfortunately I didn't have access to police or hospital emergency department records. They would have been much more helpful.

I sighed in frustration and closed out before getting ready for my date.

The afternoon had warmed up nicely and a gentle breeze seemed to waft along all the delectable scents of the street's many *boulangeries* and cafés from where I sat at the Café Bobo.

Roman and I had planned to meet at noon. As per usual, I was early. Even back home I was always early but here in France the habit was the equivalent of being about a day ahead of everyone else.

Not that French people are chronically tardy, but they don't have the same attitude toward pre-arranged engagements as Americans.

While I waited I brought out my notebook to review what I knew so far and to go over the questions I had for him.

What I now knew was that the man who broke into my apartment was the same man I saw leaving the hotel just before Bob was killed. It was the same man who Daigneault said killed Bob mistakenly and the same man Adelle and I now know killed her brother Reynard.

I wasn't going to tell Roman that I had independent confirmation that my assailant was Nico. I wanted to see how much he'd tell me first.

It was frustrating that Adelle's lab couldn't place Nico in Bob's room. That would be the cherry on the cake for a case of mistaken identity.

Inevitably my mind came back to the niggling question of the hour: *What were Daigneault's prints doing in Bob's hotel room?*

Because the one person that *could* be placed in Bob's room was the one person that for some bizarre reason I'd decided to trust. Why did I think I could trust him? Of *course* Daigneault was involved in all this, probably up to his neck.

I glanced around the café and found myself wondering if Daigneault was currently watching me, following me. A part of me hoped so.

I really wanted a word with him.

"There you are!"

I looked up to see the man I now recognized as Roman Pellé striding toward me at the café. He looked so happy to see me—and honestly so handsome with the breeze tossing his thick mop of silver laced brown hair—that I couldn't help grinning when I saw him.

He leaned over and kissed me on both cheeks. It wasn't sexual of course but it was the first time he'd done anything like that.

"You have been waiting long?" he asked as he sat down.

"Not really," I said, closing my notebooks. "I'm just chronically early."

"Uh oh," he said as he signaled to the waiter and then looked back at me. "That sounds like a classic Franco-American mismatch."

I laughed. Once the waiter came over—and he'd steadfastly

ignored me for the full fifteen minutes that I'd been there—Roman asked if he could order for both of us. I was happy to let him do it. I wouldn't have to worry about my pronunciation for a change.

He ordered our meals along with a bottle of *Châteauneuf-du-Pape* and a bottle of *l'eau gazeuse*.

"You look beautiful," he said, turning back to me. "Forgive me for not mentioning it as soon as I walked up."

"You're forgiven," I said with a grin. "I know how important food is to the average Frenchman."

We both laughed at that and I was aware of wanting to keep this lunch on a friendly level. It was true I needed information but I could also use a friend. The last thing I was looking for was to start something up romantically. I'd given this some thought on the walk over and had given myself a stern talking-to.

The fact was, everyone likes to be found desirable and honestly it had been a while since I'd felt that. But I can't even begin to think about being with someone until I sorted out what happened with Bob.

And the first step on *that* path involved the answer to the question of why and how he was no longer in my life.

"I hope you're okay with me asking you some questions about Bob's case," I said.

"I expected it."

The waiter brought a basket of bread and then poured our glasses of wine before scurrying off.

"But before that," I said, "I want to tell you something that I don't generally tell people."

I could see his face brighten at the prospect. He really did think this was a date.

"I have a brain anomaly that I was born with called face blindness."

He frowned and I went over the words in my head to make sure I'd used the right French ones.

"The medical term for my condition is *prosapagnosia*. It basically means I'm not able to recognize faces after I've seen them."

"Truly?"

"I know it's hard to believe. It's one of the reasons I took your picture a few days ago. To cement your face in my mind."

"You seriously wouldn't remember me otherwise?"

He was too mature to actually have a hurt look on his face but I have been down this road before. To imagine that your face is so forgettable that someone can't hold it in their memory is demoralizing if not devastating.

"It doesn't mean I don't *want* to remember what you look like," I said hurriedly. "It's a neurological disorder. My brain is unable to retain facial images. Have you really never heard of it?"

"Perhaps now that you mention it but I thought it was very rare."

"I think they used to think it was rarer than it actually is. Anyway, I wanted you to know. I think I've got your face secure in my mind now but just in case we bump into each other on the street and I give you a blank look, please don't take it personally."

His eyebrows shot up.

"Is this the reason you were not able to identify the man you saw at the Reynard crime scene?"

I hesitated but there was no point in lying.

"I saw him but I couldn't remember what he looked like."

"Incroyable." Unbelievable.

"For someone who doesn't suffer from it, yes, it is."

The waiter brought our food, *moules à la marinière,* which gave both of us a moment to process what I'd said.

"This looks great," I said, dipping a crust of bread into my mussels sauce.

"It is a specialty of theirs," Roman said, topping off my wine although I'd barely drunk any.

"So you don't recognize me when you see me?" he pressed.

"As I said, thanks to the photo I took, I'm doing much better with you. Detective LaRue however, no. I'd never be able to identify him if he wasn't standing next to you."

"That is quite a handicap," he said.

"Yes. Thank you. It truly is." I felt a flush of relief that he seemed to understand what a true impairment it was. It was always tricky telling someone for the first time. Usually they just didn't believe you until the fifth time you walked right past them at the grocery store or the carpool line without saying hello.

I took a large swallow of my wine. It was delicious.

"Do you know the name of the guy who attacked me yet?" I asked.

"We're still working on that. But we have some leads."

"Okay." I flipped open my notepad as if I didn't know the name I was about to ask him about. I pretended to read. "Have you ever heard of a man named Nicolas Bourdeaux? I think he goes by Nico."

Roman's body stiffened and he looked at me with outright surprise.

"Can I assume from your reaction that you know the name?" I said.

"Yes, I know it. I'm wondering how it is that *you* do."

"That doesn't matter. But since Nico was the man I saw coming out of the Hotel L'Ocean the day my husband was murdered, naturally he is of special interested to me."

"I thought you said you couldn't recognize people."

"I can't. Not their faces. There are other ways to identify people."

"Okay," he said dubiously. "So you *did* recognize Nico as the one who attacked you?"

Again, he didn't understand face blindness. The bottom line was that I was able to identify Nico, but I didn't *recognize* him.

It was just easier to go with it. "Exactly," I said.

"Why didn't you say this before? You told Jean-Marc it was too dark to get a good look."

"I recognized his aftershave," I said. "And his jacket."

I appreciated the restraint it must have taken Roman not to roll his eyes. He must really like me. Because even to my ears it sounded lame.

"Look," I said, "forget all that for a moment. Let's pretend it turns out when your people do their forensic analysis that they find evidence of Nico in my apartment."

"That is a dangerous game and ultimately useless," he said in his best policeman's voice.

"Humor me. Let's say I'm right and it was Nico who broke into my apartment. What happens next?"

"Given that you can't identify him?"

"That's right."

"The DNA is circumstantial. It would be enough to bring him in for questioning but that is all."

"I see." I could also see that this lunch was turning out to be much less enjoyable for Roman than he'd anticipated. I was sorry about that. It seemed I was on a roll as far as using people were concerned. First Adelle and now Roman.

"How well do you know Nico?" I asked watching him carefully as I took yet another healthy swig of my wine.

He sighed heavily and looked at me with an expression that could only be described as shamefaced.

"You have to understand, Claire, in this business we sometimes must work with very undesirable characters. It is necessary for the greater good. You are understanding?"

I felt my throat constrict with discouragement.

Adelle was right.

"So he's one of your snitches?"

"We have used him on occasion, yes. But that doesn't mean he turns into a good guy just because he'll help us. I mean, we *pay* him. But if we find out he was the one who broke into your apartment, he'll be arrested. I promise you that."

Pretty confident words when he knew I couldn't identify Nico. I admonished myself for being so ungenerous.

The fact was that Roman and I were working this case from two different ends. I wanted to find out who killed my husband and Roman wanted to keep his valuable CI on the street, while putting Bob's murder case to bed—and possibly me, too.

"Last question and then we can enjoy the rest of our meal," I said.

"Shoot."

"Do you know a man by the name of Paul Daigneault?"

"Never heard of him," he said as he lifted the breadbasket and signaled to the waiter to bring more.

It was a long shot, I thought with a pulse of disappointment as I reached for my wine glass.

As just about all my leads tended to be.

An hour later after saying goodbye to Roman I walked away feeling like I had an ally in the police department. I'm sure he was hoping for more than that and I wouldn't definitely say that more wouldn't eventually happen. But for now the most important thing was that he seemed willing to share at least a little information with me.

After he hurried back to work—it was still amazing to me that someone can help finish off a bottle of wine and then go back to work!— I headed in the general direction of the eighth arrondissement.

I walked slowly, my mind whirling with the feelings I felt triggered by Roman's attention to me—and incredibly, the guilt I felt about enjoying them. That made me angry at Bob all over again.

I stopped at a furniture shop and was looking in the window where I spotted a really lovely side table and thought how perfectly it would look in my *salon*—ideal for the meals I ended up eating on the couch—when I felt my phone vibrating. I stepped off the sidewalk and dug out my phone.

It was Adelle.

"Hello," I said.

"*Allo*, this is not a bad time?"

"No, it's good. I'm sorry I wasn't able to stick around yesterday at the cemetery."

"*Ça n'est pas grave*," she said. "I saw you go off with the policemen and hoped there was not a problem?"

"No, everything's fine. I might even have gotten some news. In fact, one of the detectives admitted that Nico works for them."

"How did you get them to tell you that?"

"I'm working on a contact inside the department," I said with a laugh. "Long story."

"Well, that's good if you can get information. Listen, I have the information you asked for."

My heart nearly stopped. I don't know why I wasn't expecting her to get back to me so soon on Claude's DNA. I dearly wished there was a place to sit down.

"What did you find out?" I asked, holding my breath.

"I am sorry, *chérie*. But there was no match between your DNA and Claude Lapin."

41

HELL TO PAY

"I'm sorry, Claire. Claude Lapin is not your father."

My body went completely still. It was like on some level I thought that if I didn't move, Adelle's words would remain unsaid.

I couldn't believe it.

All my life, crap father or not, I at least always thought I had one.

I needed to find a place to sit down. My head started hurting and my hands were tingling.

Claude is not my father.

I've lost everything. My husband, my father, all my money...

I was suddenly very thirsty. I looked down the sidewalk. I really needed to find a place to sit down.

"Are you okay?"

"Yes," I said, forcing myself to take in a long breath. "I guess it was always a possibility."

"What will you do now?"

I spotted a bench a block away and started for it on shaky legs.

"I have no idea. I need to call you back."

"Are you sure you're okay?"

"I'm fine. Don't worry. I'll call you later."

I disconnected and walked toward the bench. Just before I reached it I found myself looking again into the display window of the same furniture store I'd passed before and nausea welled up in me. It was all I could do not to be sick.

Just moments before I was thinking of *redecorating*.

And now I was homeless.

I turned away from the store—and the bench—and just kept walking, not caring what direction I was going in. It wasn't until I crossed the *pont Royal* that I realized where I was going.

I don't know what instinct was driving me back to this place. It was like I was totally rudderless and only had this one spot on earth directing me. This one place, the place where Bob died.

And the mystery that nobody cared about solving but me.

I stopped on the famous bridge—the third oldest in Paris—to watch a tourist *bateau* sail beneath me. The sun was still out and diamonds glittered on the rough water. I took in a long breath and closed my eyes. I was leaning against the stone balustrade of the bridge as pedestrians scurried past me.

I tried to center my thoughts and regulate my breathing to calm myself and bring me back in balance.

Nothing could help whatever would happen now. But I was in complete control of whether or not I had an anxiety attack over it.

I took in a deep breath through my nose and exhaled through my mouth. I did this several more times, deliberately not thinking of how I must look to passersby.

When I finished I felt, if not exactly wonderful, at least a little better.

I brought out my phone to check the time and found myself looking at the picture I'd taken of Roman and myself at the end of today's lunch.

He was laughing, his head near mine. His arms were longer so he had taken the picture with my phone. I looked at the photo and tried to see something in my eyes—was I happy? Was I flirting? Was I damaged goods? But all I saw were two moderately good-looking people of a certain age enjoying each other's company.

I realized as I looked at the photo that this was the first time I was seeing myself sitting next to someone who was not my husband. I studied my face again in the photo and then Roman's. I was smiling and so was he. We didn't look like friends.

We looked like two people at the beginning of something.

You could see the difference.

I think on some level that was another reason why I took the picture. If there was any chance that this friendship with Roman was going to turn into something I wanted to remember what the beginning looked like.

Except now there was no chance. I didn't know where I was going from Paris but as the most expensive city in the world, I knew I couldn't stay here.

It's true I may have to leave, I thought as I turned to continue walking.

But by God I'll make my time here count for something.

The florist was still in her kiosk across from the hotel when I walked up. It was a little after two o'clock and I could see that most of her flowers had been sold. She looked at me as I approached but that was the extent of any greeting.

I think it must have been while I was standing on the bridge looking at the photo of Roman that I got the idea to see if anybody at the hotel recognized Daigneault's picture. I was still disturbed by the fact that his prints had been found in Bob's room. Adelle tried to say that a partial could mean anything, even that time had degraded it so it might not have been left recently.

I pulled out a ten-euro bill and laid it on the wooden counter at the florist's kiosk. Her eyes never left my face. I found Daigneault's photo on my phone and showed it to her.

"Ever see this guy?" I asked.

She glanced at the photo and took the money.

It always amazed me how fast the average *normal* person can recognize faces—even those they see infrequently.

She nodded in the direction of the hotel. "Over there. Coming and going."

"A lot?"

"Yes. Many times."

I thanked her and walked across the street not at all sure what this would show. I already knew Daigneault had been in the hotel. His partial print proved that. But this is what investigators do. We relentlessly ask and re-ask the same questions until something pops.

I walked into the hotel and saw the desk clerk look up from whatever he was doing and make a hideous frown. I forced myself to smile and showed him Daigneault's photo.

"Do you know him?"

"No."

"Ever seen him in the hotel?"

"No."

He turned and went to the back office. I heard the television turn on and the sound of a soccer game. I reached down and plucked a ballpoint pen off his desk and put it in my purse. Before turning to leave I caught sight of a motion down the hallway.

It was Marie. She looked up at the same time I saw her but she was literally tethered to the spot by the vacuum cleaner. I could tell she wasn't happy to see me but I walked quickly over to her.

"*Bonjour*, Marie," I said, leaning over to turn off the vacuum cleaner.

She looked over her shoulder at the front desk but the only thing either of us could hear was the soccer match playing in Bernard's office.

I held up my phone with Daigneault's picture.

"Have you seen this man before?"

She hesitated and clearly made the decision that answering my questions would get rid of me faster than not.

"Yes."

"Where?"

"Here. In hotel."

"Do you remember when?" Instantly I cursed myself for phrasing it like that, making it easy for her to say no.

She shook her head.

On impulse I scrolled through my pictures until I came to the photo that Adelle had given me of her brother. I showed it to Marie.

"Have you ever seen him before?"

The maid blanched but she nodded.

"A lot? Here in the hotel?"

Marie nodded again.

"Alone?" I asked on impulse. I was thinking maybe he might have checked in with a woman. I wasn't expecting the answer I got.

"Sometimes. But mostly with the policeman."

I wasn't sure I'd heard correctly.

"What policeman?"

"Brown hair."

I quickly scrolled to the picture of Roman that I'd just taken and cropped me out of it. I prayed really hard and showed the photo to Marie.

She shook her head.

"No. Him I see when all police come. Not him."

I let out the breath I didn't realize I was holding.

I didn't have a photo of LaRue. I'd meant to take one surreptitiously but hadn't managed it yet. I called up a search browser on my phone and went to the Paris police website. Roman had mentioned a Bastille Day picnic they'd all attended last summer and I was able to find the link to the Facebook page for the event.

Thank goodness police all over the world were more interested in positive public relations. I didn't recognize him of course but when I went to the tags and searched I found a picture of a man tagged as Jean-Marc LaRue.

I didn't recognize him myself—he was too average looking to stick in my mind. But I could see how he might be the man I'd seen so many times with Roman.

LaRue was standing at a table and actually smiling, holding a glass of wine. I saved the photo to my phone and then showed it to Marie.

"*Oui*! That is him," the girl said. "He is here many times but that day I remember because of..." She looked at me and then dropped her eyes.

He'd been here the day Bob was killed?

"Before or after all the police came when my husband was killed?" I asked, feeling a line of sweat form on my top lip.

"Before. Just him."

I licked my lips trying to imagine what this information could mean.

"Why was he here?" I asked, feeling my excitement ramp up. I found the photo of Reynard again and showed it to her.

"Was it to see this same man?"

"*Non*. I think that day he was only here to collect his money."

42

A DOLLAR SHORT

I walked home in a fog not sure why I was surprised and trying to rewind my memory to see if the things I'd heard LaRue say in the past fit with the fact that he was secretly meeting with Reynard.

And on top of that he was taking bribes? Protection money?

Marie said she'd seen him many times receive an envelope of money from Bernard at the front desk. Always quickly, secretively. Where was the money coming from? I assumed Bernard was just the go-between.

I felt a bitter tang in my mouth.

Bottom line, LaRue was a dirty cop.

Worse, Marie said she thought she saw him strong-arming Reynard on more than one occasion.

A sudden terrible thought came to me.

Had Jean-Marc killed Reynard? But what about Nico's DNA at the murder scene? Did Nico really kill Reynard?

Or was his DNA planted at the crime scene by LaRue?

All of a sudden I remembered the interview with LaRue and Roman after I found Reynard's body. While both detectives had questioned me, LaRue had taken the lead.

Plus there had been a fresh wound on his face. Whatever had happened to him had clearly happened in the hours just before interview.

Had LaRue attacked Reynard? And had Reynard fought back?

Feeling restless and not ready yet to settle into my apartment for the night, I turned toward the Parc Monceau a few blocks from my building. This was the park I'd sat in when I first moved back to Paris.

And the park my mother took me to as a child.

I walked toward it and noticed that most people were clearing out of it. School children ran or zipped past me on their scooters with their bouncing balls, their sounds of laughter echoing down the street.

I tried to imagine the kind of amazing childhood someone would have who got to play in this beautiful historic park every day after school.

I stepped through the ornately scrolled wrought iron park gates and went to the first bench I came to. With everyone else streaming out of the park as the late afternoon gave way to early evening. The idea in the park alone was less than inviting but I was tired and I needed to rest. I looked around to see that even the ducks and the squirrels seemed to have disappeared.

I pulled out my phone and sent a quick text to Adelle telling her I had something of Bernard's that she could test. I watched the bubbles form under my message indicating that she was devising a reply, but then the bubbles stopped.

I wasn't even sure what I was hoping to find. If Bernard was in the system, that meant he was a criminal. The fact that LaRue was doing some kind of dirty business with him meant that LaRue was a criminal too.

I rubbed a hand across my face, feeling a pinch between my shoulder blades when I did. I hadn't done any stretches or even simple yoga moves since coming to Paris three weeks ago. Even with all the walking I do around the city, my muscles were tight and sore. And of course I was still achy from my wrestling match with Nico two nights ago.

I noticed the park's central carousel's lights were off and I found myself shivering. The temperature had dropped.

But something kept me rooted to the bench.

It was a memory I had of being in this park when I was eight years old. I was with my mother and I remember she was upset. She wasn't crying but not far from it. I didn't know the details of her relationship with my father at that point but I'm pretty sure her unhappiness in the park had to do with him. I didn't remember if we'd seen him that day. Perhaps we were supposed to and he'd cancelled.

Now that I think about it, Parc Monceau always felt a little sad to me.

Claude isn't my father.

I felt a chill thinking of the horror my mother must have experienced when I was conceived.

How could she even bear to look at me after that?

Suddenly my skin began to crawl and I looked around and saw that it had gotten dark and I was alone.

Nico is still out here somewhere.

Cursing the fact that I didn't even have pepper spray with me, I jumped up and hurried toward the gates, looking over my shoulder as I went.

The streets outside the park were busy with people looking for *brasseries* to eat in or cafés to enjoy their evening *apèros*. A few of the side street grocery stores were open and there was a small flower kiosk inside one where I stopped and bought a paper cone full of flowers. I'm not sure why. I think a part of me felt lonely with the idea of coming home to a quiet, empty apartment. Not that flowers were much company but at least they were alive.

I bought two bouquets, one for Geneviève, and that made

me feel better. I would look in on her and maybe she had time for a cup of tea. It wouldn't get me any closer to sorting out my problems—with LaRue or Joelle—but it would at least serve as a nice distraction. And I could use that right now.

As I walked to my building, it occurred to me that Roman might like to know what his partner was up to. I stopped in front of my apartment building door and dug out my phone.

Please don't let him already know what LaRue's up to. I don't think I can bear one more betrayal from someone I thought I could trust.

I stood with my back to the building and put the call through but it went to voice mail.

While I had my phone out I saw I was getting a call and I recognized that the number was Joelle's. I hesitated only briefly before declining the call. I didn't know what she had to tell me but I could only imagine it wouldn't make me feel any better.

I waited and saw that she'd left a voice mail. On the remote chance she was calling to say she was sorry to have brought so much anguish into my life and had decided to drop the suit to challenge my inheritance, I listened to the voicemail.

She came right to the point.

She gave me until the end of the month to vacate her apartment.

43

DEAD TO RIGHTS

By the time I stepped through my apartment building door it was early evening. My neighbors had not been pleased by all the commotion related to the break-in yesterday. Even Luc had only given me a curt nod at the mailbox this morning when I left for my lunch with Roman. I guess I was in the doghouse for allowing some brute to break into my apartment and nearly kill me.

I went to Geneviève's apartment door and knocked. I heard the faint sounds of mewing coming from inside and was surprised. I'm sure I would've remembered if she had a cat.

Geneviève opened the door and looked past me like she was checking to see if I was alone.

"Good evening, Geneviève," I said. "I have an extra bunch of dahlias I thought I'd share."

Her eyes lit up and she took the flowers from me.

"They are beautiful, Claire. *Merci.* Won't you come in for a cup of coffee?"

How the French manage any sleep at all with all the coffee they drank in the evening was beyond my ability to understand. I shook my head.

From the time the idea came to me that a visit was a good idea until the moment I walked through the building door, I'd lost my energy for socializing. The only thing I really wanted to do now was take a long hot bath and eat whatever leftover *pain au chocolat* was still in my bread box.

"Another time," I said. "I just wanted to apologize for all the commotion Thursday evening."

"That was certainly not your fault, *chérie*," she said. "If anything it is I who should be apologizing to you since Paris is my city. Are you all right?"

"I'm fine," I said.

"You do not look fine."

"I got some bad news recently."

She frowned. "Worse than losing your father and your husband in the same week?"

I nearly laughed when she said that but the French have limits even for their unique sense of irony.

"I found out today that I'm not Claude Lapin's biological child," I said, trying the words out for my own ears. "My stepmother is taking me to court to have my inheritance revoked."

Geneviève sucked in a breath and tsk-tsked while shaking her head.

"And so the courts will not recognize you as his heir?"

"Well, no. I'm not blood-related. At best I've got stepchild status which the courts do not recognize."

I'd done a little online research to see how close to the edge I could skate and still keep the money. Not close at all as it turned out.

"So I'll be moving out," I said, hearing those words too and feeling sick at the sound of them.

"Do not give up so easily, *chérie*," Geneviève said.

"I don't think it's a matter of giving up or not giving up. The law is the law. Has been for about six hundred years."

"I always liked Claude," she said, which I thought was an odd thing to say under the circumstances.

"Well, in any case, I just wanted to stop by."

"Oh, your new furniture was delivered today."

I was half turning away when she said that and I stopped to look at her.

"I don't have any scheduled deliveries," I said.

She shrugged. "He looked like a mover to me."

"Who did?" I felt my breathing accelerate.

"The man I saw going upstairs to your apartment."

There were only two apartments on the third floor, mine and a vacant apartment. Unless he got lost this man must have been heading to my apartment.

I saw Geneviève glance at her door where I saw she had a peep hole.

"I only use it to keep an eye on the apartment building security," she said defensively.

"Quite right," I assured her. "What did the man look like?"

She shrugged again. I noticed that the French do it in response to nearly any question.

"Big," she said. "Too big to fit into the elevator, I think."

"When did you see him?"

"I cannot remember exactly, *chérie.* But around my nap time, so perhaps fourteen hundred hours?"

That was two o'clock in American.

"Okay, thanks," I said, smiling my goodbyes as I hurried up the stairs, clutching the flowers and my bag of produce. When I hit the landing on my floor, the automatic light in the hall flickered on.

I slowed and then stopped because I could hear my radio clearly from my apartment.

And that was because my apartment door was open.

44

DETAILS, DETAILS

I'll never know why seeing the open door made me go through it instead of racing back downstairs. I stepped into my apartment, still holding the dahlias in my arms, my eyes looking everywhere at once.

"Hello? Is anybody here?"

I held my breath but heard not a sound.

Had whoever had broken in come and gone? Was this a burglary?

I saw the brass lamp in the *salon* tipped over on its side. My hand felt for the light switch and the room illuminated.

And then I saw the blood.

I dropped the flowers on the coffee table and inched toward a wide smear of blood on the hardwood floor. It led toward the bedroom as if something had been dragged. Instantly I felt hot and my stomach began to churn.

The scent of blood—like iron shavings—suddenly filled my nostrils. I moved as if in a trance to the doorway of my bedroom and then froze.

The body lay face up on my bed, his eyes staring unseeing at the ceiling.

My mind raced as I stared at the body.

There was no doubt he was dead. His eyes were open and he had a gaping second smile under his chin where his throat had been cut.

I felt paralyzed. I didn't think about the possibility that the killer might still be in the apartment. I honestly thought nothing. I was staring at something that shouldn't be and I couldn't wrap my brain around it.

That feeling lasted for a good five seconds before I began to slowly come back to myself and take in my surroundings. When I did, I heard my bedside clock ticking, the building pipes gurgling and the faint noises of traffic on the street.

I knew as well as anyone about the sanctity of crime scenes and the importance of not touching anything. I knew the last thing I wanted was to mess up any possibility that the police might find out who did this.

But two things came to my mind immediately and both of them took precedence over immediately calling the police.

One. I didn't know who the dead body was and I needed to find that out before the cops did and then wondered why I didn't know who was lying dead in my bedroom.

Two. I needed to talk to Geneviève before the police did. In fact, if there was any way that I could talk to her and leave her out of this completely, I wanted to do that.

I flipped on the overhead bedroom light from the doorway assuming my DNA would be all over it anyway. I knew that the crime scene techs would make a note of what lights were on, the temperature in the room, if any music was playing. But it couldn't be helped. I didn't have much time.

I went over to my bed and stood, careful not to touch anything. I looked at his face but I wasn't expecting to recognize him.

Being careful not to step in the blood that had pooled on the floor, I leaned over him and sniffed. The only thing I smelled was blood. It masked anything else that might have been there.

My stomach curdled and knowing how emphatically vomit would contaminate the crime scene, I pulled back until I could settle my nerves and my stomach.

One of the tools people with face blindness use to remember someone—and take it from me it's very nearly useless—is clothing recognition.

If I'm talking to someone at a party and he's wearing a Cerulean blue cashmere sweater and then he walks away to get a drink or use the toilet, I'll remember the blue sweater when he returns and we can pick up our conversation where we left off. But if for some reason he spills something on the sweater while he's apart from me and then exchanges it for another garment, I will never recognize him in a room full of people.

But clothes, yes. I often remember articles of clothing.

I think I've read that some people with face blindness can't even remember clothes so I guess I'm lucky.

As I was leaning over the dead man I recognized the denim jacket with the snake embroidery on the epaulets that the guy who attacked me in my apartment a day ago had worn.

So unless he loaned his jacket out to someone, this was Nico.

I felt a shimmer of relief. If the cops were eventually able to identify Nico as my assailant they would understandably be highly suspicious of my inability to identify him dead, face up on my bed one day later.

I walked to my living room where I pulled out my cellphone. My hands were shaking as I dialed Geneviève's number.

"*Allo*?"

"Hi, Geneviève," I said. "I'm afraid I've got a minor emergency. Mind if I run back down there for a minute?"

Geneviève was dressed for bed when I got to her door but she let me in without a word and only a questioning glance. I was on the phone with the police dispatch as I came into her apartment.

"Yes, that's right," I said, after having reported the death and given my apartment address. "I'm pretty shook up so I'm downstairs in the apartment of a neighbor. Apartment six."

I disconnected and went into Geneviève's living room.

"I don't have much time," I said hearing how dramatic that sounded. "But I need to talk to you about what you might have seen today."

Geneviève followed me into the living room. She looked suddenly very old to me.

"What has happened?" she asked.

"I found a man dead in my apartment after I left you a few minutes ago."

She gasped and her hand flew to her throat.

"I need to ask you exactly what it was you saw this afternoon when you thought someone was moving furniture upstairs."

She sat down on the couch and was quiet for a moment.

"I saw a man."

"Just one?"

"There is more than one dead body?"

"No, but it doesn't look like a suicide so there must have been another person."

"Oh." She swallowed hard.

I tried to be patient but with every noise I heard outside I was sure the police would soon arrive and while I didn't need to be at my door to welcome them, my time with Geneviève would come to an abrupt end.

"I only saw one man," she said finally. "He was big, as I said. Which is why I thought he was a mover or delivery man."

"And you said he didn't take the elevator?"

"No. He would not have fit."

So did Nico's killer arrive *after* he did or had he already been upstairs in my apartment waiting for him? I'd left my apartment a little before midday. The killer would have had all afternoon to arrange this.

Is this a message for me?

"Claire?"

I turned my attention back to Geneviève. "Sorry. What?"

"I'm afraid I went down for my nap not long after that. If a second man came, I would not have seen him."

"Okay. Well, at least I know the killer came after Nico did."

"Nico is the victim's name?"

"Yes. He was the one who attacked me in my apartment and I have every reason to believe he also killed Bob."

As soon as I saw her eyes, I knew I'd said too much. This was a quiet apartment building in an upscale, well-to-do part of Paris. Up until I moved in there were no hit men, killers, assailants or double murders happening on the block.

"I'm sorry, Geneviève. I'm afraid Bob's murder has opened up a can of worms."

She made a face so I assumed they didn't have that phrase over here.

Since the only person Geneviève had seen today was Nico and I already knew *he* was here since he was still upstairs on my bed, there was no point in telling the police that Geneviève had seen anything. Knowing them, they'd probably take her downtown to ruin one of the few perfectly good days she had left in her life.

"I'm not going to tell the cops you saw anything," I said.

"Is that wise? Shouldn't they know what I saw?"

"I don't think it will be necessary. They have all the information they need upstairs in my apartment. Especially since you didn't see the other guy who was clearly the one with the knife."

"He was killed with a knife?"

I must be tired. I kept upsetting her and what I was trying to do was reassure her that she didn't need to be involved.

"I really don't know," I lied. "I was just being hyperbolic."

Now we could both hear the lobby doors opening and multiple voices coming up the hall. I was surprised I hadn't heard the sirens but maybe coming to my building on a murder call had become routine.

"I need to go," I said, standing up. "If you remember anything else about today—"

"Yes, I will call the police at once."

I hesitated. "I was going to say call *me*. The police have a lot on their plate and don't tend to be all that responsive."

"I see," she said, and nodded. "I will, of course."

She walked with me to the door where I stood for a moment and watched the cops through her peep hole as they charged up the stairs toward my apartment.

"And Claire?" Geneviève said.

I turned to look at her.

"I don't at all think you have brought mayhem and calamity to our lives."

My eyebrows shot up. "Is that what the other tenants are saying?"

At that moment I heard one of the policewomen yell out something and when I turned to look back out the peephole I saw the apartment door opposite Geneviève's swing open revealing an older couple in their bathrobes huddled in the opening watching the activity.

A split second later, a dark shadow obliterated my view, followed by a brisk rapping on Geneviève's door.

"That'll be my cue," I said to her.

She reached out and gave my hand a squeeze.

"I don't care what the others say," she said, her eyes bright with stubborn determination. "I am glad you are here, Claire."

45

RHAPSODY IN BLUE

I opened Geneviève's door and greeted the policewoman standing on the other side. The officer was young and all business. She quickly glanced at Geneviève and then back at me. I stepped out into the hall.

"You are Claire Baskerville?" she asked.

"Yes. I called it in. Do you need me to go upstairs with you?"

I could hear that the police were in my apartment. I'd left the door unlocked.

"That will not be necessary. Will you come with me, please?" she said.

I'd expected this and had brought my purse and phone with me when I went to Geneviève's. Now I took the stairs down one floor to the lobby accompanied by the policewoman.

I assumed that Roman and LaRue would be the detective team on the murder. I'm sure they were wondering how it was that so many people could be dropping dead around me.

I certainly was.

I half expected to see them in the lobby or as I walked out of the apartment building. I passed two open apartment doors filled with outright hostile glares directed at me. Four people in white coats were pulling on cotton footies in the lobby. One of them was Adelle. Her eyes went wide when she saw me. I wanted to mime "call me" but was afraid someone would see and pull her off the case.

And if there was anything I needed more than someone on the inside to give me information on what had happened upstairs in my apartment, I don't know what it was.

It wasn't that late and a small crowd had also gathered outside my apartment building. Three police vans were parked on the curb and the policewoman led me to the nearest one. She put me in the backseat by myself. I wasn't handcuffed but I was fairly sure I was back in "prime suspect" position again.

Once we arrived at police headquarters I was led to an interview room although not the one I'd been in the other two times. Inside the room was a metal table and three chairs, all riveted to the floor. A pair of handcuffs hung from a chain on the table.

I was grateful nobody suggested I put the handcuffs on. But otherwise there was certainly nobody trying to make me feel better about the devastating event I'd just experienced. Surely there couldn't be that many people who killed people in their own apartment and then called to report it?

But people are strange and don't I know it. For all I know, killing people and then calling the police was a common occurrence.

I waited for about fifteen minutes before a policewoman came in and gave me a cup of coffee and a ham sandwich. I couldn't help but think that in some ways I ate better in police custody than I did in my own apartment. I thanked her and was surprised to find I had an appetite. I ate everything and was half surprised she didn't come back with a *crème brûlée* and demitasse.

Since I still had my phone, I went on one of my people search sites to do what I would've done if I hadn't come home and found a dead body in my bed. I typed in the name *Paul Daigneault* in the search window to see if anything came up. I didn't really expect to find anything and I didn't.

For one thing I was pretty sure my search sites are restricted to people in the US. I'd meant to do some research to find the French equivalent to the skip tracer's friend—something I didn't feel my little smart phone could comfortably handle—but of course hadn't gotten the chance to do that tonight.

I didn't have to wait long before both detectives joined me in the interview room.

To be perfectly clear, I didn't totally recognize either of them but I'd studied Roman's picture enough times so when he walked in the first thing I registered was that he looked vaguely familiar. That was a huge improvement.

"Before you say anything," I said to them, "I can tell you the name of the dead guy and also state categorically that he was the one who attacked me two nights ago."

"I thought you couldn't identify your attacker," LaRue said.

"Not by his facial features, no," I said. I took in a long breath. "I suffer from a brain anomaly called prosopagnosia. I'm not able to remember faces but I make up for it with a heightened sense of smell."

The two of them looked at me exactly as I feared they would—even Roman who had been trying so hard to be the good cop and who I'd already explained my condition to.

"Prosopag...?" LaRue said doubtfully.

"It doesn't matter," I said. "The bottom line is I'm not able to remember faces but I remember his aftershave. It was the same man."

"His aftershave," LaRue said, with an ugly twist to his mouth.

Have I mentioned how much I hate this man?

"Anyone could wear the same aftershave," Roman said

reasonably. I suppose he didn't want to look like a fool in front of his partner but I could see he was trying to throw me a bone.

"Yes," I said. "But it smells different on every man. It's subtle but I'm sure it was the same man who attacked me."

They both sat down.

I debated reminding them that my attacker was also the same guy who ran into me at the hotel the afternoon Bob was killed but I could see they weren't open to hearing it.

"How was he killed?" I asked.

"That's not how these interviews go," LaRue said dryly.

But Roman answered me.

"A knife across the throat."

"So, like the others."

"You can't have it both ways, Madame Baskerville," Roman said with faint frustration. "You can't insist this man is your husband's killer and also that he was killed by your husband's killer."

I assumed the comment was for LaRue's benefit but still, I didn't appreciate it.

"What time did you return to your apartment?" LaRue asked me.

"Seven o'clock." I had of course told the policewoman all of this.

"And your apartment door was open?"

"Yes."

"Why did you go in? Most sane women would not have."

"I don't know why I did."

I didn't want to say *because I had an armful of dripping flowers.* That really did not sound sane.

"And you called the police as soon as you saw the body?"

"Of course."

Nobody was writing anything down nor had they flipped on a recording device that I could see.

LaRue's phone buzzed and he stood up to take the call at which point Roman leaned across the table to me.

"Are you all right, Claire?" He moved his hand to touch my wrist and then clearly thought better of it.

"Not really. Can you tell me anything else about the dead man or who you think might have done this?"

"His name is Nicolas Bordeaux. We're sure now that he was the one who killed the man you found in the alley. His DNA was found at the scene."

"I thought LaRue said there was no DNA found."

Roman frowned. "No. There was. We just hadn't identified it."

That wasn't true. Adelle said her company's report had specifically named Nico. But I found myself nodding my head.

"Nicolas Bordeaux is a known contract killer," Roman continued. "We now believe your husband's murder was a case of mistaken identity. Especially since you switched hotel rooms at the last minute."

"But you didn't find Nico's DNA at Bob's crime scene?"

"He must have worn gloves."

"But he wasn't wearing gloves when he killed Reynard? Isn't that weird behavior for a professional killer? He left DNA in an outdoor crime scene but not in the indoor one?"

Before he could answer me—and I could see he was a little annoyed that I wasn't jumping up and down with joy at the tidbit he'd thrown my way—LaRue came back in and told him somebody wanted to see him outside.

Roman gave me a patient look and left me alone with Jean-Marc.

The cop who hates me.

The cop who lied about being at the hotel the day my husband was killed.

The cop who was taking bribes.

"Detective Pellé just informed me that you think my

husband and Reynard were both killed by the man found dead in my apartment today."

LaRue frowned fiercely, clearly not a fan of Roman having told me anything.

"Except I don't believe it," I said.

"Believe what you like," he said. "I'm sure my partner thought you were so eager for answers you'd appreciate hearing what we've discovered."

"So was Nico your confidential informer?"

"No. He was just a thug."

LaRue was definitely lying. Roman had already told me they used Nico as a CI which according to Adelle was the sole reason his DNA wasn't released before now on Reynard's murder.

"Did Nico use the same weapon in both crimes?"

LaRue hesitated just a hair as if trying to make up his mind about answering me at all.

"Yes," he said finally. "The call I just took confirmed that a knife was found in his apartment. It matched both crimes—your husband's and Reynard's."

And that's when I knew for sure he was lying.

46

SHINE ON

Roman ended his phone call in the hallway outside the interview room and looked up to see Jean-Marc coming out of the room, his face red with agitation.

Roman was like any other policeman when it came to trusting his gut. There was a place and a time. And every cop he knew trusted that feeling deep inside that told him what his other senses failed to.

And what Roman's gut was telling him was that Jean-Marc was losing it.

Roman had to admit that Claire had a tendency to be tenacious and he could see how that could be frustrating.

Especially to someone with something to hide.

Especially to someone who had a problem with Americans.

"Are you okay?" Roman asked him.

Jean-Marc turned on him, his eyes blazing, his face flushed.

"Take her to Hotel Matteo," Jean-Marc said. "Put a policewoman on the door and then meet me back at the crime scene."

"Hotel Matteo? That's not a great area of town."

"Did you hear the part about putting a policewoman on her door?" Jean-Marc barked, his eyes flashing.

"Okay, fine. No problem," Roman said, bewildered at why Jean-Marc was so angry. "How did you leave it with her?"

"She's a problem, Roman. I'm just telling you she's a problem."

"Okay. But does she know anything? About why Nico was in her apartment?"

"No. And she refuses to believe he killed her husband."

"But why?"

"I don't know, Roman," Jean-Marc said sarcastically. "I was going to ask her but I thought she might say it came to her in a dream. What difference does it make?"

"Did she ask who killed Nico?"

"Now that you mention it, she didn't."

"Is that significant?"

"That she doesn't ask who killed the guy in her apartment? Don't you think?" Jean-Marc said in frustration. "I no longer have any idea what her end game is."

"She doesn't have an end game. She just wants to find out who killed her husband."

"*No*, Roman. She doesn't. *We told her who killed her husband*. She wants to find out—"

Jean-Marc stopped and turned away.

"What?" Roman asked him. "What is it you think she wants to find out?"

"Nothing. Just get her out of here. The hotel is two blocks over. Put her on the second floor and clear the floor so it's only her."

"*D'accord*."

Jean-Marc turned away and then stopped. "And Roman?"

Roman stopped and looked back at him.

"Quit acting like she needs your help. She's a hell of a lot harder than you are."

I was sitting in the downstairs police headquarters waiting room when Roman and LaRue finally appeared. LaRue didn't even look at me but went straight down the corridor toward the outside entrance as Roman came over to me.

By this time it was a little after eleven in the evening.

"Have you eaten?" he asked as I stood up.

"No, but I'm not hungry. Am I free to go?"

"You can't go back to your apartment. Jean-Marc found a hotel for you to go to. I'll take you there."

I hesitated when I saw a policewoman appear.

"Am I under arrest?" I asked, suddenly feeling overly warm.

Roman glanced at the policewoman and then back at me.

"No. It's for security purposes only. Officer Pagel will be positioned outside your door."

I looked at the policewoman who gave me a blank stare in return. Roman touched me on the back to guide me toward the front doors of the building.

I rode with Roman in what I assumed was his private vehicle which I have to say was much less stressful than the way I'd arrived a few hours earlier. He pulled up outside the hotel and I could see that Officer Pagel was already standing there, her eyes sweeping the sidewalk in front of her.

Roman walked me in and spoke to the desk clerk before turning and directing me to the elevator. We went up to the second floor and down the narrow hall to my room.

Hotel Matteo wasn't any nicer than the Hotel L'Ocean but there seemed to be a few more people bustling about at least.

Roman unlocked my room and came inside and looked around. He poked his head in the bathroom before coming back and handing me the room key.

"I don't have anything to sleep in," I said. "Or a toothbrush."

"There is an all-night *pharmacie* not far from here. I'll pick up a few items and drop them off." He paused. "You know I would stay if I could but—"

"Don't be silly. You have an active crime scene and every minute counts. Believe me, I get it."

"I'm sorry all of this is happening to you."

"You finally see that it's all connected, right?" I said. "My husband is killed and the guy who killed him tries to kill me and is then killed in my apartment?"

"I do. I just don't see *how*. Why you? You are not, excuse my bluntness, important in that way. You are not a drug dealer or an arms dealer or a celebrity. You didn't witness the attack yourself. It makes no sense."

"Not to toot my own horn," I said, "but it's possible I was attacked by Nico this week because I was getting close to the truth about who killed Bob."

"Possibly," Roman said doubtfully, "but then why was Nico killed? And why in your apartment?"

"All good questions. I have no idea. I'm just glad you're taking it seriously now."

I could see he was about to defend himself.

"I didn't mean it like that," I said hurriedly, although a part of me was annoyed I had to placate him when of course what I said was the absolute truth.

"It's just that I never felt the answers you came up with were right," I said. "And now I feel better knowing you'll take a new look at it."

He smiled wryly. "That is I think the famous backhanded compliment you Americans are known for?"

I smiled tiredly. It had been a long day.

"I should go," he said. "I'll have someone drop off a toothbrush to you."

I walked him to the door and then hesitated.

"What is it, Claire?" he asked. "You are safe here. *Absolument*. The policewoman is right downstairs."

"It's not that," I said. "It's about Detective LaRue."

He frowned. "I know he is rude with you, Claire, but he is a good detective. He is very thorough and—"

"No, it's not that." I took in a big breath. "I have a source that says he's taking bribes."

He looked at me with surprise but honestly not the kind of surprise that would have indicated he didn't know about the bribes.

"You knew?"

"There's been talk," he said. "My question is how do *you* know?"

"The maid at the hotel told me she saw him taking money on more than one occasion. So if you know he's dirty, why don't you report him?"

"I wish I could make you see what I see."

"I see plenty! Your partner is taking bribes! Which is not okay no matter how many people run over his wife."

"Okay, but look at it a different way. Chloe—that's his wife—is demanding and unreasonable. While it's true her drugs are paid for by the state, there are other things that Jean-Marc tries to do to ease her suffering that he can't afford on his detective's salary."

"What kinds of things?"

"Trips to the UK, to the beach, to EuroDisney. Jewelry, expensive clothing, plastic surgery. Even though she can't walk, she's vain about her appearance. Jean-Marc is trying to make up for what happened. He feels responsible."

"Why in the world would he feel responsible?"

"The night of the accident he was to have taken her to a play but he chose instead to work late on a case."

"So he feels guilty and he assuages that by taking money from people who are afraid of him—people who are basically at his mercy as a policeman."

"It's more complicated than that."

"Is it *more complicated* when a man breaks into a jewelry store and steals a diamond bracelet? Is it more complicated when *anyone* breaks the law but has a good reason for it?"

"I don't know what to tell you," he said in frustration.

"So you won't report him?"

"No! He's a broken man! He has nothing left! Would I strip him of his job? Maybe throw him in jail? I can't do it. And if that makes me a bad cop then so be it."

I could see I'd upset him but honestly I was a little upset myself.

"The maid said she saw him being physically aggressive with Reynard. The money is one thing but..."

"I know. I know." He looked completely miserable. I'm sure he hated looking weak in front of me and possibly a part of him was afraid I'd tell someone what I knew.

But maybe, just maybe, he'd go off and think a little more about it and end up doing the right thing.

"I know you need to go," I said, "but I have one more question. It's about what happened tonight."

"I'll answer if I can."

"LaRue told me Reynard and my husband's murders were done by two different knives."

That of course is the opposite of what LaRue told me.

A look of annoyance crossed Roman's face. "Jean-Marc said that?" He swore.

"So *were* they done by two different knives?" I asked innocently.

"The medical examiner said the knives used on Nico tonight and Reynard were not the same. The knife used in your husband's murder was not the same as the knife used on either of the other two homicides."

"So *three* different knives were used. And none of the knives have been recovered?"

He narrowed his eyes at me. I fear I must have looked a little too jubilant at having wheedled the information out of him.

"Jean-Marc never told you they were all done with different knives, did he?"

"No, he lied to me, Roman. Just like you were prepared to do."

He could have been angry with me. After all, I'd tricked him with a lie.

But to his credit, his shoulders sagged with shame.

"I'm sorry, Claire. I don't want to lie to you but it's just easier."

"I get it. It's easier than answering my questions and putting up with me."

"I have no trouble putting up with you. Quite the opposite. But surely you can see that just because Nico didn't use the same weapon on both men it doesn't mean he didn't kill both men."

"Except his DNA wasn't found in Bob's room."

"How do you know that?"

"Detective LaRue told me."

That was another lie. It was Adelle who told me.

"He's been telling you a lot lately," he said, clenching his jaw. "I suggest you don't believe everything you hear."

"Because he's lying?"

"No, he may feel he's protecting you."

"That would surprise me greatly. You know he hates me. Honestly how well do *you* know him?

"He's well-respected on the force. It was an honor for me to be teamed with him."

"So you don't really know him."

"Not personally, no."

"But you trust him."

"With my life."

"But that's what you *would* say. He's your partner."

"Tomorrow, when I have more time," he said, leaning tantalizingly close to me, close enough that I was almost positive he was about to kiss me, "we'll go through this all over again if you want, okay?"

"Okay," I said. "Thank you, Roman."

"*Pas du tout*," he said, pulling away at the last moment. "Lock the door behind me."

I closed the door and stood there for a moment. I'd come very close to telling him how LaRue had lied about not using Nico as a CI.

I'd come even closer to telling him how Daigneault believed there was a mole in the police department. And why I now believed that mole was Jean-Marc LaRue.

If I had thought that Roman was in danger I know I would have spoken up.

Honestly, I'll never know why I held back.

47

TOOTH AND NAIL

The first thing I did when I was alone in my hotel room was to text Adelle to ask her to meet me tomorrow so I could hear what she found at the crime scene—although I had a pretty good *Cliff's Notes* version.

What I didn't know was *why* Nico was killed in my apartment. Or by whom.

Or why he had attacked me two days ago.

What I'd said to Roman was still my main conundrum. I knew all the murders were connected—Bob, Reynard and Nico. But for the life of me I couldn't see how.

I debated turning on French TV for a moment since I was too wired to fall asleep any time soon.

I checked my social media feed on my phone and saw there was a message from Lillian.

<Please call me, Claire. After rereading my message to you I think I didn't express myself well. Your mother wasn't raped.>

Well, that got my eyes open.

It was nearly midnight in Paris so it would be almost six in the evening in Jacksonville, Florida. I called the number she included in her message.

"Hello?" the voice that answered was gravelly from a lifetime of smoking.

"Lillian? This is Claire Baskerville."

"Who?"

"Helen's daughter?"

There was a pause before she said, "Oh, my goodness! Claire! You're calling from Paris! Oh, I'm glad you called! I felt so bad after I wrote you."

"So are you saying my mother *wasn't* raped?"

"Oh, I knew you'd gotten the wrong end of things after I reread your first message to me. No. She was not raped."

Then why the hell doesn't my DNA match up with the man she was married to? I wanted to say.

"But there *was* something?" I prompted.

"Just the love of her life," Lillian said. "That's all."

"Who? My mother's?"

"Let me start at the beginning, dear. Your mother met someone while she was married to Claude."

I nearly groaned out loud.

"And got pregnant with me," I said.

"Yes, dear. She was over the moon about it. She and Philippe both were."

"His name was Philippe? Do you have a last name?"

"I...you're not thinking of contacting him, are you? He's probably dead by now but I'm sure he has a family who would be upset at—"

"No, of course not."

"Philippe Moreau. A handsome devil and you look like him. Your mother would often say how sometimes just looking at you she saw compensation for all the misery of her life."

That made absolutely no sense to me.

"So she was in love with him? Why didn't she leave Claude for him?"

"Philippe was married too."

Naturally. Not sleazy at all.

"I see. Well, thank you, Lillian. It's a relief for me to know the truth."

"I was sure it would be, dear. Sorry for the misunderstanding."

"No worries. Take care of yourself now."

"And you too, darling. Goodbye."

I hung up and for a moment I sat in the spare chair in the hotel room and stared at the wall.

*Well, at least I'm not the product of a rap*e.

Not that it mattered as far as my future poverty was concerned. Of course I would track down this Philippe Moreau.

After all, finding people is what I do.

Impatient with not getting a response from my text to Adelle I tried calling her but the call went to voicemail. I assumed she must still be knee-deep in plucking DNA bits out of my bedroom carpet.

Just as I was about to pick up the TV remote control, my phone rang.

I looked at the screen but it only showed that the caller was unidentified.

"Hello?" I said.

"Madame Baskerville?"

"Hello, Monsieur Daigneault," I said immediately recognizing his voice. "How did you get this number?"

"I need to see you, Madame. I watched the detective bring you into the Hotel Matteo. I am nearby."

A needle of unease pierced through my shoulder blades.

"I'm not sure that's a good idea," I said, trying to keep my voice calm.

His fingerprints were found in Bob's hotel room.

"I must see you. You are in danger."

With Nico dead I was tempted to tell him that the one thing I was no longer in was danger. Unless it was from *him*.

"I must speak with you," he insisted.

"We're speaking now."

"I was wrong about Nico. He didn't kill your husband."

There was literally nothing else he could have said that might have gotten my attention. Before that moment I hadn't realized that my gut was telling me it wasn't Nico who killed Bob.

For one thing, I'm pretty sure contract killers don't use a different knife every time.

"I can't tell you the rest over the phone," he said. "It's not safe."

"Okay. Where?"

"There's a policewoman at the door. You'll need to get past her."

Even contemplating what he was saying sounded mad.

That policewoman was there for my safety! And now I was listening to someone I didn't trust tell me how to give her the slip?

"Go to the stairwell on your floor. Walk down to the next floor. There's a laundry room with access to the outside. It will take you to where the garbage cans are. I'll be waiting for you there."

"Give me five minutes."

Even to me it sounded dangerously like the dumb teenager who goes into the basement after hearing the radio report about an escaped mental patient in the neighborhood.

But one thing I know if I know anything is that you don't find answers sitting in your hotel room waiting for something to happen.

It was pretty clear after my conversation with Roman that the police were as baffled as I was. If I wanted answers, I needed to go find them.

I picked up my phone and saw that the battery was nearly dead. I didn't have my charger with me so I left the phone on the dresser. I slipped out of my room and crept down the darkened hall to the stairwell and then down the stairs to the floor below mine.

As soon as I opened the stairwell door I saw a door in the hall labeled *blanchisserie*. It was unlocked and I stepped inside. When I did, I saw a dark shape coming toward me. My heart leapt to my throat and I turned to try to go back the way I'd come.

"Madame Baskerville! It's me!" Daigneault whispered.

I stopped, my back to him, my heart thundering in my ears.

"I thought you were going to meet me outside," I said hoarsely, my lips and chin beginning to tremble.

"I realized you needed a disguise," he said. When I turned around I saw he was holding a hoodie. While he didn't look at all familiar to me, I registered that he was good-looking with dark brown hair.

I reminded myself that Ted Bundy was good-looking too.

I reached for the garment he held out to me and tugged it on over my head.

"Follow me," he said.

What am I doing? I thought feverishly as I followed him out a door on the far side of the room that opened up onto a dark and narrow alleyway and which did nothing for my nerves. Once more I found myself wondering why we couldn't have this conversation in my hotel room.

But it was too late for that.

As soon as we were outside, I felt the cold and was grateful for the sweatshirt. Even so, I shivered as I followed him down the alley. We emerged at the end of it. He paused and then signaled for me to follow him across the street.

I looked both ways before crossing. As I did something struck me about the front of the hotel.

The policewoman guarding the entrance was gone.

48

THE ONLY THING TO FEAR

I followed Daigneault across the street and felt my growing fear and doubt like a throbbing mass in my chest.

He paused at the door of a *brasserie* across from the hotel. He turned, looked meaningfully at me, and then entered. I hurried after him feeling briefly better.

Meeting a suspicious, possibly dangerous character in a public restaurant was better than a darkened alley any day.

As soon as I entered the *brasserie,* I could see Daigneault was talking to the *maître d.* He motioned for me to follow him. It was warm in the restaurant and I dropped my hood to my shoulders. I expected Daigneault to lead me to a table at the back of the restaurant but instead he walked over to a four-top positioned by the front window. The front view of the hotel filled the window.

I counted only three other diners in the room.

Daigneault sat at the table and I sat down across from him. A waiter came over with a carafe of red wine and a basket of *pommes frites*.

The policewoman still hadn't returned.

Roman had said he'd send someone to get me a toothbrush.

Maybe that's where the policewoman was? Maybe Roman sent her to the drug store? I kept my eyes on the front door of the hotel expecting to see her appear any moment.

"I know Nico was killed in your apartment tonight," Daigneault said.

I turned to observe him.

This man was a total conundrum. There was no rhyme nor reason for why he was continually contacting me under the guise of warning or protecting me.

And of course there was the little matter of his fingerprints at Bob's crime scene.

"Your DNA was found in my husband's room," I said.

He nodded and took a healthy swig from his glass of wine.

"I'm not surprised. I've used that room as well as several others in the hotel for the last year."

"Used it how?"

He looked a little uncomfortable.

"That is irrelevant. I am no angel but I am not a killer."

"Why are you helping me?"

"Again, irrelevant. What is important is that one of the detectives you are trusting is taking money from the Big Boss."

"I know that already." I got a sudden irrational urge that I was sure I was going to hate myself for later but I couldn't resist.

"Which detective?" I asked.

"I do not know. I only know about him from Nico."

"Do you know who killed Nico?"

"Word on the street is that he disappointed the Big Boss."

"Disappointed him in what way?"

"I do not know."

"So he was made an example of?"

"C'est ça." That's it.

"You said you knew my husband wasn't killed by Nico after all. What is it you know?"

"Forgive me, Madame Baskerville," Daigneault said,

finishing off his wine. "I had to think of something to get you to meet with me."

"So that was a lie? You don't know who killed my husband?" My muscles were quivering in pent-up fury.

"I have my doubts about Nico being his killer," Daigneault said. "The detective taking bribes out of Hotel L'Ocean was running a confidential informant there. That informant was killed three weeks after your husband."

"I know all of this." But I didn't. The fact that Reynard was a CI for the cops—if true—was news to me. But it made sense the more I thought about it. It dovetailed nicely with the information Marie had given me about LaRue meeting with Reynard and bullying him.

"Ah, yes, but did you know that the informant feared that his own handler would kill him?" Daigneault asked.

I frowned. "How do you know that?"

"He spoke with my girlfriend about it. He told her—"

"Wait. You knew Reynard personally?"

"No. He was my girlfriend's ex and they remained friends."

"What did Reynard tell her?" I asked.

"He said his boss wanted him dead because he knew too much."

"Why do you assume it was his *cop* boss who wanted him dead? Doesn't it make more sense that it was this Big Boss who thought Reynard was about to squeal on him to the cops?"

"Except his cop boss as you call him," Daigneault said, "works for the Big Boss. Why do you think he was being paid bribes?"

"Wait, wait." My head was spinning. "So Detective LaRue is working for the Big Boss?"

Now it was Daigneault's turn to blink in surprise.

"You know the name of the policeman taking bribes?"

"I know LaRue is taking money from the desk clerk at the

Hotel L'Ocean and that he met with Reynard frequently at the hotel."

Daigneault nodded. "Then, yes. It is him. The desk clerk Bernard Santé works for the Big Boss. He was paying the detective for information. Or possibly to murder the snitch, Reynard."

I felt a sickening twisting in my stomach as his words sunk in. Some part of me had not wanted to believe it. Even though I didn't like LaRue and I knew he took bribes, this was a whole different thing.

This was *murder*.

I felt nearly as betrayed as when I'd found out about Bob and Courtney.

I also felt betrayed by my own lack of awareness. Because fooling me to this degree meant I could no longer trust my instincts about people.

I had to get to Roman and tell him what I knew and I had to force him to report what LaRue was doing. If he didn't, I'd need to do it myself.

I still didn't know who killed Bob but one thing was certain —LaRue knew a whole lot more than he was saying.

I reached for my wine glass and saw that my hand was shaking. I have to say in retrospect that the next few seconds would have been infinitely more devastating for me if not for the fact that the waiter showed up at our table at that moment to take our order.

Because I turned my body to address him, I was facing away at the moment the front of the hotel across the street exploded in a blizzard of wood and plaster and glass, shooting projectile debris across the street and through the window where we sat.

49

ONCE BURNED

I found myself on the floor of the restaurant, Daigneault on top of me. I remember smelling burning rubber and hair. My ears weren't working except to thrum ominously. I felt glass beneath my hands on the carpeted floor and struggled to get out from under Daigneault.

As soon as I managed to squirm free of his body I sat up and saw the waiter was sitting stunned on the floor with his back to the wall, an ugly cut over his eye which was bleeding down his face. I turned to see Daigneault sit up and look at me, his eyebrows arched in a frantic expression.

I was shocked to realize he cared if I was okay.

"I'm fine," I croaked. "What the hell just happened?"

Even from where I sat on the floor I could see the flames and billowing smoke that came from the hotel across the street. I was well aware that if it was a terror attack it might not be over but I was too astonished by what I was seeing to hide.

The whole second floor of the hotel was gone.

The floor my room was on.

My body began to tremble as I realized the implication of what I was seeing.

"We need to get out of here," Daigneault said, squatting down beside me. "Are you okay to walk?"

"What happened?" I asked, knowing full well what had happened but hoping beyond hope that there was a different way to interpret it.

Daigneault glanced over his shoulder at the inferno at the front of the hotel and looked back at me helplessly. By now we could hear the sirens getting louder and louder.

"The policewoman," I said.

"Come, Madame Baskerville," Daigneault said, pulling me to my feet. "We must go!"

"You don't understand," I said as he began to tug me toward the front door. "The policewoman was supposed to be out front but she left! She *knew* the place was going to blow."

Daigneault wasn't listening but looking both ways as he stood near the door.

Another waiter was kneeling by the waiter on the floor and held a cloth to his head. The two men were talking, and thankfully neither seemed seriously hurt.

Had the policewoman known the hotel was going to blow up?

A cold chisel of pain drilled into my gut.

LaRue chose the hotel.

Daigneault was back by my side.

"Not the front door," he said. "There is a back way." He gripped my arm.

"Wait," I said breathlessly. Everything was moving too fast.

"No!" he said, fiercely. "We cannot wait! The police are already here!"

I looked past his shoulder and saw two police vans with lights flashing pull up in front of the hotel. A firetruck had arrived too.

Two men in plainclothes got out of the van and walked to the middle of the street facing the hotel. They weren't twenty feet away from the restaurant but between my affliction and the dark it was impossible to tell for sure who they were.

One of the men held a bag loosely in one hand. I could see the big green cross on the sack that identified it as from one of the local pharmacies.

Roman. With my toothbrush.

My first inclination was to run to him and tell him I was okay. In fact the urge was so powerful I must have taken several steps in the direction of the front door before Daigneault grabbed me and physically dragged me away.

"Let me go!" I shouted.

"No!" he said and before I could twist away from him I felt him lean down and throw me bodily over his shoulder.

The world tipped upside down as I hung shocked and disbelieving as Daigneault ran toward the back of the restaurant.

50

TWICE SHY

As firefighters brought coughing and terrified hotel guests out into the street, Jean-Marc leaned against the police van facing the burning hotel. Even on what had become a cold November night, the heat from the blaze gave both him and Roman a glistening sheen of sweat on their faces as they stood and watched.

"You're sure she was inside?" Jean-Marc asked.

"Yes! I escorted her there myself," Roman said angrily. "I just left her! It couldn't have been an hour ago!"

"Calm down, Roman. We don't know for sure she's dead."

Roman looked at him as if he'd lost his mind.

"The whole second floor is gone!" Roman practically shouted.

Jean-Marc was seconds away from reminding Roman that getting personally involved with a person of interest had never been a good idea but from the look of his current reaction he decided that now was not the right time to mention it.

He looked back at the smoldering hulk of the hotel and felt a nauseating eruption form in the pit of his stomach.

"If only she had gone home," he said. "She would be alive now."

"I can't believe it," Roman said, shaking his head in utter bewilderment. "I *literally* just left her. I can't believe it."

"Do you want to take the rest of the night off?"

Jean-Marc hated to ask but the man looked as though it was all he could do not to push past the firemen and climb up one of the ladders reaching up to the upper floor windows himself.

"And do what?" Roman said, whirling on him. "Watch television? Read a book? *You* were the one who put her there, Jean-Marc. This is on you."

Jean-Marc's mouth fell open.

"What are you saying? This...this was just a terrible coincidence."

Jean-Marc curled his hands into fists in a picture of maligned indignation.

But Roman suddenly seemed to get a grip of himself.

"No," he said. "I didn't mean that. I apologize. I know it's just an accident. Of course it is. But I need to investigate it with you. I can't be sidelined on this one."

"Of course. But there's nothing much for us to do here tonight. The fire marshal will be able to tell what kind of bomb it was and where and when it was set. We should have his report in a couple of days."

They both watched as the team of CSI investigators in their white jackets and booties stood back and waited and watched the place burn. *They* would be the first ones in after the firefighters got the rest of the hotel guests out and succeeded in putting out the blaze and ascertained there were no more bombs inside.

Then the CSI team along with the medical examiner and his techs would go in to find and remove the bodies.

"Honestly, in a way I'm not sure she would be satisfied with any other ending but this one," Roman said sadly, looking at the *pharmacie* bag in his hands. "I'm sorry you didn't get to know her, Jean-Marc."

Yes, well, I'm sorry you did, Jean-Marc couldn't help but think.

"She was so passionate," Roman said, watching the fire burn, his face wet from the sweat reflecting the dancing flames. His eyes were wet with unshed tears. "She was a bulldog to find the answers she wanted about her husband's murder."

"Well, she's out of her misery at least," Jean-Marc said giving Roman an awkward pat on the shoulder.

"Yes, at least there's that," Roman said, wiping his face and clearing his throat as if suddenly embarrassed.

Jean-Marc looked away to give the man time to pull himself together.

He focused for a moment on Roman's comment when he'd intimated that the bomb exploding—and Jean-Marc's involvement—was bizarrely coincidental as far as timing was concerned. It would be natural for people to ask if this hotel was any kind of terrorist target.

While he knew terrorists didn't tend to have a reason for the targets they chose, still, it would warrant looking into the possibility. If nothing else to at least have available a suggestion of an answer to the why-question.

Especially if, like Roman, my superiors find themselves asking why it was that I put Madame Baskerville in this particular hotel on this particular night.

51

HOMELAND SECURITY

The place Daigneault took me was in a nasty part of Paris but the apartment itself was clean and orderly. Daigneault's girlfriend Eva was sitting at the kitchen table with me and Daigneault and listened to a seriously truncated version of what had happened tonight from Daigneault, who had already told me that Eva did not know the full truth about what he was up to. Then he and I watched the hotel fire on the nightly news while Eva made ragout and pasta and opened a bottle of wine.

While I'd been manhandled out of the restaurant and nearly threatened with my life to get in the dilapidated service van that Daigneault then drove with one eye on me and one eye on the narrow backroads that led to his neighborhood, I still insisted on giving him a hundred euros I had in my pocket for tonight's bed and meal. I got the impression that he hated to take it, but knew Eva could use the money.

Regardless of the fact that Daigneault had forced me to go with him to this apartment, I'd already seen that moment of relief in his eye after the explosion when he saw I was okay. That made me believe he didn't mean me any harm.

I can't say I felt exactly safe. After all, I was pretty sure that the senior cop who had been working my husband's murder was dirty and very possibly out to kill me. But nobody knew where I was at the moment and that gave me at least a certain degree of comfort.

Except when I thought of Roman.

I hated the fact that I hadn't shared with him what I knew. But on the other hand it occurred to me that that ignorance might keep him safe. He was either in on whatever dirty dealings Jean-Marc was into—in which case telling him would be a waste of time—or he was going to have to blow the whistle on his partner which could very well get him killed.

The next time I saw him there would be a decision to be made and I hoped very much that the man I thought Roman was would be able to step up and make the right one.

The next morning I woke to the scent of brewing coffee. I'd slept in my clothes in Eve and Daigneault's bed. Where they'd slept I'm not sure. Even so I woke up feeling like I'd fallen down a flight of stairs.

When you get to a certain age it's hard to adjust even to minimal change. You like your routines. I didn't want to ask for a toothbrush last night but I was seriously regretting not doing so now.

I found mouthwash in the bathroom and swished and spit before dabbing a little on the cut on my knee that I'd gotten when the *brasserie* window blew out and threw me onto the floor.

I found my way into the kitchen where Eva was pouring coffee.

"Good morning," she said handing me a full mug.

"Good morning. Where's Daigneault?"

"He went out."

A note would have been nice. Even after everything that had happened and after everything that had been said didn't remove the niggling doubt I still had that he was someone I could trust.

"May I turn on the television?" I asked. I was keen to see how the police were painting last night's explosion.

Eva looked guiltily toward the TV set.

"It isn't working properly," she said.

It had been working fine last night.

"May I borrow your phone?" I asked.

Eva went to the far side of the kitchen and returned with her phone. I quickly used it to open up Google News. The explosion story led the news in Paris.

Terrorist bombing, as yet no responsibility claimed. Three dead.

All on the second floor.

I felt briefly sick at the thought of those people dying in that hotel—all because Jean-Marc LaRue needed to keep his dirty little secret.

I pushed the thought out of my mind and dialed Adelle's phone number.

One of the few upsides to this brain anomaly of mine is that I have a remarkable memory for names and numbers that I've even briefly heard or read.

When Adelle's line began to ring I knew the call would show up on her screen as *Unidentified Caller* and prayed she would pick up anyway.

"*Allo*?" Adelle said.

"Don't react in case anyone's watching, but I'm alive."

"Oh, yeah, that's cool," Adelle said, although I could detect a splinter of astonishment in her voice. "What's up?"

"I need to see you."

"Bit busy here. But when and where?"

52

SOUNDS LIKE A PLAN

Daigneault returned a few minutes later with a bag of croissants and a half dozen *pains aux raisins*. I was amazed at how differently people did things in France. Even on the run from the cops after surviving a police assassination attempt, it was important to have your morning *pain beurre*.

Adelle was not going to be able to meet me until lunchtime which was still a couple of hours away.

As the three of us sat down at the laminate dining room table in their apartment, I couldn't take it any longer. I put my hand on Daigneault's as he reached for a croissant. He looked at me in surprise.

"Why are you helping me?" I asked.

He shrugged and plucked the croissant from the plate.

"Because you helped me."

When I didn't respond, he said, "That day in the alley? You looked right in my eyes and when the cops grabbed me, you refused to make an identification."

I nearly groaned out loud. He thought I'd seen him and

refused to identify him in the line-up. Should I tell him I only refused because remembering his face after one brief glimpse was impossible for me?

"You were the only eyewitness," he said. "They had to let me go. So when I heard that Nico had targeted you, I thought warning you was the least I could do."

"Why did they pick you up?"

"I have a record."

"What kind of record?"

"Is any kind good? It doesn't matter. I would have gone down for the attack in the alley if you had confirmed I was there. And so I owe you."

"Did you see who killed Reynard?"

"No. I got there right after you did."

So all this time, he thought I knew he was in the alley. But until this moment I had no idea that the man I'd briefly seen was Daigneault.

I had to bite my tongue to keep from asking him *why* he was in the alley that day.

I'd arranged to meet Adelle at a café near the Rodin Museum which wasn't too far from Daigneault's apartment. It had been drizzling on and off since lunch and I didn't know whether to be glad if it helped put out the hotel fire or sorry in case it complicated the Fire Marshall's investigation.

There was no doubt in my mind that LaRue had put me in the hotel and then had a bomb planted. Just like there was no doubt he was working for the Big Boss and either killed Nico himself or arranged for someone to kill him.

I still didn't know where he fit in with Bob's murder, but I had the beginnings of a plan that I was starting to feel was going to show me exactly that.

Adelle must have been held up because it was nearly two o'clock in the afternoon before I saw her coming around the corner. I stepped out of the alcove where Daigneault and I stood ready to wave to her, but Daigneault stopped me.

"Not yet," he said. "She may not be alone."

It was hard waiting for Adelle to walk down the long block, her eyes sweeping from side to side looking for me but Daigneault was the expert in these matters. If he said hold back and wait, I would do just that.

The second she passed me, Daigneault gave me a gentle push and I stepped out of the alley and slipped my arm around Adelle's waist. She jumped but kept walking.

"Claire!" she said. "What is happening?"

"There's a park a block away," I said. "We can talk there. Meanwhile, pretend to make small talk."

"*D'accord*," Adelle said tartly. "So! Who is trying to kill you, *chérie*?"

"That's small talk?"

"First I am at your apartment because there is a dead body in your bed, yes?" she said, ticking off the item on her fingers. "And then my whole team is called in to be on stand-by at the Hotel Matteo."

We came to the park entrance. It was early afternoon on a Monday so the nannies and the smaller children were already inside the park. I hurried Adelle through the gates to the first bench I came to.

As I turned and sat, I saw Daigneault loitering by the entrance. He lit a cigarette and every once in a while he turned to look in our direction.

"How did you know I was staying at the hotel?" I asked.

"It's all the police are talking about! I could not believe what I was hearing when they mentioned your name."

"You were right about not trusting them," I said. "I think the cops are in on this. One in particular in fact."

"This is very scary, Claire," Adelle said, wringing her hands. "What will you do?"

"What are they saying is the reason for the explosion?"

"They're saying it's a terrorist bomb, but as of yet there is no claim of responsibility."

"And there won't be," I said grimly. "None that won't be fabricated by the police. How many were hurt?"

"They have found remains so far of three people and are expecting to find one more."

"Is that supposed to be me?"

"I guess so."

"I imagine it will look suspicious when they don't find a body in my room."

Adelle winced. "They are not expecting to find a body, *chérie*. The bomb detonated near your room."

"I see. So, no body. Convenient. Are you working it?"

"Everybody's working it. It's a mess."

"How long before they realize I'm not there?"

"Probably by tonight. Tomorrow morning for sure."

"Will you help me?"

Adelle never even hesitated. "Of course," she said.

"I'm going to need a laptop. I think I'm safe where I am for now."

"Where are you staying?"

"With someone who warned me last week about Nico trying to hurt me."

Adelle pursed her lips and looked worried.

I definitely didn't want to mention to her that this particular someone was the one whose prints were found in Bob's hotel room. I thought I could trust Daigneault but I would understand completely if based on the facts Adelle couldn't bring herself to.

"I feel like I'm finally closing in on some answers, Adelle."

"If you survive," she said, making a face. "But yes, I'll bring you the laptop. What exactly are you looking for?"

"I'm not sure. I'll only know when I find it."

53

COME TOGETHER

Adelle and I walked as far as the corner of the boulevard Saint-Germain and then split. I watched her walk back down the sidewalk in the direction of the hotel. Daigneault came up silently behind me.

"Will she help?" he asked.

I nodded and rubbed my arms. I was cold and in dire need of a hot shower and a shampoo. Daigneault and I turned in the direction of his apartment.

"Eva said there was a problem with your Wi-Fi this morning," I said. "And I'm going to need it for whatever plan I come up with."

"I'll make sure you have working Wi-Fi," he said.

We walked nearly a whole block without talking. I didn't want to tell him that I couldn't have identified him even if I wanted to but I hated that he was thinking I was better than I was. On the other hand, I needed him. Maybe there was time for honesty when this whole thing was over.

"You don't have to continue helping me," I said in spite of myself.

"Perhaps I am helping you for my own reasons."

"It might get...dicey. I don't want you to get hurt."

"Do you need my help?"

"I do."

"*D'accord.*"

I don't know what his personal reasons were for helping me beyond just being grateful I didn't identify him for Reynard's murder. But I did need his help. I decided to stop trying to send him away.

When we got back to the apartment, I smelled garlic and onions as soon as we hit the stairwell. Eva had obviously taken some of the money I'd given Daigneault and bought groceries.

In the hour before dinner I took a shower and washed my hair. I have mid length hair that requires coloring and regular trimming not to mention lots of product and at least an hour with a styling brush and a blow dryer. Eva gave me some hairpins and I twisted my wet hair up into a chignon. Since we were both the same size, I borrowed a pair of jeans and a shirt of hers while soaking my clothes in a tub of cold water with dishwashing liquid.

More than once I thought longingly of my apartment bathtub and my own closet.

Better known now as a crime scene.

Was that really just yesterday?

I prayed that Geneviève hadn't heard from the police about my likely demise. I hated the thought of upsetting her. I also hated the thought that Roman didn't know I was alive but the tendrils of my plan were coming together and I was pretty sure that the fewer people who knew about what I was doing the better.

I was confident he would forgive me when it was all said and done.

I came out to the living room just as Adelle showed up at the front door. I'd texted her Daigneault's address before I'd gone in for my shower. If it weren't for the fact that I had no more money on me I would've asked her to run by Monoprix and pick up a few personal items for me.

Thinking of my apartment made me wonder where I would go if my plan worked and I were somehow able to resolve all of this tomorrow. My apartment was off limits but the idea of going to a hotel literally sent shivers of horror through me.

Worry about it tomorrow, Scarlett, I told myself as I walked across the living room to greet Adelle.

After introducing everyone, we sat down to dinner. Adelle had brought a bottle of Cote du Rhône and Eva had several bottles of Prosecco.

The meal was stupendous. The dish Eva made was like nothing I'd ever tasted before. She used ground and mixed spices I'd never even heard of.

By the time we all pushed away from the table, it occurred to me that whole minutes had gone by where I hadn't been thinking about my plan for tomorrow or worrying about whether I was going to get innocent people hurt.

Or about those three people at the hotel who died last night because of me.

Because of LaRue, I reminded myself sternly. *Don't put that on yourself.*

As we were clearing the table after dinner I asked Adelle if they'd given up on finding any pieces of me in the hotel yet and she said no. They would keep looking. The police were sure my remains would be recovered soon.

"Ready, Madame Baskerville?" Daigneault said as he stood by the cleared dining room table.

"Call me Claire, Daigneault. Or should I say Paul?"

His eyebrows shot up. "You have done your research."

Adelle handed me her laptop and I set it up on the table. Daigneault gave me the Wi-Fi password that I was sure belonged to someone in the building.

It didn't matter. I just needed it for a few hours.

Adelle settled in next to me and I opened up a Google search window.

"Okay," I said. "What problem do we have that we're trying to solve?"

"Find out who killed your husband," Adelle said automatically.

I smiled at her. "Yes. But that is not our immediate problem."

"How to keep the police from trying to kill you?" Daigneault asked.

I nodded. "Exactly. And it occurred to me that I might be able to accomplish both. *How* you may ask? By taking my biggest threat by the horns, so to speak."

I turned to Adelle. "My purse and phone got burned up in the hotel fire. Can you loan me three hundred euros? If not, I can ask my neighbor."

"I have the money," Adelle said.

"Good. If all goes according to plan, I can pay you back as soon as the bank issues me a new debit card."

I typed in the browser window and searched for surveillance cameras in Paris. Immediately several webpages were presented to me for selection. I went through them and ordered what I needed, indicating I would pick them up in the morning and pay at that time.

"Surveillance cameras?" Daigneault asked. "I think it is time you told us your plan."

"My plan is a little bit old-fashioned," I said. "And a little bit high tech."

"I like it already," Adelle said with a grin.

I turned to Daigneault. "I need you to find me a remote space where we can meet tomorrow afternoon. Ideally it will have phone reception but be soundproof."

"You sound like a serial killer."

"I'll need you to help me position the cameras I've just

purchased. We'll need a ladder and mounting tools. I want two placed inside the space and one over the door on the outside leading into it."

"No problem."

I turned to Adelle. "I'll need you to be someplace safe on your laptop monitoring the video feeds of all three cameras."

"Okay," she said, frowning. "What am I looking for?" Before I could answer she said, "Never mind. I know. I'll know it when I see it."

"You have one other vitally important task," I said, my voice as serious as I could make it. "If things go wrong I need you to call Roman Pellé and tell him what's happening. Do not call anyone else. Do not let them redirect you. Got it?"

"In what way do you think things may go wrong?"

"I don't think they will go wrong. I just like having a safety net."

Then I turned to Daigneault. "I'm going to get LaRue to agree to meet me and I need you to bring him to the place you find for me."

He frowned. "Should I disarm him first?"

I thought about that for a moment.

"I don't think it will be necessary. He won't shoot me if that's what you're worried about."

"Why wouldn't he, *chérie*?" Adelle asked. "He tried to kill you once that we know of. And if he is the one who sent Nico to your apartment, that's twice!"

"I know but that's where you come in. I'm going to make him an offer he would be a fool to turn down. I'll tell him that Roman Pellé is scheduled to be notified of what's going down if anything happens to me."

"I don't like it," Daigneault said.

"Do you have another idea? The only real weapon I have is the threat to reveal him. He'd have to kill all of us and destroy the videos if he chose not to cooperate."

"Those do not sound like very big barriers," Daigneault said.

"I am an American national. My government would not let my murder go unaddressed."

Except of course that's exactly what they did with Bob.

"But I'm sure it won't come to that," I said hurriedly.

I could tell Daigneault and Adelle weren't as confident about my plan as I was and, to be honest, that was probably because they didn't have as much riding on it. Oh, Daigneault had some physical danger involved but I had *everything* on the line—the answers about Bob and therefore my sanity going forward, as well as my future safety in this country, the one place on earth I could still at least temporarily afford to live.

As Adelle packed up her laptop, I went over with her one more time exactly what I needed her to do. After she went to the store and picked up the cameras, she was to hand them off to Daigneault at an agreed-upon rendezvous point and then go on to work—back to the hotel fire scene.

She'd keep me apprised of anything they found via Daigneault's phone since I no longer had mine, then go back to her apartment and get ready to test and monitor the videos.

Once he delivered LaRue to the remote area we'd agreed upon Daigneault would notify Adelle of the precise time when the cameras would be rolling. From that moment on, we had exactly ninety minutes to get the information from LaRue and his agreement to our deal.

If Adelle didn't get a call from me by the end of ninety minutes, she was to call Roman on the personal number I gave her and tell him everything.

Before she left Daigneault's apartment Adelle gave me a steady gaze.

"You are a brave woman, Claire," she said. "I've never met one braver."

"An obsessed woman, more like," I said. "But thank you. I guess it doesn't feel like bravery when you're driven to do it."

She gave me a brief fierce hug which I very much appreciated since I know that French people don't hand out hugs willy-nilly, and then turned and hurried down the stairs.

That night I found it impossible to sleep. I kept running through my brain all the things—scripted and spontaneous—that I intended to say to Jean-Marc tomorrow.

All I wanted was a verbal confession and the answers about Bob's murder. If he insisted it was Nico who killed Bob when my gut told me it wasn't, I would threaten to reveal what I knew.

If he came clean with the name of the killer, I could be reasonable.

If on the other hand *he* was the killer ...well, I wouldn't think about that right now.

I intended to tell him he could run away but I needed to know the truth about what happened to Bob.

One way or the other, it would all be over by this time tomorrow.

54

WINGING IT

The next morning Daigneault went out to meet Adelle and pick up the cameras. Just to be safe, we decided not to travel together to the space he'd found—a warehouse not too far from his apartment. Not that I thought LaRue was clever enough to track me down, in fact I had very little respect for the man's detection abilities. After all, how smart do you have to be, to be fifty-five years old and still a detective second-class taking bribes as the highlight of your career?

But it never hurt to play it safe.

Before leaving the apartment I thanked Eva for everything she'd done for me and was surprised when she too gave me a hug. As I said, the French don't hug and so this moved me. But it also made me a little uneasy.

It was as if she knew I wasn't coming back in one piece.

The warehouse that Daigneault found was easily reachable by the Metro. It was a Monday morning and the commuters on the train were stuffed in cars going from Saint-Denis to Champ de Mars which was my stop.

Daigneault had shown me the address of the warehouse on

a map. 23 *rue de Emile Zola*. As soon as I saw it, my brain—useless in so many ways—automatically photographed the map image to be called up when needed.

As I looked around at the shop girls and office workers and even a few tourists on the train, I couldn't help but wonder how I'd found myself on this mission to confront a dirty Paris detective and very possibly endanger my life in the process.

I was astonished to see that the Eiffel Tower was in plain view when I came up from the Metro dungeons and, for no reason I can think of tears sprang to my eyes.

Maybe because for one split second I remembered that I was in Paris, the most romantic city on the planet and what I was about to do shouldn't be thought of in the same breath as romance and happy walks through the City of Light.

I walked away from the Eiffel Tower into the fifteenth arrondissement, passing more and more streets with boarded up shops and offices. I hadn't seen a café in at least ten minutes of walking. So unusual for Paris.

I continued to walk, passing narrow alleys that seemed impossible to fit the width of an average man until I came to *rue de Emile Zola*.

I hesitated when I turned down the last alley. It had started to rain and it was a very cold rain. The light had faded considerably by then for midmorning, and the alley seemed dark and uninviting.

It was incredible to me that this alley was just a few blocks away from the most famous sightseeing landmark on Earth. Someday as the terrorists grew bolder this whole neighborhood would likely be cordoned off such that it was impossible to get close to La Tour Eiffel without one's whole dossier being revealed to security forces.

But that day was not today.

I turned down the alley and reminded myself what I might face today.

Jean-Marc LaRue was a dangerous crooked cop and I would be meeting with him without benefit of police protection—only Daigneault for muscle and Adelle as a remote witness. If my plan failed catastrophically, at least this time Catherine wouldn't have any questions about what happened to her remaining parent.

I know. Cold comfort.

Daigneault stepped out of a doorway where he'd been hidden from sight. I gave a startled scream and clapped my hand to my mouth.

"You are nervous, Claire."

"Yes," I said, trying to get my heartbeat to slow down again. "Of course I'm nervous."

"Come. This way."

I followed him down the lane to the third recessed doorway and saw not a soul the whole time. I have to admit it was exactly what I'd asked for. I was just astonished that such a desolate and unwelcoming place existed so close to the heart of Paris.

He waited for me at the door and then opened it with a key. That bothered me a little because it meant he wasn't breaking into the place and I knew for a fact he couldn't possibly own it himself.

Which meant he'd gotten the key from someone. Which meant someone else knew we were here.

I forced down my doubts and mounting fear.

Once inside I saw the warehouse space was a large triple bay garage area. Empty wooden shelving lined the walls up to a twenty-foot ceiling. Naked bulbs hung in a row across the space causing distorted shadows as we walked.

Not ideal for video recording.

Daigneault led me to a wooden table under a frame of wooden beams latticed across the ceiling.

"I thought we could position the two interior cameras there, yes?" Daigneault pointed to the middle of the rafter overhead.

I walked to the center and looked up.

"Good idea," I said. "Drag the table under them so he'll think standing here makes sense when he comes."

While Daigneault set up a step ladder under the lattice work, I went to the box he had gotten from Adelle that morning and looked through the camera equipment. I'd used the brand several times back in Atlanta when I used to do surveillance before I had Catherine.

These cameras' microphones were much better than the ones back then. At ten plus feet over our heads the hanging framework should easily pick up our voices.

I was satisfied. The space was just dark enough to hide the cameras—provided you didn't know they were there—but the naked bulbs should illuminate us enough to afford a decent picture.

Daigneault and I worked silently to position the two cameras over the space and situated the table beneath them.

"Should we get chairs?" he asked.

"No one will be sitting. The table is just a prop to get him to stand in place."

"You are sure this will work?" he asked as he handed me the third camera and picked up the step ladder to move outside.

"Absolutely," I said.

I'm the kind of person that once I've committed to a course of action I don't like to second guess myself. I think that's the first step toward losing your nerve.

And I've never seen anything good come from *that*.

I held the ladder for him in the alley while he brought the camera up to a ledge over the door and positioned its lens to take in the street. He cursed.

"What is it?"

"Damn light won't go on," he said.

"Hand it down to me."

He stepped down and gave me the camera. I saw right away it was broken. I wished I'd asked Adelle to check the equipment before she picked them up but it was too late now.

"Never mind," I said. "We have enough with the two inside. I'll text Adelle not to expect a feed from the alley camera."

I took his phone and went back inside the warehouse to confirm that there was decent reception and then came back out and locked the door behind me. In spite of the cold, Daigneault was sweating. We began to walk back toward where I could once more see the Eiffel Tower in the distance peeking out at the ends of various streets.

The plan was for me to call LaRue and get him to meet Daigneault at a specific café. From there Daigneault would lead LaRue to the warehouse where I would be waiting. Daigneault would then serve as lookout while LaRue and I met.

That was the plan.

As we walked, I slipped my arm inside his. The move surprised me and I know it did Daigneault but frankly I was feeling a little vulnerable. Whatever was going to happen in the next couple of hours would be the culmination of this whole wretched mess.

I thought things would go my way. I thought LaRue would see sense. But of course you never knew how people would react.

Especially dangerous, desperate people.

"When he shows up at the café," I said, "if he tries to arrest you, tell him I'll expose him on the evening news tonight. And I'll still be at the police station with an attorney to bail you out."

"What if he doesn't come alone?"

"Then try to run. If they catch you, same thing. He's exposed tonight on TV France 2 and I'll come bail you out."

"I guess that just about covers everything."

"It's going to be fine."

We walked in silence to the café and took the first table we came to. I ordered coffees for both of us.

He put his phone on the table between us. In exactly ten minutes I would call LaRue.

The butterflies in my stomach suddenly felt like vampire bats.

"What makes you so sure it wasn't Nico who killed your husband?" Daigneault asked.

That was a good question. And one I didn't have an answer for that most people would understand.

The fact is, I'd met Nico. I'd smelled the bedroom where Bob died when I walked in. There was no scent of Nico in there at all.

But I couldn't tell Daigneault that.

"It's hard to explain," I said. "Let's just say it's a gut feeling."

Daigneault picked up his coffee and frowned.

"I try not to trust those feelings," he said grimly.

55

HELLO DARKNESS, MY OLD FRIEND

Jean-Marc watched the activity as the fire brigade personnel continued to go in and out of the hotel, dragging hoses, carrying out depleted oxygen cannisters.

Roof tiles were scattered across the street although smoke no longer seeped out of the black jagged hole that had once been the second floor. Debris littered the street and dogs with their handlers sniffed every piece.

At this point the dogs weren't looking for any more bodies. The ambulances had gone. They were looking for clues as to who did this. Dust continued to cling to the air in front of Jean-Marc, hovering like a question.

Where the hell was her body?

He bit his lip and rubbed his ears. He couldn't stop fidgeting.

She asked for this! She wouldn't have it any other way!

His chin quivered and he put his hand on his face to stop it, angry at his own body for betraying him with the tell-tale signs of guilt.

Had there been another possible ending to this?

One of the dogs started barking and Jean-Marc felt his stomach heave. Had the animal found something?

Roman had neglected to clear the second floor as Jean-Marc had instructed. As a result there were more bodies than there should have been.

God! This was interminable!

Roman walked over to him and handed him a paper cup of coffee.

"Thanks." Jean-Marc noticed his hand shook when he took the cup. Roman couldn't have missed it either.

"Any idea when they'll let us inside?" Roman asked.

Roman's affect was flat and deflated, his face grim. Jean-Marc noticed because the man was normally ebullient. For the first time in his association with him he was seeing a Roman Pellé who wasn't always smiling.

As they stood next to each other watching the fire brigade and the emergency medical services start to pack up Jean-Marc knew the things they'd said to each other earlier could not be unsaid or forgotten. They would continue to work together. They would also commit to taking a bullet for each other if need be.

But he would always remember Roman suggesting he'd deliberately put Claire Baskerville in that hotel. That wasn't something a partner couldn't *not* think of in the back of his mind. And that kind of doubt would turn corrosive before too long.

Jean-Marc stared at the scene before him, his eyes stinging with the smoke that still hung in the air.

Roman had only said what everyone else would be thinking once they had a moment to reflect and analyze.

The detective renowned for hating Americans had been given the case of a murdered American tourist.

And now the widow of the man murdered dies in police custody?

At the direction of the same American-hating detective who'd sat on his hands during her husband's murder case?

No. He would not be hearing the last of this.

And the worst of it was, he had no defense. Just as Roman had warned him, he'd let his emotions run away with him.

And this time they'd run him right into his last dead end.

The dog handlers were conferring now. One of the dogs had burned his paw and was being taken away. The *Sergent-Chef* of the firefighters was directing his men to bring yet more equipment into the hotel.

Jean-Marc glanced at his partner. The fact that Roman still wasn't speaking was testimony to the diminished level in their relations.

I don't care how many cups of coffee he fetches for me. We're done.

Jean-Marc's phone rang in his pocket and he felt a twitch of unease as he felt for it. It was probably too early for headquarters to be asking questions related to him and Claire Baskerville's death. But it might not be too soon for him to be taken off the case.

Hell, if it were me, that's what I'd do.

He squinted at the phone screen. It read *Unidentified Caller.*

"Detective Jean-Marc LaRue," he said.

"Good morning, Detective Douchebag. Do *not* react. Do not let on it's me or I won't meet with you."

Jean-Marc blinked in confusion. At first he thought he must be hearing her voice because he'd been thinking of her just before the call.

"Who...?" he said in bewilderment.

Jean-Marc looked at Roman who turned to him and frowned. Instinctively, Jean-Marc walked out of Roman's earshot.

"Who is this?" he said, his voice lowered. But there was no

doubt. Her voice was distinctive. Her accent, her inflection so very American. Unmistakable.

"I'll make this simple, Detective. I need to talk to you privately. But if you alert your pals, the hostage I am holding dies. Did I mention I have a hostage?"

Jean-Marc cleared his throat. "*Non.*"

"So you'll need to come alone," Claire said. "That is, if you *care* if she dies. Do you care, Detective LaRue? Oh, did I mention this call is being recorded? So if you let her die, the world will know—among other things—that you let it happen. *Comprenez-vous*?"

"Where are you?" Jean-Marc said as he glanced over at Roman who had turned from the hotel fire and was openly frowning at him.

"I need an assurance from you that you will not tell your police pals where you're going. I'm pretty sure you're used to keeping secrets so this should not be difficult for you."

"*Oui, d'accord.*" He covered the mouthpiece and said to Roman, "It is Chloe. More drama."

Roman nodded.

"Go to the Café Denzel on the *Avenue Emile Acollas*," Claire said. "Do you know it?"

"I can find it."

"Be there in fifteen minutes. A friend of mine will meet you. Remember *come alone*." She disconnected the call.

Jean-Marc looked at his phone and took a moment to register that she had not died in the fire after all.

Roman walked over to him. "I'm sorry, Jean-Marc, perhaps I shouldn't say anything. But what kind of life is it to be constantly at her beck and call like this?"

"It is what it is," Jean-Marc said. "But I need to go."

"You need to do something about that woman,"

"I was just thinking the same thing," Jean-Marc said, tucking his phone away.

56

TIME'S UP

It didn't take me long before I wished I'd worn more clothes. Except of course I didn't have more clothes. The warehouse smelled of diesel fuel and bleach and I found myself walking the perimeter of the interior to keep warm.

I looked at my watch every few minutes.

I'd called LaRue thirty minutes ago. It would take him at least fifteen to get to the café where he would meet Daigneault and another ten to walk to the warehouse.

So if he'd hung up and left right that minute, he should be walking through the warehouse door any second now.

I turned and stood by the table, leaning on it with my arms, my eyes on the door. I glanced up at the cameras and saw both of their red recording lights on. Again, if you knew they were up there, you could see them. I intended to keep LaRue's attention firmly on me during our encounter.

Bottom line, I was counting on him not looking up.

You'd think I'd be used to the waiting by now. Or perhaps I was used to it when I did this sort of thing for a living but I was so much younger then and I'd gotten out of the habit.

I shook out my hands and did another lap around the space

hoping to warm up before coming back to the table. I listened for any sounds of someone coming but heard nothing and reminded myself that this space was soundproof—as requested.

Daigneault and LaRue could right now be battling to the death outside the warehouse door and I would have no inkling.

A sheen of perspiration formed on my top lip.

I was hot and cold at the same time. Worse, I'd forgotten to take any ibuprofen this morning and now my hip and shoulder were beginning to simultaneously ache. And the cold was really getting to me.

I felt a wave of discouragement. That was not something you ever heard Wonder Woman having a problem with—the cold getting into her bones just before a big showdown with a super villain.

But then Wonder Woman wasn't sixty years old.

I'd debated keeping the lights off when LaRue came but decided I had enough tricks up my sleeve and besides it might make the camera recording lights that much more visible.

The door swung open on hinges so loud and creaky that I jumped.

I felt excitement and fear tremble up my arms as I realized LaRue was finally here.

I saw him silhouetted in the doorway for a split second before Daigneault slammed the door shut behind him. I had the satisfaction of seeing LaRue jump when that happened but he recovered quickly.

He marched over to me.

"You will go to prison for this," he said, his face flushed red with fury. "Your embassy won't be able to help you. You've really done it now."

I needed him to come a little closer in order to be fully in the camera frame.

"Explain how it is you were seen with Reynard at the Hotel L'Ocean," I asked, crossing my arms on my chest.

That did the trick. He walked over to me as if to intimidate me.

"Who says I was?" he said belligerently.

"I have a source. One who says she's seen you with him twice."

He frowned. "The maid?"

Damn. I shouldn't have given away her gender.

"Her testimony is as valid as anyone's. She said she saw you with Reynard the day my husband was killed."

"She's mistaken."

"Well, I'll guess we'll just have to put the two of you on the witness stand and see what crawls out from under the rocks."

"You do know you'll be arrested for this?" he said.

"You can threaten me all you want but unless you answer my questions you are not going anywhere."

He looked around the space. "Where is your hostage?"

"You'll find out in due time. I'm still waiting for you to answer my question."

He bared his teeth and spoke in a strained voice. "I'm not saying she was mistaken about seeing me with him," he said. "But she got the day wrong. I can account for my whereabouts on the day of your husband's murder. I met with Reynard the day before."

"Why?"

"He was my CI."

So far he was at least partially telling the truth.

"When your husband was killed it was clear to me that Reynard had escaped a near miss. I told him to lie low which he did for about three weeks. But he panicked and came back to town and contacted me saying he needed to see me. He said he had the name of someone big—someone we have been trying to identify for nearly a year of investigation."

"Why didn't he just tell you the name on the phone?"

"CIs often think they can get more money if they stretch it out. It's a common tactic. So I agreed to meet with him."

"Alone?"

"Reynard was the nervous type. We always met alone."

"So what happened?"

"I was followed on my way to meet him and attacked. When I came to, Reynard was dead."

"How do I know it wasn't you who killed him?"

"How would that benefit me?"

"It might if you killed my husband and he knew it or if *you* were the Big Boss."

He laughed. "You have been watching too much American television."

"And you are an officious French twat." I took in a breath to calm myself. Getting angry would not get me the answers I needed.

"So you have no idea who might have wanted to kill Reynard?" I asked.

"Aside from someone working for the Big Boss who discovered he was working for the police? No."

He walked directly under the wooden grid and stared up at the cameras overhead.

"You know this wouldn't hold up as evidence," he said as he pulled his smartphone out of his jacket pocket.

I watched in horror as he called up a website on his phone, pointed it at the camera, and then I watched the red recording light go out.

He turned and did the same thing with the other camera.

"Any more I should know about?"

"How did you do that?" I asked in dismay.

He nodded at the cameras. "It's a common brand. Probably the cheapest you can buy. The disarm code works remotely from any smartphone."

"I have someone with instructions to call the police if they don't hear from me at a certain time."

He regarded me with impatience. "I'm not going to hurt you. I'm going to make sure you don't bother anyone ever again."

"Sounds like the same thing to me," I said, my eyes going helplessly to the now darkened cameras overhead.

"Then let me be clear. I'm going to arrest you and charge you with kidnapping a police officer."

"Did you kill Reynard?" I blurted out.

"Again, what possible motive would I have had?"

"Well, I don't know but you're a big liar so it could be anything. Where does the little weasel behind the registration desk at the Hotel L'Ocean fit in?"

"I have no idea who you're talking about."

"The desk clerk! Bernard somebody. When I went to talk to him a week ago you and Roman showed up two seconds later."

"I got a call that there was some trouble. And we happened to be nearby."

"Weird that *homicide* detectives would respond to what was essentially a nuisance call, isn't it? Bernard called you directly, didn't he? His call didn't go through police dispatch."

LaRue looked uncomfortable.

"Are you on the take?" I asked.

"What? No."

"Except I have another source who witnessed you taking money from the Hotel L'Ocean desk clerk on two separate occasions."

LaRue blanched.

"So to save time, here's what I know," I said, using my fingers to tick off the items. "I know you take bribes. I know you're dirty and I believe you know the truth about what happened to my husband."

"You're insane. You should know that even your American

embassy can't help you after all this. You are illegally detaining a French police officer. You will go to prison for years."

"So you've said. Did you not hear me? I have proof that you take bribes. So if I go to prison so do you."

"What is it you want?" A visible vein throbbed in his neck.

"I told you. I want the truth."

"And in return, what do I get? Your promise that you will not tell what you know?"

"Unless you killed my husband, yes, I promise not to tell."

"You think *I* killed him?"

"I don't know! Maybe! I know you were at the hotel and you lied about it! I know you hate Americans! I know you've been lying to me every step of the investigation and you showed up right after Reynard Coté was murdered with a big purple bump on your face! And let's don't forget the bomb that blew up as soon as you put me in a hotel *you* chose!"

He looked at me as if totally bewildered. But again, detectives have to be great actors. His expression was nothing to go by.

"The bomb was from a terrorist group," he said.

"That is complete bull shit. Unless you set the bomb yourself to get rid of me—which is what I'm going with—there's no way you'd have confirmation from a terrorist group this early."

"What else could it be? I didn't arrange it. Perhaps it was a gas leak."

"When are you going to start telling me the truth?!"

"I didn't kill your husband! Your husband was killed by mistake by Nico Bordeaux—"

"You're still lying!"

"I am not lying. I can't tell you what you want to hear! Your husband was killed by mistake by a contract killer who—"

"I swear I'll turn you in. Is it worth it to you? Or are you lying because *you're* the one who killed him? And don't even think about trying to silence *me* because I have no fewer than five people who know I'm talking to you right now and who will be calling Detective Pellé within the hour if they don't hear from me."

"This is a very dangerous game you're playing, Madame Baskerville."

"Do you know Paul Daigneault?"

He frowned again. "The name sounds familiar but I can't place him."

"So he's not your CI?"

"No."

"Is he Roman's?" I was basically just hoping to catch him in another lie. I was fairly sure Daigneault wasn't anyone's CI.

"Roman and I are partners. We know each other's CI's. So he's not Roman's CI either."

"So you're saying that *Reynard* was also Roman's CI?"

LaRue stared at me as if trying to figure something out.

I repeated the question. "Detective? *Was Reynard also Roman's CI*?"

"No."

"But you just told me—"

"Roman only joined the homicide division six months ago. Reynard had been my CI for over a year."

"Can I ask you a really offensive question?"

LaRue laughed in spite of himself.

"Why stop now?"

"When Reynard told you there was a cop on the force feeding information to the Big Boss, did you tell Roman?"

I could tell by LaRue's face that he'd hit on that same question about five seconds before I asked it.

Now there was the possibility that LaRue was just an amazing actor but I swear by everything I've seen in my life—and yes that's coming from a woman who was being cheated on by her husband for over a year—that LaRue's sick expression was the real deal.

Which meant that there was every reason to believe that the mole in the police department was Roman Pellé.

I was starting to feel a little sick myself.

"I think I've made a very big mistake," LaRue said, raking his hand across his face.

He looked at me and then at the door. "I told Roman," he said.

My heartbeat took off at a gallop.

"Told him what?" I managed to say.

"That I was meeting you." He looked at me, a slick sheen of perspiration on his face.

The next thing we heard was a muffled popping sound that sounded like a car backfiring in the alleyway.

Suddenly all my senses came alive. The popping sound must have made more sense to LaRue because within a second of hearing the noise, he lunged at me.

Just as the door opened revealing Roman Pellé.

With a gun in his hand.

Pointed at me.

57

HELL TO PAY

I barely had time to register that Jean-Marc had grabbed me before he released me just as fast—as his body spasmed violently…

…in time with the sounds of two gunshots reverberating loudly in the warehouse. His head snapped backward knocking me in the face as the bullets thudded into his body. I went down hard underneath him as he crumpled to the floor.

It was then that some part of my conscious brain registered that Jean-Marc hadn't been attacking me.

He'd pulled me behind him.

To protect me.

Jean-Marc was a heavy dead weight across my hips and legs. I was sweating as my body took in the situation and began to shake violently.

"Are you still alive, *chérie*?" Roman called out. "Show yourself, please."

I stopped struggling and for one mad moment thought

about playing dead. But I was pretty sure Roman wasn't that stupid.

I freed one leg from under Jean-Marc and watched as Roman walked over to me. In some insane part of my brain he looked exactly as he had that afternoon when we met for lunch, open faced and charismatic, his brown eyes dancing and focused on me.

I finally completely recognized him.

His gun was still in his hand but he held it loosely, not really pointed at the ground but not aimed at my heart either.

Not yet anyway.

The shot I'd heard a few seconds ago must have been Roman killing Daigneault. I forced myself not to think about that right now. Thinking about that made it harder to think clearly about anything.

Roman was looking around at the interior warehouse space as if appraising it.

I freed my other leg and turned to kneel beside Jean-Marc. The cold cement floor beneath my knees was slick with blood and I could see it was pooling by his head. My heart sank.

"So you thought Jean-Marc was the mole, right?" Roman said as he turned to glance down at me. "You never suspected me?"

I could see his gun was a Glock 19. Paris police department issue. That told me he intended to make what happened next look like a tragic accident.

"Are you the Big Boss?" I asked as one hand went to Jean-Marc's neck to try to find a pulse. I didn't expect one. There was just too much blood.

"I don't care for that appellation," Roman said, losing his smile. "Let's just say I run a consortium and I have people who answer to me."

"Like Nico?"

The thing about a certain kind of man and by that I mean

all men is that they tend to underestimate women. I'm sure it comes from never having to feel seriously threatened by a woman.

And certainly not by a woman of a certain age. Even in France.

Roman relaxed his stance and leaned his weight on one hip. He crossed his arms, his gun still held loosely in his hand. He didn't act for a minute liked he wasn't completely sure that he was going to kill me. On that point he was confident. He'd already shot his only two possible threats—both males. He could take his time with me.

"Nico was one, yes. But I have dozens more. Some even you haven't met." He laughed at his own joke.

"Since it looks like I'm not leaving this warehouse," I said, "I wonder if you could tell me the truth about my husband's murder."

"You still want to know? You truly amaze me, *chérie*. I would've thought begging for your life would be uppermost in your mind right about now."

So he's a complete sociopath, I thought, feeling the cold certainty of his words in my gut. *There's nothing I can say to talk him out of this. He has no human feelings I can appeal to.*

"I'd like to know the truth, please," I said. I'd actually felt a pulse in Jean-Marc's neck, although I wasn't sure it mattered. After Roman killed me he would surely put another one in his partner's head to be certain.

Roman made an exaggerated shrugging motion.

"The truth was staring you in the face the whole time," he said with a grin. "I found out that Reynard was selling secrets. I sent Nico to deal with him. I knew Reynard sold drugs out of the hotel so I sent Nico there and he went to the wrong room by mistake—your husband's room."

"You're telling me Nico killed Bob?" I said feeling an irrational pulse of anger. "You have literally nothing left to lose by telling me the truth."

"Will you let me finish?" he said, his face suddenly flushed with anger. "No. Nico didn't kill your husband. He found your husband dead and left."

Hearing the news that I'd been right—even though I still didn't know who killed Bob—was like a kick in the stomach.

"I would've sent him back to do the job properly but by that time Jean-Marc had sent Reynard into hiding. Then when you kept kicking up dust—and getting Jean-Marc asking questions I'm sure he would never have asked if not for you—I sent Nico to visit you."

And all the while he was flirting with me.

He grinned wryly. "Nothing personal, *chérie*."

"And when Nico failed to kill me you killed him."

"*C'est ça*. I can't have my people seeing such incompetence go unpunished. I hated to lose Nico but the man was an idiot."

"How did you get inside my apartment without being seen?"

"Well, I didn't do it myself. If you'll remember, I was busy having a very nice lunch with you on the *boulevard Haussmann* during the time of Nico's murder."

"Why was he killed in my apartment?"

"Nice touch, don't you think? I thought at the very least it might make you leave—you see, *chérie*, I was still hoping not to have to kill you."

"It was you who put me in the hotel that blew up, wasn't it?"

He laughed. "Actually, no, Jean-Marc picked the hotel. But *I* sent the man to plant the bomb."

I had a brief flash of memory of Roman standing in the doorway of my hotel room. I pictured him smiling, promising to pick me up a toothbrush, telling me to be sure and lock the door behind him when he left.

And all the time he was planning on calling one of his henchmen to come blow up the hotel with me in it.

"Did you shoot Daigneault?" I hated to ask. I didn't want to know. I had to know.

He glanced at the door and shrugged. "I don't even know why he got involved with you at all."

My stomach churned.

"How are you going to explain his death? Or Jean-Marc's or mine?"

"I'll say that Jean-Marc and I interrupted Daigneault trying to rape you—we'll have to get those clothes off you in a minute. When Jean-Marc tried to stop him, Daigneault grabbed his gun and shot him and then you. I eventually shot Daigneault but by then, sadly, it was too late."

In that moment I suddenly remembered that Adelle was supposed to call Roman at a set time. Without the camera feed would she assume something had gone wrong and improvise or would she stick to the plan?

My mind raced as I watched Roman rocking on his heels, his back to the now useless cameras. Because the alley camera wasn't working Adelle wouldn't have seen what happened to Daigneault.

She doesn't know that the person she's supposed to call is the same person holding me at gunpoint.

Just then Roman's phone rang. I prayed he wouldn't take the call.

He pulled his phone out, glanced at the screen and frowned. And answered it.

"This is Detective Roman Pellé."

I watched him listening to the voice on the other end and when he looked at me with a hard smile carved onto his lips, I knew it was Adelle he was speaking to.

And my heart fell at my feet.

"By all means, Madame," he said. "I will go there immediately. Thank you. Where are you so that I may take a statement afterward? Yes? I know the place. Yes. Thank you again."

He hung up and looked at me.

"So clever, *chérie*. Now, thanks to you I will be able to reach out and find that one last loose end."

"I hope you rot in hell," I said as I saw every one of my options disintegrate around me.

"And now you will disrobe, *chérie*," he said, waving his gun at me. "Your clothing is ruined anyway, *n'est-ce pas*?"

"How can you be so heartless?" I said, my voice trembling. "This man was your partner."

I turned to look at Jean-Marc's body and put my hands on his chest. He was warm but very still. I'd been right about a lot of things about him, but wrong about the main things. He might have been dirty but he wasn't the killer and he wasn't the mole.

He was just some duped schmo who'd taken a few bribes and probably knew less than I did about why Bob was killed.

"I will shoot you where you sit and strip your corpse if you make me," Roman said. "But I was looking forward to seeing you naked while you were alive."

Tears streaked down my cheeks. "You're a monster," I choked.

"Tears do not affect me, *chérie*," he said. "Even as a child they didn't bother me. Zut! You should ask my first wife. The woman cried over everything. I'm afraid it was just white noise to me." He laughed. "You should have heard her carry on! Never could I have imagined that someone could weep so much over so little. Why one time when we were first married..."

Roman was so busy talking about himself and I was doing such a good job of crying and looking terrified that it never occurred to him that the ending to this little episode might turn out differently. It never occurred to him I might try to fight for my life.

In the end he really did have a very poor opinion of women.

So when my probing fingers found the gun in Jean-Marc's shoulder holster Roman was not expecting what happened next.

I pulled the gun out—the same Glock model I had shot many times before.

And even then—even looking at me with the gun now in my hands Roman was so disbelieving that I might actually be doing this that he simply gaped at me in confusion.

I regret to say I didn't tell him I would shoot if he didn't put down his gun. There seemed no point since I was determined to shoot him in any case.

I squeezed the trigger three times aiming for the tight cluster pattern as I'd been trained to do during all those hours at the shooting range on Peachtree Road in Atlanta.

And unlike how Roman shot Jean-Marc, all three of my shots hit center mass.

58

A DAY LATE

The sounds of the gunshots echoed loudly in the warehouse. Once I saw Roman fall I dropped the gun and wrenched Jean-Marc's phone out of his pocket. I was on my feet and hobbling on shaky legs toward the door.

I knew there was phone reception inside the warehouse. But I had to get out of there. I couldn't breathe. I tripped once on my way out abrading my knee, before wrenching open the door and immediately falling over Daigneault's body where he lay on the threshold to the warehouse.

I scrambled to my feet again. One look at Daigneault told me there was no point in looking for a pulse. Still staring at his body, I backed away until I hit the garage door opposite the warehouse. Tearing my eyes from Daigneault's corpse, I looked at Jean-Marc's phone and saw it was password protected. I knew the bypass code for emergencies in the US, and keyed it in, praying it would work here.

The call went through.

I sputtered out, half in tears, "Hurry! Policeman down! Two dead! Can you triangulate my location?"

The dispatcher assured me she could. I set the phone down

on the street so the police could use it to find where we were and stepped around Daigneault's body to the warehouse door which I propped open with a large brick that seemed to be there for that reason.

It took every bit of bravery I ever hope to have in this lifetime to go back inside that building. But I couldn't leave Jean-Marc there. I knew Roman had to be dead but that didn't stop me from fearing he somehow wasn't, that he was waiting for me.

My jaw clenched, I ran to Jean-Marc's body but slowed before I reached him.

I'd left him on his stomach. He was now on his back.

Holding my breath I turned to look at Roman but he hadn't moved. I dropped to my knees by Jean-Marc and his hand reached out and grabbed my wrist hard.

I gasped. His eyes fluttered open and I stared into them. There was blood everywhere. He was literally swimming in it. There was no way he wasn't seriously hurt. But he was watching me, his eyes stunned and unfocused.

"They're coming," I said to him. "The ambulance. The police."

And then I felt a shiver of apprehension.

"Unless...is there...are there more like Roman?" I asked.

It hadn't occurred to me until just that moment that the cops might show up, decide to eliminate the problem that Roman had been unable to, and then go on their way.

Mess cleared up, problem solved.

Jean-Marc groaned. I put my hands on his chest and felt what I should have felt before. He was wearing a vest. That accounted for why he wasn't seriously dead right now. But the blood...

I touched his head. He had a head wound. With all the blood I couldn't tell how bad it was but I knew that going to sleep was generally regarded as a bad idea. His eyes rolled back into his head. I could hear the sirens now.

"Hey, Detective," I said loudly. "Wake up."

He didn't open his eyes. I grabbed him by the lapels and shook him. "Wake up!" I shouted.

His eyes fluttered open. "Stop," he said.

"No. You can't go to sleep. You want me to slap you? Wake up!"

His eyes widened. "I'm awake." And he closed his eyes again.

I slapped him. I hated doing it. The man had a head injury! Who wants to slap someone who's been shot in the head?

The slap barely fazed him. But he did open his eyes.

"They will be here in literally thirty seconds," I said. "You can sleep then."

"Okay, okay."

He licked his lips and tried to focus his eyes. I could see him struggling.

"I didn't know," he said.

"I figured that as soon as he shot you."

"I'm not dirty."

"Except you are. Don't close your eyes."

He groaned. "You're right. I took the bribes."

The sounds of people coming through the warehouse door took my attention then. I felt immense relief that the responsibility of keeping Jean-Marc alive was soon going to be someone else's problem.

"I'm sorry you got shot," I said.

"You Americans," he said, with the faintest of smiles, "so strange." His eyes drifted closed again just as the EMTs came running toward us.

59

LIFE ITSELF

It was hard to believe it had been a whole week since the nightmare in the warehouse. From the minute the place was swarmed with cops roping off the area and EMTs packing up—Jean-Marc to the hospital and Roman and poor Daigneault off to the morgue—I was treated by everybody with kindness and kid gloves.

I was treated, dare I say it, like a hero.

I had not only revealed a mole in their ranks, but I had saved the life of one of their own. And regardless of how badly I felt Jean-Marc must have bungled his career, surprisingly it turned out he was very fondly regarded by his peers.

Since I couldn't go back to my apartment—live crime scene and all that—I spent the night at Geneviève's and then went to the bank to get a new debit and credit card and checked into the Premier Deluxe guest suite at the George V Hotel.

A part of me needed major pampering after what I had been through but another part of me knew that all my money was going to go away very soon and pinching pennies at this point would not make a lot of difference. I was never going to be able to pay Joelle back what I owed her in any case.

Remarkably, within hours of the whole nightmarish warehouse scene, my life settled down. Nobody was warning me about hits put out on me. Nobody was breaking into my apartment. Nobody was trying to blow up hotels I was staying in.

I stayed in my hotel suite for five days and slept most of the days, reading books on my new phone, eating room service, watching cable movies and waiting until my apartment was released back to me.

I did surface at one point during this time. The day after the showdown at the warehouse I went to Saint-Denis to visit Eva. I have to say that, as soon as she saw me, she knew. Daigneault had obviously not come home the night before and since she wasn't related to him nobody contacted her.

She was sad but not terribly surprised about what had happened. I personally felt absolutely sick about it. I felt like Daigneault had wanted to help me and he lost his life in the process. I felt completely responsible. If I'd guessed sooner that it was Roman, and not Jean-Marc—well, no use going down that road.

Once I moved back into my apartment, I was immediately swamped with love and attention by Geneviève and even to a certain extent by Luc, who found an excuse at least once a day to drop by to see how I was doing.

Geneviève was so delighted to see me that, since leaving the Georges V, I have either spent most of my time at her place or she at mine.

On this rainy November day, we were having an early *apéro* and just enjoying being together. She had already offered her guest room to me for as long as I needed it after I was booted from my apartment and I had accepted with gratitude and relief.

"*Chérie*, you do know that Luc watches you in a special way, no?" Geneviève said as she nibbled a *gougère*.

"I'm *not* dating Luc, Geneviève. He's like eighteen years old."

"*Très amusant, chérie*. He is forty."

"Still twenty years my junior."

"And your point?"

"You are so French."

"Ah, you must be a detective! I knew you would discover that sooner or later."

The idea of having a roommate in her old age was one that clearly delighted Geneviève. And honestly I was pretty happy about it myself.

Adelle was of course horrified to learn she'd called Roman as he was holding me at gunpoint and asked me no fewer than five times why I didn't just yell out while she was on the phone with Roman. I don't have a good answer for that, beyond the fact that I didn't think of it.

Maybe at some level I thought it would trigger him to shoot me right then.

It had only been a week and Adelle was so busy with all the assorted crime scenes associated with me that I'd only seen her once in all that time. She came to visit me at the Georges V having never been inside the famous hotel before.

I think she felt like she got answers regarding everything that had happened but more importantly she and her mother would now get justice for Reynard. I'm glad about that anyway. It made me feel less guilty about everything I put her through to know that she and her mother at least knew why and how he died.

Geneviève kept looking at the door like she was expecting someone but when I asked her she only shrugged—that shrug that everyone in France knows how to do and all of us foreigners are helpless to interpret.

My phone rang and it was Adelle.

"I just have a minute, Claire. But I wanted to know if you are interested in helping a friend of mine—Canadian expat—whose wife ran off. He needs to find her."

I sat down and reached for a notebook without realizing I was doing it.

"Sounds like she doesn't want to be found," I said.

"Does that matter? Are you interested in talking to him? He'll pay."

Of course those were the magic words. Once Joelle took all my money, I would need a source of income.

"Yes, I'll talk to him," I said. I jotted down the details she gave me and then hung up.

"Perhaps you have a new business, yes?" Geneviève said.

"Maybe," I said. I still hadn't decided how I was going to make a living back in the States. Back home on the job market, being sixty was tantamount to having a criminal record.

Would it be any easier in France?

There was a knock at the door and I got up. Nobody visited me at my apartment unless I buzzed them up—something that had yet to happen—or they lived in the building.

"It must be Luc," Geneviève said. "I told him when my present arrived to please bring it up to you."

"What present?" I asked. "Geneviève, you didn't have to get me anything."

I opened the door and saw Luc standing there, an embarrassed grin on his face, and an adorable French bulldog puppy in his arms.

"Oh, no way," I said looking at him and then the dog.

"That is not very friendly," Luc said, leaning over to kiss me on the cheek.

"It's not you," I said still shaking my head.

Geneviève rushed over, her hands outstretched to take the puppy.

"Oh, *c'est charmant*! Do you not think so, *chérie*? And you, Luc?"

He grinned. "She pissed on my sleeve on the way up."

"Of course she did! Clever girl!" Geneviève kissed the puppy's head and turned to look at me. "You cannot decline the gift," she said. "After all, *chérie*, given who you are, you must of course have the proverbial hound, *n'est-ce pas*?"

60

LA BOHÈME

The next morning when I took the as-of-yet unnamed puppy on our first walk together, it was cold but sunny.

The little dear seemed to realize she was on probation because she didn't whimper all night (although I did allow her to sleep with me so she had little cause to) and only had one accident. As much as I'd argued with Geneviève about taking the dog, my arguments sounded weak even to my ears.

As we walked from my apartment to Parc Monceau, the puppy strained at her leash at the sight of the children we met. I had to admit she served as a nice icebreaker for meeting the children's handlers and I spent a pleasant hour chatting to complete strangers whose children were in thrall over my dog.

I hadn't intended to bring the puppy along on my errand afterwards but we were both enjoying the sunny weather so much that I decided to see how she'd behave in a café setting.

It seemed I still can't stay away from the Latin Quarter. As I walked to my afternoon appointment, I stopped and looked in a perfume shop window. Checking my watch to see that I had time, I tucked the puppy into my tote bag and went inside and spent money I no longer had on the most incredible fragrances I have ever smelled in my life.

Once back out on the sidewalk, I let Puppy out to sniff and wet the pavement and wrapped my pashmina around me against the chill. I glanced again at my watch. My appointment was two blocks down Saint-Germain-des-Prés at the Café de Flore. As I approached the famous café I realized I'd never actually gone here for a drink. It struck me as funny that Jean-Marc would choose it as a place to meet, but maybe he saw me as the perennial tourist.

I'd visited him in the hospital the day after they brought him in but they only kept him two nights and if he'd had his way it wouldn't have been that long. His scalp wound had required dozens of stitches but ultimately rest and time would heal him.

It was still hard for me to believe that he'd lived through the warehouse nightmare with no serious injuries to show for it.

The significant phrase being of course *to show for it.*

When I walked up to the café Jean-Marc was sitting outdoors under the iconic white awning with green letters. He waved when he saw me. He was wearing a baseball cap which I thought incredibly out of character for him but when I got closer I could see that one side of his head had been shaved.

"You have a dog," he said unnecessarily, standing as I joined him at the table. "Have you always had a dog?"

I laughed at how bemused he seemed.

"No, she's a recent acquisition. Actually she's also a living breathing example of the French sense of humor—something frankly I wasn't sure existed before now."

We sat down and he signaled to the waiter.

"You will have your hands full now," he warned. "Dogs are a lot of work."

"No, *puppies* are a lot of work. Dogs are lovely to snuggle up with at night and bark when someone breaks into your apartment."

"I thought that's what a husband was for—" He stopped himself nearly in mid-sentence and turned red. "I'm sorry."

"You don't need to screen your words with me, Jean-Marc."

"You are so American," he said, not for the first time. But he was smiling when he said it.

After the waiter brought our drinks—hot mulled wine for me, an ice-cold beer for him and a dish of water for the puppy —I leaned back in the chair to feel the sun on my face.

We didn't speak for a moment and then I was ready to begin.

"Okay," I said. "How did you know Reynard?"

I knew Jean-Marc was prepared for my questions. He'd already promised he would answer them all. But there were things I needed to know from him that I didn't have questions for. I'd need the answers to those too.

"Reynard approached me a year ago. He wanted money for information and he said he had something on the one they called the Big Boss."

"Why didn't he just tell you that Roman was the Big Boss?"

"Because Roman wasn't the Big Boss."

"He told me he was."

"And of course Roman always told the truth."

"Good point. Go on."

And so Jean-Marc told me everything. He told me that Reynard had been discovered giving information to Jean-Marc and for that he was marked to be killed.

The day before Bob was murdered, Jean-Marc had arranged to meet Reynard at the hotel. Reynard told him there was someone on the Paris police force arranging hits and facilitating drug drops. At first Jean-Marc didn't believe it but Reynard said he'd get closer and come back with a name. Unfortunately, the next day Bob was killed and Reynard panicked, assuming it had been a case of mistaken identity and the hit had really been meant for him.

"I told him to get out of town and I would reach out when things cooled down," Jean-Marc said. "He stayed gone three weeks and when he came back I arranged to meet him at a café near the Hotel L'Ocean."

"Did you tell Roman you were meeting him?"

Jean-Marc pulled off his cap and started to run a hand through his hair and then winced. He gingerly replaced the hat.

"I didn't. It wasn't that I didn't trust him..."

"But on some level you must not have."

"Maybe. Anyway, he must have had me followed because I was attacked on the way to my meeting with Reynard. When I came to, ambulance sirens we're going off everywhere." A sad reflective gaze came over his face and I knew he was thinking of Reynard.

Reynard had been not much more than a kid, not even twenty-one. I could see that Jean-Marc had felt some responsibility for him.

Adelle told me that she and her mother had gotten a visit from Jean-Marc a few days ago. He wanted to tell them he was sorry he didn't protect Reynard. And that he always thought Reynard might be able to break free and do something else for a living someday since he was such a bright young man.

"If the idiot had just done what I told him to do and stayed gone!" he said now.

His feelings for Reynard also explained why he was at Reynard's funeral. It wasn't to look for Reynard's possible killer as I'd thought.

It was to pay his respects.

"I can't tell you how surprised I was to hear that it was you who discovered his body," he said now, narrowing his eyes.

"Don't get sidetracked," I said. But I couldn't help adding, "You made me feel as if *I'd* killed him."

"I was only doing my job. It was of course not believable that you might have seriously been involved in his death."

"Just like you didn't believe I was able to get Nico's knife away from him that night in my apartment."

"It is still hard to believe."

"I've had marital arts training."

We let a moment of silence go by where I focused on the puppy happily gnawing on the side of my favorite Fendi flats.

"Tell me about the bribes," I asked softly.

He sighed and took a swig of his beer.

"I took bribes. I don't know what else you want me to say."

"The maid said she saw you manhandling Reynard."

He frowned. "Manhandling? No. She's wrong, I swear it. I liked Reynard."

"Can I ask why you risked your career like that?"

"You know about my wife?"

I nodded. "Unless Roman lied about that too. He said she was run over by a drunk American tourist and was confined to a wheelchair."

"Correct," he said tightly, his face unreadable.

"He said you took the money in order to buy her luxury items to ease her pain."

He snorted. "Well, that's nearly true." He looked at me. "I'm not making excuses. I took the money but not for information. I was only tasked with keeping police focus off the Hotel L'Ocean."

"Was something happening at the hotel that might otherwise have demanded the focus of the police?"

"I never saw evidence of it firsthand," he said, looking down at his hands. "I was told—"

"By Bernard?"

He looked up at me in surprise.

I'd not been able to get the ballpoint pen that I'd stolen to Adelle because it was in my purse that got burned up in the fire.

But from the look on Jean-Marc's face, there could be little doubt that Bernard existed in one of the international crime databases.

"Yes. He had a business he wanted not to show up on the Paris police's radar."

"What kind of business?"

When Jean-Marc hesitated, I spoke more sharply.

"Come on, Jean-Marc. I can't imagine you didn't find out what it was you were giving a free pass to."

"Skirting immigration laws," he said.

"You mean Bernard wanted to use people without proper papers to work in his hotel?"

"Yes."

But he still wasn't looking at me.

"Look, you don't have to tell me the truth. I don't intend to rat on you to your superiors. But I would have thought after everything we've been through that you owed me the truth."

When he still didn't answer, I said, "Is it possible what you were protecting Bernard from wasn't breaking immigration laws but human trafficking?"

He looked at me with a sick look on his face and I have to say I realized two things right away.

One, he hadn't allowed himself to go down that road. Two, now that he was going down it, he was remembering clues to support it.

Bernard Santé was using people for enforced labor. And he was giving money to Jean-Marc to turn a blind eye to what was happening.

Oh, and Three: If Jean-Marc tried to turn in Bernard the desk clerk would most certainly have stockpiled evidence to prove that Jean-Marc had taken bribes.

So doing the right thing now would cost Jean-Marc his career.

He picked up his phone and made a call. His French was

very fast with so many colloquial expressions that I didn't catch all of it.

But I caught enough to know he was calling in a raid on the Hotel L'Ocean.

He put the phone down and looked at me.

"One way or the other Bernard is out of business," he said.

But so are you, I thought sadly.

"How will you get out of this?" I asked, surprised at how sorry I felt for him.

He shrugged. "I still have friends."

The rest of our hour together was pleasant and relatively noninformative. In retrospect I can't believe I ever thought Roman was the handsomer of the two. Plus it turned out that Jean-Marc wasn't fifty-five. He was sixty. The same age as me.

After untangling the leash from my chair leg a few dozen times, I decided both Puppy and I could use a nap. The sun had been steadily dropping and I was officially cold. I asked Jean-Marc if I could take a photograph and although he agreed, he rolled his eyes when I took it. So I had to take another one since that was not how I wanted to remember him when we were not together.

When I stood up to go, he did too and took my hand. For one crazy moment, I thought he was going to kiss my hand, but he just held it. I think he wanted to say something more to me, perhaps *I'm sorry* or *please, leave Paris*. I don't know. But whatever it was it was personal and it never came.

"What about your husband?" he finally asked as I pulled my hand away to deal with the puppy's leash. She'd been very good napping and gnawing my shoes from under the table but now she was ready to walk. "You never found out who did it."

"Didn't I?" I said and arched an eyebrow at him. Then, impulsively, I leaned in and kissed him on the cheek. As far as I was concerned, we'd survived a life and death situation together. Surely that warranted a goodbye peck on the cheek.

He must have thought so too because he kissed my other cheek.

"*Au revoir*, Jean-Marc. Be sure and mind what the doctors tell you. Head injuries are nothing to play around with."

He shrugged.

The perennial French response to every situation.

As I turned to walk down Saint-Germain-des-Prés with Puppy pulling insistently on her leash, it occurred to me that if I were to stay in Paris and Jean-Marc was to somehow keep his job after the hotel raid, I probably had a very useful inside contact in the Paris police department.

And how nice would that be?

61

UNMASKED

Whether it was the wine or the recent unburdening or the fact that I felt pretty sure I'd just made a friend, I walked away from the Café de Flore feeling buoyant and happy.

I let Puppy pull me relentlessly down the sidewalk, side-stepping school children and shoppers. In my mind I had the idea that I would go home to a nice bath and begin packing up. I still had nearly two weeks before I needed to be out of Joelle's apartment but there was no sense in waiting until the last minute. Geneviève would be only too happy for me to move in early.

As I walked down the street, my phone pinged and I pulled it out to see I'd gotten an email. I slowed my pace, forcing Puppy to stop pulling and settle for sniffing a nearby streetlamp and opened the email on my phone.

It was from Claude's attorney's office giving me the date and time I was to appear in front of the magistrate in the case of *Lapin vs Lapin*.

Weirdly the case was set up as Joelle vs Claude and not Joelle vs me because it was Claude's estate that needed to be modified now. A part of me wished I could just tell her—"go on and take it, just leave me out of it." But nothing was ever going to be that simple.

I put my phone away and continued walking.

I'd tried to figure up how much money I'd spent from Claude's estate. It was a lot. Paying it back would be nearly impossible. If Joelle decided to charge me rent for the time I'd lived in her apartment this past fall, it would be even worse.

Looks like I was in crushing debt on two continents now.

By the time I reached the Hotel L'Ocean I could see there was nothing to indicate that a full-blown immigration or human trafficking raid was going on. Still, I had been sitting right there when Jean-Marc called it in.

*It doesn't do to start doubting my brand new fri*ends, I told myself. Even if I do personally have the absolute worst record in the history of the world for judging people.

I crossed the street and entered the hotel. There was nobody in the lobby or behind the desk. Since Bernard was the last person I wanted to talk to, I didn't call out or ring any bells.

Neither did I intend to go down the hall knocking on doors either. I glanced at my watch. Three o'clock in the afternoon. This was roughly the time I'd caught Marie the other times I'd come here.

I settled down on one of the sofas in the lobby. There was a tourist magazine on the table with the headline *Discover Paris,* dated 2010.

I didn't have to wait long.

Marie appeared in front of the registration desk with a packet of cigarettes. The puppy barked at her and she looked up in fear. I stood and walked over to her.

"I need to talk to you. Let's go outside so you can smoke."

Marie looked around nervously but seemed to come to the

quick conclusion that outside with me was better than inside with me.

The *with me* part being the inescapable common denominator.

I followed her out the front door and she immediately turned to the same little alley where I'd talked to her before. I waited for her to light her cigarette.

"Trini attacked somebody at the hotel, didn't she?" I said. "That's why she left."

Marie didn't look at me or answer.

"I found the towel," I said. "The one that somebody used to clean up the mess. As soon as I track down the guy who was stabbed—which will be easy to do since he was a registered guest here—I can match his DNA to the towel."

That of course would be nearly impossible to do since I had no hope of knowing which guy at the hotel had bled on the towel but Marie didn't know that.

I saw the moment she gave up the effort to lie to me.

"Trini said she wouldn't go with the men anymore," Marie said. "She told Bernard that."

So I'd guessed right. It *was* a sex trafficking operation.

"But he set her up with one of them anyway," I said. "Is that right?"

She nodded. "When Trini went to his room he tried to take her, but she was ready."

"Trini stabbed him," I said. "But she didn't kill him. And then she was sent away?"

Marie nodded.

"So you decided the next time Bernard sent you to a guest, you'd do the same thing."

Marie looked at me for the first time, her eyes swimming with tears, her expression tortured.

"I didn't mean to kill him."

And there it is.

For one heartbreaking moment the world spun away and I felt the truth like a punch in the stomach. Even though I'd guessed what must have happened it still took my breath away to hear it.

The maid killed Bob.

"Does Bernard know what you did?" I asked, trying to keep my voice steady.

"No. He thinks I am a doormat for men to wipe their feet on. It would never occur to him I might do this."

"What weapon did you use?"

"A steak knife from the kitchen. I washed it and put it back with the others."

And of course the police didn't bother doing any forensics in the kitchen—where, washed or not, they would have found Bob's DNA on the knife—because the Hotel L'Ocean was protected by Jean-Marc. He would have made sure the case was restricted to the hotel room and wrapped up as soon as possible.

"I didn't mean to kill the man," Marie said desperately. "I just wanted to tell him, *no*."

I didn't dare ask if she attacked Bob *before* he reached for her. Maybe she came to the door and before Bob had a chance to tell her *no thanks*, she attacked him. But if it was all a mistake or I gave her reason to think it could possibly have been a mistake then she would be tortured her whole life thinking she'd killed a man who hadn't intended to buy her after all.

But if she truly did fight him off, well, that was an image I could go my whole life without seeing in my head. Either way, it was a question I thought we could both live happier not having answered.

"How did you know it was me?" Marie asked, lifting her face to me. When she did I detected the scent of lavender in her hair. Probably her shampoo. Or maybe her body soap.

"I didn't for a long time," I said.

But when everyone else fell out who could possibly have done it, I started looking at other things.

Like a bloody hand towel which indicated *somebody* in the hotel had had a serious accident. And the maid Trini leaving mysteriously. And then there was the faint, niggling scent of lavender buried deep in the back of my brain.

The horror of stepping into that crime scene with Bob's body on the bed was so overwhelming that my senses had gone into a virtual hibernation. And because I didn't want to remember that awful moment, I allowed myself not to revisit it in my brain.

But when I forced myself to remember the moment that I walked into that room, I was eventually able to piece together the gossamer memories and recollections of that moment.

The sun was coming into the room through the half-open blinds. But Bob would have closed them if he were taking a nap *—or preparing for an assignation.*

The scent of a strongly citrus cleaning product hung in the hotel room.

But under that, faint but insistent, was the unmistakable fragrance of flowers.

When there were no flowers in the room.

Lavender.

Like the scent Marie wore.

It wasn't much but what was it Sir Arthur Conan Doyle said? Eliminate the impossible and whatever you're left with, no matter how improbable, must be the truth?

Well, that barely-remembered hint of lavender, improbable as it was, led me to Marie.

But only after I knew that Roman, Nico, Daigneault and Jean-Marc didn't do it first.

Some detective I am.

. . .

After assuring Marie I didn't hate her or have any animosity toward her, I left and walked across the street. I stopped at the florist and bought all the flowers she had before turning to make my way back to the eighth arrondissement.

It truly seemed that I have spent half my time in Paris these past weeks walking its famous streets numb and unseeing to the beauty around me. This afternoon was no different.

I wasn't a half a block away from the hotel when I saw a squad of five police cars come roaring down the street to pull up in front of the Hotel L'Ocean.

In spite of the cold day a warm glow spread through my body at the sight.

Well done, Jean-Marc.

As I walked home from there, the puppy tugging my arm out of its socket nearly the whole way, my mind kept coming back to what Marie had said about the hook-up that she thought the desk clerk had arranged with Bob.

I'll never know whether that was all a misunderstanding or whether Bob really was going to take a chance that I was out for the afternoon and buy sex.

I don't know and I don't want to know.

I was pretty sure Jean-Marc would be fine with keeping Bob's case an unsolved murder and now I have to decide whether I'm okay with that too.

Probably yes. For Marie's sake.

I let my dog pull me home to the safety and comfort of my apartment, the last few leaves of autumn fluttering to the ground around me.

Karma, Bob.

It is certainement a bitch.

62

PRICELESS

One thing I know about French fashion is that you cannot err on the side of being too formal. So on the morning I was to stand in court next to my triumphant and always impeccably arrayed stepmother to witness my future being ripped out of my hands, I knew it would be important to dress for the occasion.

Not that what I wore would make a difference but I think one should dress for major life events. And being impoverished in the space of an hour definitely qualifies.

Before dressing I pulled on sweatpants and a jacket to take Izzy out to the interior courtyard downstairs. I named her Izzy, short for Isabelle, because I couldn't keep calling her Puppy. Izzy was already proving herself to be exceedingly smart and at four months was nearly completely house trained. From what I'd read on the Internet, that's advanced for a small dog.

It was three weeks before Christmas and many of the apartment doors in my building had small fir wreaths on their doors. There was nothing around the city to rival what American Christmas enthusiasts did—gaudy garlands and blinking lights—but it looked lovely and festive to me.

I was still living in my apartment because Joelle had been on holiday for most of November and allowed me to stay until after the court hearing. That was fine with me. I could be packed within the hour. All my possessions that weren't in a small storage unit back in Atlanta—mostly just photo albums and mementos—could fit into two suitcases.

After Izzy had done her business and we were hurrying back upstairs, I noticed that Luc's door was open. He stood in the hallway holding a steaming mug of coffee.

"Today is the day, yes?" he said.

I appreciate that he knew the significance of today but was hardly surprised. In the last couple of weeks we've spent more and more time together.

"Today's the day," I said. "I already know the verdict. This is just a formality."

He nodded at Izzy.

"I am happy to watch her while you're gone."

I gave him a grateful smile. I knew he hated the thought that I might move back to the US. And I appreciated that too.

"I'm leaving her with Geneviève," I said.

"Lunch then? When you get back?"

"Maybe," I said. "Can I call you?"

"*Bien sûr.*" He smiled encouragingly at me and I hurried upstairs, my stomach already heaving at the prospect of my day.

An hour later I was back in the stairwell dressed for my morning in court in a Chanel by Karl Lagerfeld wool suit that I'd found at one of the consignment boutiques in Montmartre. I stopped at Geneviève's apartment and she made over Izzy as if she hadn't seen her in years instead of just the night before.

"You look stunning, *chérie*," she said appraising my outfit. "Is that Chanel?"

"Is it too much? Will the judge think I've been blowing through Claude's money?"

She snorted. "I'm sure he will think you look like a beautiful woman as will anyone else with eyes." She held up her finger to have me wait and then went to a side table in her living room where she brought back a rose and freesia corsage.

"This will be the finishing touch," she said.

I struggled not to cry as she pinned it to my lapel.

"Thank you, *chère* Geneviève," I said and kissed her.

"Good luck, *chérie*," she said from where she stood in her doorway, Izzy in her arms. "Izzy and I await your return no matter what happens!"

I turned and walked toward the stairwell and the taxi waiting to take me to the judicial buildings downtown.

After the taxi let me off, I walked purposefully into the imposing façade of the Palais de Justice on the Boulevard du Palais on the Île de la Cité. The double doors leading to the Court of Appeals—*Cour d'appel de Paris*—looked like they'd been there for centuries. I tried to imagine all the years of cases and decisions that had been determined behind those doors.

And all the resulting lives that had been forever affected.

I took a deep breath and let it out, then straightened my shoulders and walked through the doors.

There were only seven people in total in the cavernous room. They were seated at a long table in front of a tall podium where a man sat in a dark robe.

Knowing I had literally nothing left to lose, I walked purposefully to the table in front of the magistrate, who was a thin sour-faced man with mean eyes.

Unlike last time, Joelle turned to look at me, her lips pulled into an evil smile.

I nodded at the magistrate and took my seat and decided for once in my life to just let whatever was going to happen, happen.

I left the court an hour later totally numb.

I stumbled unseeing down the broad stairs of the Palais de Justice and walked into the crowds of lunchtime office workers and tourists swarming Notre-Dame and the Quai de Saint-Michel. At that moment I wouldn't have registered whether the weather was warm or cold, the skyline clear or full of V2 bombers.

I walked nearly five blocks before I stopped at a sidewalk café, bowed my head and sobbed openly on the street.

I can only imagine how much I must have horrified the French passersby and café clients.

The French do not typically show emotion.

But I couldn't help it. All those weeks of being strong and brave just crumbled away with a few succinct, bloodless words from an impersonal French magistrate.

I cried in gut-wrenching sobs.

I cried for all the loss I'd suffered in the last months. Of missing and hating and loving Bob every day and of having my trust in him trampled into the dirt and flung in my face. I cried for how I'd taken my hands off the wheel my whole life long to let Bob direct me where we would go.

And now in the last decades of my life *with no experience whatsoever* it was all up to me.

I cried at how alone I was in the world. No parents, no husband, my child thousands of miles and six time zones away.

I cried for having killed a man.

And finally I cried in relief and disbelief because in the end the judge said it was his considered view that Claude had recognized me as his daughter during his lifetime and so the inheritance would stand.

Unrelated or not, I was Claude Lapin's legal heir.

Not in any of my wild imaginings did I think that was possible.

And clearly neither did Joelle. She left the court before I did. Somewhere in the back of my brain I registered that I might not know much but I knew when I'd made an enemy for life.

After I turned away from the corner of the sidewalk café—much to the diners' and waiters' relief—I dug in my purse for a tissue to mop up the most obvious evidence of my emotional breakdown and hurried toward the first Metro entrance I came to on the *boulevard Saint-Germain*.

I went first to the large colorful map outside the ticket machines, found the Metro line I needed, and bought a round trip ticket.

When I emerged thirty minutes later from the uncrowded train trip on the boulevard de Ménilmontant, it had started to rain. I thought that was appropriate. After all, have you ever been to a cemetery when it wasn't raining?

I crossed the street to the majestic gates of *Père Lachaise*, unmindful of how the rain was flattening my hair and dripping down my neck.

A maze of lumpy cobblestone pathways wound through the massive eighteenth century cemetery shadowed by oak and maple trees that had yet to drop their leaves of gold and vermillion. Jim Morrison was buried here and Abelard of Abelard and Heloise fame, but I'd been surprised to recently discover that normal people were interred here too.

As soon as I stepped into the cemetery, the towering trees protected me from the shower and I was able to shake out the rain from my jacket. I wandered around on my own for a while enjoying the peace and tranquility of the place. I'd read it was busy in the summer with tourists but in early December, not so much.

I took a picture of a few headstones and sculptures that I thought were particularly beautiful with the idea that I might post them to Instagram or send them to Catherine. The thought of my daughter made me smile. She would be happy to know I wasn't going to be impoverished after all and that I could continue my adventure, as she called it, in Paris. But I knew she would be sorry I wouldn't be coming back to the US.

That thought surprised me because until that moment I didn't realize I'd decided to stay. Now that I could keep my apartment and had the possibility of a little work coming my way from the expat community, I actually had options. I could choose to go or stay.

And it looked like I was choosing to stay.

I saw an old man shuffling along the cobblestone path toward me. He was carrying a rake so I figured he must work here.

"Who are you looking for, Madame?"

"I'm looking for a grave," I said. "It would have been last August."

He nodded and pointed me in the right direction.

My father's grave had a marker on it with the simple inscription: *Claude Lapin Ne 1933 et Mort 2019.*

Because of the natural landscaping surrounding all the graves at *Père Lachaise,* there was no lawn to be tended, just bushes and patches of dead flower beds. Pea gravel was banked around Claude's raised tomb.

It wasn't just the fact that the grave had been tended that surprised me. I'd already seen the man with the rake so I assumed he must keep the gravel tidy.

It was two things, really. First, the fact that my father had a headstone at all meant that Joelle must have spent the money to do it. And second, there was a small etching of a rabbit carved into the headstone.

Rabbit. *Lapin.*

The headstone alone was more than I would have expected of Joelle. But the addition of the hand-carved rabbit—which had to cost a good deal in itself—told me something about Joelle I hadn't realized before.

She'd loved him.

Maybe it was easier to think she was just a money-grubbing second wife than to think she was someone who'd loved and cherished my father and had then been spurned at the end.

The headstone must have been erected after she knew she'd inherited nearly nothing from him.

People are always surprising me. And at my age, that's not a good thing.

As I stood in front of Claude's grave, I felt an overwhelming desire to make peace with him. And also with Bob.

I'd done a good job of not thinking of Bob and what he might or might not have been up to with the little maid Marie. But I knew I couldn't go forward if I didn't forgive him. Really forgive him.

That might still continue to be a long process but at least I had a goal. I wasn't determined to stay mad at him my whole life long.

And as for my father—or the man who was willing to be considered my father—him I forgave for all those tepid invitations (at least he'd made them) and for his disinterest in getting to know me or his granddaughter while he was alive.

"Thank you, Claude," I said in a voice catching with emotion. "Thank you for leaving me the money when you didn't have to."

I felt a tear streak down my cheek.

We were not blood-related and he'd always at least suspected that. But he'd stepped up anyway.

Suddenly my phone rang and I jumped at the sound in the quiet air. I answered it without looking at the screen.

"Hello?"

Jean-Marc's voice came on the line.

"Claire? Are you all right? You sound strange."

I wiped the tear away and cleared my throat.

"I'm fine," I said. "What's up?"

I hadn't seen him since our meeting at Café de Flore a month earlier but he'd texted me last week when he went back to work.

"I wasn't sure whether or not to tell you this," he said, "but I just learned that Marie Cho is no longer in custody with French Immigration Services."

It took me a moment to mentally put all the players into place. After the police raid on the Hotel L'Ocean, Bernard had been held on human trafficking charges and Marie had been detained long enough to get her a French identification number so she could find a proper job. Jean-Marc assured me that the French government would work to see her located and settled somewhere in France.

"Do not tell me she was deported," I said. "She has suffered enough, Jean-Marc."

"She wasn't deported. In fact there doesn't seem to be any consensus on what exactly happened to her. One minute she was in custody and the next she wasn't."

I sat down hard on one of the stone benches lining the gravel path.

"How is that possible?"

Instantly my thoughts went to the possibility of other people in the trafficking ring who might want to hurt or enslave her again.

"That is a very good question and one I can't answer," he

said. "I do have something else to tell you but I'm going to need you to forget I was the one who told you."

"I'm listening," I said, taking in a huge breath.

"It seems Marie has several other aliases as well as a record with Interpol."

For a minute I didn't think I'd heard him correctly. Why would Marie have more than one name?

"For prostitution?" I asked.

"No. Murder. In Dubai. And before you jump to any conclusions of her defending herself she's wanted for the assassination of a local Dubai political figure—the death of whom allowed a multi-billion dollar building deal to proceed."

My mind was whirling.

"It can't be the same person," I said. "Marie is a victim of a human trafficking ring."

"That is what we all believed anyway."

He means that was what we were all led to believe. By Marie.

I shook my head in disbelief. It wasn't just the fact that Marie had confessed to me, but my own senses had led me to the unmistakable conclusion that she was the one who'd killed Bob. And I'd been right about that.

It was the question of why she'd killed him I'd gotten wrong.

"I'd appreciate it if you'd keep me in the loop," I said stiffly.

"You still have closure. You know who killed your husband."

"I have to go, Jean-Marc. Please let me know if she resurfaces."

I disconnected and sat on the stone bench, numb with shock.

I'd asked the wrong questions with Marie. I'd assumed I knew *why* she'd killed Bob and she let me believe I was right. And now she was gone. Would I ever find out why?

My phone was buzzing and I looked down to see I'd received a text.

<Just remember I am always looking out for you>

I stared at the text and then at the number. I didn't recognize it. I read the message again and again, my confusion growing.

And then I just sat there in the now deserted cemetery and felt the chill of the day and the vaguely threatening message creep relentlessly up my arms.

AUTHOR'S NOTES

There are a few places mentioned in this book that you might want to visit the next time you're in Paris.

Café de Flore—Opened in 1880 during the Third Republic, Café de Flore was then and is now frequented by famous writers and philosophers. The nearest underground station is Saint-Germain-des-Prés which is served by line 4 of the Paris Métro. The menu offers typical café fare. But you don't go there for the food. The people-watching on Saint-Germain-des-Prés is incomparable.

Café le Triomphe—this café was described in Chapter 2 and has a brilliant view of the Arc de Triumph. It serves classic Parisienne food—duck *confit*, omelets, *croque monsieurs* and of course the omni-present *foie gras.*

Parc Monceau—Claire goes to this park a lot because it's very near her apartment. Created in the 18th century for Philippe Egalité, cousin of Louis XVI and father of King Louis-Philippe I Parc Monceau is a stunning retreat from Paris's urban streets, complete with ducks, ponds, flowers, wide stretches of lawn, a carousel, charming stone bridges, ice cream vendors, and lots of adorable children running around. A pastoral respite from all your cares. Guaranteed.

Bakeries/Patisseries—Eric Kayser's *boulangerie*. Yes, it's a chain. That doesn't mean it's not amazing. It just means you'll have a better chance of finding a location near you. The one near Claire's apartment in the 8th arrondissement is at 85 Bd Malesherbes, Saint-Augustin.

Père Lachaise—Not just a great place to set a last chapter in a book, but this cemetery is a must-see all on its own. One of the most beautiful—and most visited—cemeteries in the world, Père Lachaise is considered a living gallery due to its many beautiful tombs and headstones. Located at 16 rue du Repos, take the number 2 or 3 metro line and get off at the Père-Lachaise stop. Open daily from 8 until 6 pm.

ABOUT THE AUTHOR

USA TODAY Bestselling Author Susan Kiernan-Lewis is the author of *The Maggie Newberry Mysteries,* the post-apocalyptic thriller series *The Irish End Games, The Mia Kazmaroff Mysteries, The Stranded in Provence Mysteries,* and *An American in Paris Mysteries.* If you enjoyed *Déjà Dead*, please leave a review saying so on your purchase site. Visit my website at www.susankiernanlewis.com or follow me at Author Susan Kiernan-Lewis on Facebook.

Made in the USA
Coppell, TX
30 August 2020